P9-DCO-666

# PAINTED DESERT

## OTHER BOOKS BY FREDERICK BARTHELME

### NOVELS

Second Marriage

Tracer

Two Against One

Natural Selection

The Brothers

### SHORT STORIES

Moon Deluxe

Chroma

FREDERICK BARTHELME

# PAINTED DESERT

*A Novel*

VIKING

VIKING
Published by the Penguin Group
Penguin Books USA Inc., 375 Hudson Street,
New York, New York 10014, U.S.A.
Penguin Books Ltd, 27 Wrights Lane, London W8 5TZ, England
Penguin Books Australia Ltd, Ringwood, Victoria, Australia
Penguin Books Canada Ltd, 10 Alcorn Avenue, Toronto, Ontario, Canada M4V 3B2
Penguin Books (N.Z.) Ltd, 182-190 Wairau Road, Auckland 10, New Zealand

Penguin Books Ltd, Registered Offices:
Harmondsworth, Middlesex, England

First published in 1995 by Viking Penguin,
a division of Penguin Books USA Inc.

1 3 5 7 9 10 8 6 4 2



PUBLISHER'S NOTE
This is a work of fiction. Names, characters, places, and incidents either are the product of the author's imagination or are used fictitiously, and any resemblance to actual persons, living or dead, events, or locales is entirely coincidental.

LIBRARY OF CONGRESS CATALOGING IN PUBLICATION DATA
Barthelme, Frederick, 1943–
Painted desert : a novel / by Frederick Barthelme.
p. cm.
ISBN 0–670–86469–2
I. Title.
PS3552.A763P35 1995
813'.54—dc20 95–6769

This book is printed on acid-free paper.
(∞)

Printed in the United States of America
Set in Palatino

For my mother

Helen Bechtold Barthelme

# PAINTED DESERT

# one

We started carrying a TV in the car because Jen liked tiny TVs, liked the pixelated two-and-a-half-inch screen and the idea of watching whatever you wanted wherever you were, liked the idea of never being out of touch with things, liked being able to swoop in on stuff electronically from beach, mall, restaurant, movie theater. We went to all the pawnshops in town, and she found a handheld LCD color for under seventy dollars at a place called Lomo's Pawn and Pistol, so we had this Pocketvision set in the car when my brother Bud got us on the cell phone to say O.J. was making a run for it, and we just clicked on and watched as we cruised the beachfront highway, headed for a restaurant in Pass Christian. It was dark and we got a good picture, though the antenna shot off sideways and banged into the windshield whenever I turned the Walkman-size TV so Jen, who was driving, could see better what was on the screen. We watched the tail of the chase and the driveway scene, and it was clear even then that this was one of those shake-the-earth deals, like Kennedy or the moon shot or something—you knew right away the world was changed. The tower was turned and facing another direction. We came in on it just about when the light started to go down in L.A., and the helicopter shots were hard to see on the little screen, but we could make out the Bronco in the driveway, and the argument with Jason, and the cops in the doorway.

"This is one of those remember-where-you-were-when-it-happened things," I said. "People are going to ask."

"Duh," Jen said. "Earth to Del. That's not how it works anymore, buddy. Must be a generation deal. So much stuff happens now you couldn't ever remember where you were each time, anyway."

"Yeah, that's probably right."

"You just stick with me," she said. "I'll explain everything as we go along."

So we got to the Blue Lobster and took the TV inside because we figured they wouldn't have a TV in the restaurant, which they didn't, and we kept ours low on the table, flat on its back, so it would be inconspicuous, but that didn't work at all since the waiter saw right away what we had and he started bending over our shoulders to see what he could see. He had the breath. It wasn't long before we had a crowd, and everybody had an opinion about the murder, about Nicole, about the supplementary victim, the bloody glove, the Bronco—everyone was well informed.

I hadn't paid much attention to the murder, but I love a crisis on TV. The excitement is catching: the fever in the announcers' voices, the way they recap every couple of minutes for those of us just tuning in, the cuts to different reporters at different places picking up different threads of the story, the interviews with witnesses and passersby, and just the look of tragedy—flashing lights, people running around, flames, firemen in their slickers, the crumpled fuselage or car carcass if it's that deal, newspeople with their careful hair blowing, chopper shots, police tape, gawkers—it's wonderful stuff. Car wrecks with more than fifty cars are good, especially on fog-shrouded highways, and plane wrecks are good too; train crashes are usually not so hot unless they're in water, in which case they're great for the misty-steamy look and the weird places they happen, in the middle of nowhere; hostage situations are interesting, especially if the setting is a little exotic so you get palm trees and rain-spattered streets and swarthy natives; riots are beautiful, of course, with the collective action, the people darting around, the broken glass and homemade weapons and upturned cars, big smoke rising; and multiple murders are great, like when they're wheeling the evidence out of the guy's apartment, or if they get a perp holed up in some small building, maybe a sniper scenario or a standoff; urban and suburban fires are O.K., though kind of limited unless it's a hotel with jumpers on high floors.

At the restaurant, one of the waiters eventually brought in a bigger TV, a thirteen-inch job, and we lost our audience. We couldn't really eat at this restaurant, because everybody was too busy with the chase, so we left, picked up some fried chicken at a drive-through, then parked down by the beach to follow the capture. I started eating a big drumstick, and Jen called her father in Baton Rouge to be sure he was tuned in. He was way ahead of her. "He's recording it," she said to me, lifting the mouthpiece high.

They went on talking, and I went on eating and watching the little TV.

Jen and I had been together three years, in my tiny high-rise condo fronting the beach in Biloxi, living on my salary from the junior college and some money she had from her father. I was close to twice her age, forty-seven to twenty-seven, but the big difference wasn't really a problem. Things were fine. Jen spent lots of time on CompuServe and the Internet, sending packs of information to people she didn't know but who shared her interests, redistributing news stories stolen from the wire services, or things she keyed in or scanned from newspapers and magazines, even books. Some were typical horror shots—guys throwing their two-year-olds off second-floor balconies into swimming pools to teach them to swim—but others were just things she liked or thought people ought to know: corruption, stupid speeches, UFOs, tattoo dreams, gonzo publishing, sneaky political crap, warnings, cartoons, wild stories. She was a small-scale cybermuckraker with an off-center idea of what muck needed the work. She read a lot of lists on the Internet, so she had plenty of fringe source there, and she tracked electronic and overland zines, so she had them for fodder. Her hard-copy broadside publishing had slowed to a trickle in the three years we'd been together. She wasn't putting stuff on bright flyers and stapling them all over town anymore, but she was peppering the Net with e-mail and forum messages, and posting files on bulletin boards all over the country, so she figured she was doing her part out on the electronic frontier.

I had worked up the computer myself and used her notebook for telecommunication stuff, calling CompuServe and some boards, but mostly I just taught my classes at the college and got over my last divorce, which was also my first and which had taken me too many years. The job my brother Bud had lined up was working out better than I'd anticipated, and I was beginning to think I was back on track.

Jen's father, Mike, had been trying hard to get us to visit him in Baton Rouge. He and Jen's mother had divorced ten years before. Lida had remarried and moved to Maryland, and now nobody ever heard from her. Jen's father lived alone. Jen had been a bad girl as a kid and probably seemed to him to be straightening out. Even though I was way too old, which couldn't have made him happy, he figured I was a step up from her last boyfriend because now Jen called every week or so.

She was about ready to take me over to meet her dad in spite of my being almost as old as he was and not nearly as successful.

Usually when I talked to him on the phone we did weather, or cars, or gambling in Biloxi. Mike liked gambling and was always saying he was going to come over for a weekend tour of the new casinos. I encouraged him to hurry up, but secretly I wasn't eager to get more friendly. He was charming on the telephone—funny and wry, maybe a little parentlike. He'd had three children. A son had died in a highway accident and the other daughter lived in California. Jen was the difficult daughter. Before we got together she'd finished college and then gone Greenpeace, Save the Whales, Seals, Trees, whatever, then hooked up with this guy who called himself Itch and sold bathing suits out of the back of his van. Jen had lived with him a year or more. He was the guy Mike thought I was an improvement on. Jen was just splitting up with this guy when we met, and we'd been together since.

We'd run into Itch a few times in our three years. His real name was Larry, and he'd bettered his lot considerably, expanding the bikini business by branching out into snow cones and rentals—flotation devices, umbrellas, Sunfish, Rollerblades, volleyball equipment, water wings—plus entrepreneurial deals like beachfront valet parking, sunscreen delivery systems, small foods, and so on. He had a new Chevy van with an aftermarket nine-thousand-dollar paint job featuring severed Medusa heads being pulled from strange boxes swamped in elegant lime-and-teal flames.

Jen put me on the phone with Mike and started rustling around in the box of chicken.

"So, when are you guys coming over?" he asked me.

"He wants to know when we're coming to visit," I said to her.

"Jen says soon," Jen said.

"Now," Mike said.

"Well, I guess that's it, then," I said.

"You got anything else planned?" he said.

"We don't plan," I said. "We don't do a lot of planning."

"I envy that," Mike said. "So what're you? Out in the car somewhere?"

"We're at the beach," I said. "We were at this restaurant, but that didn't work."

"You're not teaching this summer?" he asked. Mike had a healthy respect for professors, even those of us working the junior-college circuit on the Mississippi Gulf Coast.

Jen snapped the phone back and said, "O.K., Dad, we're really doing it this time. We're on our way, no stopping us. You going to behave when we get there?"

A pretty smile ran across her face as she listened to his answer. She held up a strange-shaped fried chicken wing for me to see or eat. I couldn't tell which.

# two

Mike had prickly gray hair that shivered as he talked. He was a tubby guy, couldn't have been more than five six, five seven, and must have weighed one ninety. He was the same size as my father, but stockier, and had a squarish face and head, like a small stereo speaker on his shoulders. His hair stuck out an inch in all directions in this crew cut from the fifties that I got the feeling was going to retain its viability right through the turn of the century. He was nice, a retired insurance guy who had plenty of money and lived in a well-kept subdivision in Baton Rouge.

"What's this new look?" Mike said when he let us in.

"My new look," Jen said.

She had dyed her hair black and cut it short like a boy's, and she didn't use a lot of makeup, but other than that there wasn't much new. Sometimes she went for body stockings and miniskirts, the Olive Oyl look, but mostly she wore jeans and T-shirts and combat boots. The hair made a difference though. Her features were chiseled and she looked a little foreign, a touch of the Eastern Bloc plain. I could imagine that it was a shock.

"It's great," Mike said. "It's different, though. You look older."

"I'm younger than ever," she said, poking a finger in my ribs. "This is my friend Del."

"Hi," I said. "This is *my* new look."

"It's good to meet you," Mike said, shaking my hand.

He showed us in, but I stopped just inside the door and pointed to the car, and went out to get the bags. He and Jen went on.

This was a community planned to the hilt. There wasn't anything unplanned about it. Once inside the main gate you could see how hard the designers were working to make it neat. They'd built sunken covered guest parking areas, landscaped caves that dotted the development like burial mounds. I dropped our bags on the slip of grass in front of Mike's house and moved the car into the nearest mound.

We'd driven over shortly after the Simpson arrest, so there was lots of news, lots of television to watch, though we couldn't get much on the trip, usually just one station on the Pocketvision when we were out on the highway.

Arlene was around all the time. She was a neighbor he saw occasionally, mostly as a friend, he told Jen. Arlene was a woman who had blown up like a balloon animal, too many curves in all the wrong places—stomach curve, abdomen curve, hip curve, rump curve—and she wore gaudy sweater-and-slack outfits so everybody got a clear view of every curve she had, which seemed to be bad planning. She was two years older than I was.

We had a room of our own. There had been talk about separate rooms—Mike had a four-bedroom town house, so there was plenty of space—but that talk sort of fizzled into laughter in the kitchen between father and daughter, so we ended up in a large second-floor room with a peaked roof and miniblinds, looking out over the front yard and one of the parking grottos.

We had a TV in the room. Sometimes I could escape up there to take a rest. I did that often in the first couple of days we were there. I did that before dinner and after dinner and in the afternoon and late at night when Arlene and Mike were watching TV downstairs, which they did a couple of nights a week. Mike had an elaborate system for recording things on videotape for time shifting. He used the super-long-play setting so he could get three movies on each tape. I suggested one night that if he used the two-hour setting the picture would be a lot better, but he argued vigorously that the advantage of having three movies on a tape outweighed the possible advantage of better picture quality.

"Besides," he said, "who watches them? We just sit here and stare at the screen together while we think things over—isn't that what everybody does?"

"I don't know," I said. "Maybe."

"Sometimes I even stare at the wall behind the set," Arlene said. "The screen's too bright."

"Picture quality's not a big issue when you're staring at the wall," I said.

"Nope," Mike said.

"Maybe it's an age thing," Arlene said.

That's when I went to take my nap, leaving Jen with Arlene and Mike to stare at the television. In the bedroom I put the TV on CNN, turned off the sound, then cranked the brightness almost all the way off so I couldn't see much of anything, except some dark spots and light spots moving around. Even that was annoying, so I got a towel and draped it over the screen, put a couple of books on top to hold the towel in place. That was better. Just enough flexing light to keep the room occupied. Then I took a rest that eventually turned into a nap. It was pleasant. I felt like I was stealing from everybody, nobody could touch me. It was the most pleasant thing that'd happened since we'd arrived.

Jen woke me up around eight that night, asking if I was going to sleep straight through. I said I wasn't. I asked her what she'd been doing.

"Watching television with Arlene and Mike."

"Why'd you stop?"

"They turn the sound up real loud. You can't hear yourself think," she said. "Dad's got this bad hearing. And that stuff about not watching is bogus. They were watching."

"I know about the sound thing. My father makes the walls rattle."

"That's it," she said. "So are you going to sleep or what? You're killing me with all this sleeping."

"You want me to come down?"

"That wouldn't be bad," she said. "They need somebody to talk to. Dad's checking you out, remember."

"What does he think so far?" I said.

"Not talking," she said. "But I can tell he's O.K. Maybe we're a little freaky, but he's doing fine."

"Did I pack my plaid pants?"

"Grab a bite, will you?"

"I want to get up early and get out on the links," I said.

"Cute, Del. He wants you to play golf with him, so what? I told him you hadn't played golf since you were seventeen."

"How would you know?" I said.

"You told me," she said.

We went downstairs and sat in the living room, and a few minutes later Mike and Arlene, one after the other, came out of the TV room and sat with us. It was one of those awkward family-style meetings, the kind where people think about what they need to say but can't get close to saying it.

Mike said, "So how's the educating business?" This was just the opening, I figured, but it wanted an answer. Nothing too detailed.

"It's good," I said. "I like it. I like the idea I might help somebody a little. Doesn't work, mostly, but we don't hurt many."

"That's it," Arlene said. "Do no harm."

"Damn right," Mike said. "Arlene used to teach in the high schools here."

"No kidding?" Jen said. "That's great."

"She was the madwoman drama teacher," Mike said. "All the kids loved her."

"Well, you can't really ask for a lot more than that," I said.

"So you give them an education over there, huh?" Mike said. "They come in, and they leave with an education."

"Sometimes they don't even come in," I said. "Sometimes they just call."

"That's his brother Bud's joke," Jen said. "Bud teaches at the school, too."

"That right?" Mike said.

"Yeah," I said. "Close enough. We're brothers, after all. We get along."

"How do they feel about having brothers on the faculty?" Arlene said.

"I guess they don't mind," I said.

I noticed that there was a lot of octagonal furniture in the room. The coffee table was octagonal, the side tables by the sofa were octagonal, and there was a kind of octagonal table alongside a chair where Mike was sitting. That was Mike's chair. It was green. The walls in the house were dusty pastels. Not bad colors, just slightly more active than you'd want. Shadowy pinks and washed-out browns. They weren't the kinds of colors I would have chosen if I were choosing, and I guessed that Mike hadn't chosen them either, that they'd come ready-made with the house. The furniture was his fault, though. I wasn't going to give him anything on the furniture.

"So you think he did it or didn't do it?" Mike said, gesturing toward the TV in the next room. It was still on, showing a Simpson special, but now the sound was real low.

"Did," Jen said.

"Don't know," I said. "But I can imagine the killing, the Bundy house, the court, the gate. Nicole and Bernard, or whatever his name is, getting carved up on the flagstone. I can sort of see it in my head, the way it happened, the struggle. I've been dreaming about it."

"No kidding?" Arlene said.

"Yeah," I said. "It's not like I wake up sweating or anything, but I can feel this murder, see it happening. Maybe I just never bothered to imagine one. This one's very graphic. The space is small and kind of half enclosed, overgrown with ficus and some short, barbed shrubs, and there's the sound of clanking metal gates, this pale milky light, quick movements. I see what the night's like. Everything."

Arlene said, "So who's doing it?"

"Well, when I see it, I am," I said. "But I don't think it makes much difference who's doing it."

"It made a difference to Nicole and Ron," Jen said. "That little nick on her spinal column."

"Now, don't start," Mike said. "All of those freaky stories of yours. You're always so gruesome."

"I've expanded my horizons," Jen said. "I'm not just doing gore now. You won't have me to kick around for that. I'm doing human-interest stories, warm, touching, meaningful stories about people who succeed, people who manage to overcome great obstacles, people who do the right thing."

"Is that true?" Mike said. "I haven't seen those."

"Haven't sent any," Jen said. "They're new."

I shook my head at her.

Arlene laughed. "What are you shaking your head about? Not so?"

"She started doing those stories a couple years ago," I said. "But she's drifted back to the mangled, beheaded, and delimbed. I'm not sure she believes in hope."

"Rat," Jen said.

"So they put these things up at your school?" Mike said. "These posters she makes?"

"Sometimes I see them around school," I said. "When she does them. She doesn't do so many these days. I don't post them, but kids pick them up other places and post them at school."

"I'm putting most of the stuff out with a modem—

telecommunications," Jen said. "I have a wider circulation, even if they are all geeks."

"Geeks? Now, what does that mean, exactly?" Arlene said. "Kind of fruitcakes?"

"Yeah, it's fruitcakes with a dinosaur twist, some kind of sexual problem," Jen said.

"Sounds great," Mike said. "What's for dessert, Arlene? Are we having dessert?"

"Why don't you have a peach?" Arlene said. "A peach would be good for you. Grow hair on your chest, make a man out of you."

"It's about time," Mike said, waving a fork in the air. "But if you just want to grow hair, I can grow hair." He was brandishing the fork as if it were some kind of magic wand, as if by itself it would grow hair. He waved it in my direction.

"I have plenty, thanks," I said.

"I don't know," Arlene said. "You look like you're about three-quarters forehead to me."

Jen made a sweep of CompuServe and the Net through the server back at the university to get her e-mail and pick off newsgroup messages aimed at her. She saved everything for later, and then we went out to take a look at Baton Rouge. She hadn't been there in years, and I had never been there, to speak of, just traveled through it, so we went out for a drive, first by the lake in the center of town and then out to the river. It was a pretty town—some old buildings covered with sandstone pockmarked with shells, a southern tradition, and a nice metal bridge over the Mississippi. When we got close enough to the river, we noticed that it made a peculiar noise—soothing, gentle, persistent. We drove into a little park that overlooked the water near the city side of the river, the downriver side of the bridge, and sat there for a time watching the cars go by, looking at the lights flicker on the water, at the boats, the barges. It was a lovely time, warm but with a constant wind that kept the mosquitoes away. "So how do you like him?" Jen said. She had the little TV out and was scanning to see what channels she could pick up. The green line slid across the screen, stopping at ABC, then CBS.

"I like both of them fine," I said. "They're old but harmless. Sweet."

"They're oddly dressed."

"I noticed that," I said. "Him especially—are those clothes made out of plastic or something? How come his stuff is so stiff?"

"That's what he's like," Jen said. "He likes the way everything is real neat. Notice how neat the house is? The neighborhood? He's deeply neat."

"Pleasure from the small stuff," I said. "I understand that. Enriched by the orderly. At least there wasn't anything colored in the toilet bowls."

"I think there *is* something in the toilets," Jen said. "But it's clear. It smells funny. Did you smell it?"

"What? The toilet?"

"Yes."

"No, I didn't smell it," I said. "Did you?"

"Well, sort of. I didn't mean to, but I sort of did. I think there's something in there, but I'm not sure. Something clear."

"That wouldn't be so good if he had a dog," I said. "What if the dog went in there and drank out of the toilet and it had this clear poison stuff in the water?"

"Dad doesn't have a dog."

"Yeah, but if he did, that would be a terrible thing," I said. "It might kill the dog."

"Yeah, but he doesn't."

"I know. That's not the point. It's the principle of the thing. What if a dog comes over to visit with one of his friends?"

"He doesn't have any friends with dogs," Jen said. "If a person has a dog, Dad doesn't want to know them."

"Oh, is that so? That's the way he is?"

"Pretty much," Jen said. "A dog isn't tidy."

"It's very affectionate," I said. "It's big and physical. It's substantial."

"Yeah, I know, but he doesn't want anything big and substantial. He wants neat things. Really tidy things."

Cars were ringing by on the bridge above and to the right of us. Tires on the gridded pavement made a singing noise. The steel girders were silhouetted against the sky. A few cats were sitting down below us at the edge of the river. There were actually more than a few, half a dozen or more. A small herd of cats. When we first arrived, they had darted away from us, but they decided we might not mean any harm, so they were back, sitting in a dusty clearing around a metal hoop the size of a septic tank. There was a solid black with a yellow blaze, a white-chested one, a three-colored tabby and a pair of gray-and-white tabbies, some other gray ones.

"How long are we staying?" I said. "Is there a minimum requirement?"

Jen popped me on the ear with her finger. "I don't know. A few days. I don't think it's all that bad. Dad seems to like you well enough."

"He thinks I'm a little old for you," I said. "Twenty years. I was a hippie when you weren't quite born—you know, rock 'n' roll forever, peace and love, beads, patchouli, the rest of that. You were in the womb, you were an accident waiting to happen."

"Hey, Woodstock Nation," Jen said. "You're way real."

"I didn't mean it that way."

"What way *did* you mean it?"

"I don't know," I said. "Some other more friendly way."

"Whatever you do, stay away from politics. I don't want you and him comparing views, you hear? 'Cause if you do, then we've got trouble. We've got a week's worth of bad road."

"I'm starting with Whitewater," I said. "Then I'll cut to one of those women—I can't remember the names—one of those our president was purported to have given a poke or two."

"The big blond woman or the black-haired woman?" she said.

"Either one. Anyway, what is he, a Bob Dole fan? Or does he like that groundhog guy from Texas?"

"No, neither of those. But he's got views. Just leave him alone. That's my advice. But hey, don't take my advice. Do whatever you want. Enter into a covenant with him, for all I care. Discuss the nature of man, postmodernism. Unpack your issues together."

"O.K., forget it. What about Arlene?"

"What about?" Jen said. "She's fine. She doesn't want to hurt anybody. She doesn't want to force anybody to do anything. It's like she's found some little thing she likes, some way of living that she likes and that's comfortable and provides for her. I admire that, even though all she does is chatter and weird hair. Somehow that doesn't matter. She could be anything, she could be the hippest person on the planet, and it wouldn't make any difference if she felt the way she does, if she liked what she did. I mean, if she were the hippest person on the planet, she'd probably look down on herself the way she is, but if she were really, really hip, then . . . you know what I mean?"

"Sure. Chinese boxes. You never get out."

"You want to try to catch the last news? See what they did in L.A.?" She waved the TV at me. "Maybe he tried to escape."

"Nope," I said. "I'm guessing they found blood running from his Bronco to the police station, up the steps and into the elevator and into Detective Vannatter's office. You never know."

We got up and brushed off our clothes and got into the car and drove back through Baton Rouge and out to the suburb where Mike lived—a Stepford community. We parked our car behind Mike's big Lincoln Town Car and went inside. Arlene and Mike were sitting in the den watching the television, a CNN special report he'd recorded—the upcoming moon shot anniversary. We sat down to watch with them.

After the special, Arlene packed up her purse and said good night. Mike walked her to her car. Sometimes she drove over, even though she lived only two houses down. Jen went upstairs to read her e-mail. That left me in the den with Mike when he came back inside—not particularly where I wanted to be. These moments when you're supposed to have these conversations always arrive. You can't avoid them, but you can usually dodge the questions, or just truck up some weird answers to the questions when they come. Usually the people leave you alone after that. I figure they don't want to ask the questions any more than you want to answer them. They're not really interested, they're just acting out, doing their jobs. That's what Mike was up to, I guessed. So we had an awkward time.

Mike slapped the arm of his chair. It was a designer chair, not modern, but it was clear that it wasn't something he got at Sears. He was very proud of this chair. It was an ugly, really expensive chair.

"Well," Mike said. "I've been looking forward to having a chance to get with you one on one. You know what I mean? You know what I mean, Del?"

"I've been looking forward to talking to you too, Mike."

"You're teaching over there in Biloxi? And teaching is something you want to do, is that right?" Mike said.

"I don't mind it," I said. "It's good work. It's worthwhile work, sort of. In a small way. It's time-consuming and it pays the bills."

"It's a good, honest career," Mike said. "It's a commitment to society. You shouldn't hang back about this."

"I'm not hanging back."

"Well, I mean, it's important."

"Yeah, it is," I said.

"Those kids need to be educated. Jen needs to be educated, you know. She's got her degree, but she could use another one. Another degree never hurt anybody."

"We talked about that," I said. "About her going back to school, getting a graduate degree."

"You did?"

"Yep. Yep, we talked about it. She can't figure out what she wants to get a graduate degree in, though, and the areas she's thinking about—art, journalism—are not big moneymakers."

Mike laughed and patted his chair. "Yeah, she never was bound for glory that way. That's for sure." He sighed real large and smiled and patted the chair again.

I noticed there was a spot on the arm of the chair where he'd patted some of the finish right off.

"Well, we can't all be tycoons like you, Mike," I said. "Some of us just stick to the shadows and sneak by. Skirt the edges, economically speaking."

"It's not economics I'm worried about," Mike said. "I don't know how to get into this, but perhaps I'll just, well . . . Now, as I understand it, you're about . . ."

"Just turned forty-seven," I said. "But I obscure my birthday."

"Right," Mike said. "That's what I was wondering. You see, I'm fifty-three, and there you are with my daughter, who's twenty-seven. Doesn't that seem a little odd to you? I don't want to be forward about this, and I'm not making any big problems, but it worries me, I don't mind telling you. I mean, I hoped we could go straight at this, man-to-man."

"That's like retail-to-retail, wholesale-to-wholesale?"

"What?"

"Nothing. It's just car dealer talk."

"Well," Mike said. He pulled his pants out of his crotch. "I don't know. I'm retired, so I don't know about that."

"Jen and me was a surprise. Good surprise, but still. I'm divorced, and at first it was just a friendly sort of thing, and then—"

"That's not the way Jennifer said it was," he said.

"What's that?"

"The friendly thing."

"Well, I meant it wasn't serious. I didn't know it was serious," I said.

"Quickie?" he said. "You and Jennifer?" He winked at me then, one of those self-conscious winks where the message is "See this fake wink? Know what it means?" I was not doing as well as I would have liked.

"No, that's not what I meant. I just didn't know what was going on. Now we've been together a couple of years and we're comfortable. She seems comfortable, and I am too."

"Well, the both of you are comfortable, then," Mike said. "That's worth something."

He was up and around behind his chair now, leaning on its back, his arms folded. He was picking at his teeth with the nail of his thumb. "Comfortable. I like to see that, but I'm not sure—I mean, see, I'm wondering if you ought to, I don't know, get to one side there, so that Jennifer can go on with her life. Unless you see yourself as, well, you know . . ."

"Permanent?"

"Right."

"Well, I think we see me in her life. So that's why I don't get off to one side—we're sort of keeping company in a serious way."

"Keeping company. Now, I haven't heard that since I was a kid, when my pappy used to talk about that. I think he used to talk about keeping company. That's nice, the way you use that," he said.

"Well, thank you," I said.

There was a long pause while he picked his teeth and looked down into the seat of his chair. Then he straightened his arms and looked at the TV, which was still on, though the sound wasn't.

"That Simpson thing's a mess out there, I'm telling you. I don't like it. You think he did it?" he said. "The police seem to think he did it."

"Yeah, that's right," I said.

"I don't know—you know that dog and everything, that dog found them."

"Yep."

"Wailing there," Mike said, doing a little tight stretch with his shoulders, trying to move them forward. "I guess I'd better go over and say good night to Arlene. I'm glad we had this talk. I feel better. Maybe we could have another one."

"Sure," I said. "That'd be good for me."

"Let's schedule that. Let's pencil that in. Right after golf. You play golf?" he said.

"No, I don't really play golf," I said. "I played golf when I was a kid, as Jen may have told you. I was on the golf team in high school. We were pretty fair golfers there in Houston at high school. But since then I haven't played much. Golf's not my game, really."

"So what is your game?"

"Well, I don't really have a game," I said. "When I was younger I liked various games. I liked archery."

He gave me a look when I said archery.

"Well, I can't help it. I liked it," I said. "Shooting those arrows, that was fun. Football and baseball, of course. I played Little League. Played grade school football."

"You didn't play high school?" he said. "You're a big boy. Probably a big kid, weren't you?"

"Well, yeah, I was, but I didn't."

"Why didn't you?"

"I didn't want to," I said. "I had an idiot coach in eighth grade."

"Everybody has an idiot coach," Mike said.

"This guy was Vince Lombardi with that gay-jock conflict thing going. He had us smack each other in the face before games—that sort of thing. Slug each other in the stomach as hard as we could. Got one kid to jump on another kid who was easing up and twist his helmet, bend his head back. That was always me, the one easing up."

"So that's when you turned to archery?"

"I didn't turn to archery. I was just interested in archery."

"Were you any good at it?" Mike said.

"No," I said. "Bowling. I was pretty good at bowling. Now, there you go. That's my game—bowling."

"I never was any good at bowling," Mike said.

"Well, what're you going to do?" I said.

# three

Jen was in the tub when I got upstairs, so I turned on the television and climbed into bed. When she finished she came out and stood in the doorway with a towel wrapped around her waist, her breasts bare. She was dripping wet, rubbing her hair with a second towel.

"You and Dad had a chat?" she said.

"Yeah," I said. "He said I was really old."

"You are," she said. "Too old."

"He didn't exactly say that. He was sort of suggesting that I get out of the way and let you go on with your life," I said.

"You going to do that?" she said.

"I don't think so."

"Good." She went back into the bathroom. "I got weird e-mail."

"What?"

"A guy named Durrell Dobson, lives in Las Vegas. He's seen my stuff out there on his favorite BBS, so he found me on the Net and now he's sending me this rant deal where he goes on for pages and pages telling me how he hates everything, hates everybody, about how everything bothers him—the world and its inhabitants."

"He's mad as hell, etc.?"

"That's him. He sounds sort of reasonable, though. Plus, he's a fan. He remembers the Box of Heads story I posted in alt.medical.research last year, when we first got on."

"He's a stand-up guy," I said.

I clicked through the channels on the old RCA television that was in our room, catching bits of war in black and white, British actors chatting, that *Silk Stalkings* show that never quite made it, news, congressional repeats, four or five religious channels, *The Best of Arsenio Hall,* sports, home shopping, some Discovery program on mites, the usual history-of-aviation stuff that's endlessly fascinating to somebody—me, sometimes.

I got a show about violence in America on A&E, and I was sort of watching that, my pillows propped up behind me. The speaker was squeaky, but I could make out what was being said. I half listened to a segment in which some movie reviewer was mad at Oliver Stone for being neck-deep in what he was supposed to be parodying, "a part of the problem," the reviewer said, and then there was a segment about the Los Angeles riots. The riots were pretty, even on that old TV. The flames, the excitement, the helicopter shots. It was *The Year of Living Dangerously* in real life. I figured that was the reason the rioters had done it in the first place. They were as desperate as the rest of us for something to happen, something big, something significant. The King verdict was chickenshit, of course, but it was just a key to the door. When they got started out here in the street, they said, Hey, we can do this. We can ravage this fucking city, this fucking shithole. We can tear it apart and burn it down. What the fuck? They can't do anything worse to us than they've already done. You could see their minds working there on the TV, see them getting more and more excited, getting the thrill of smacking people with boards, yanking people out of cars, standing in the middle of the road where you don't belong and pissing like there was no tomorrow. It was day and night drama, something to tell the kids. I wasn't being cynical, either. The riot guys felt bad about their lives. You got a sense how bad looking at them work.

Jen came out of the bathroom, dressed in a T-shirt this time, and crawled into bed alongside me. On-screen the guys were beating up Reginald Denny, the truckdriver. The one guy drop-kicked him and another guy hit him with a rock. Denny wasn't looking too good. He was kind of splattered on the road there, didn't know where he was, his big truck was right there with its door open, but it didn't offer any protection at all. They showed the attack on him four or five times, and it was hard to watch over and over. I understood it and it still made me angry, like I wanted some avenger to swoop in and kick these kids' asses.

Then they showed some video I'd never seen, about a guy named Lopez, a Guatemalan guy who lived in L.A. and was delivering a dishwasher or something; he had some kind of delivery service he was running by himself. So they were beating him up, and the same guy who beat up Denny, the guy in the calf-length shorts and the high-tops, was beating on Lopez. Somebody hit Lopez with a boom box or maybe it was a big stereo speaker, I couldn't tell. This guy Lopez was down on the ground, and they were kicking him, and he was out, gone, so just then the guy with the black high-tops pulls Lopez's pants down and pulls his underpants down and spray-paints his dick and balls. All over them. The guy was using a can of black Krylon paint; you could see the label real clearly on the videotape. He soaked Lopez's crotch. They showed him doing it on this TV special.

"Jesus Christ," Jen said. "Jesus fucking Christ." She took the remote from me and upped the volume.

"I know, I know."

"Did you see this?" she said, waving the remote at the TV to cut the sound of a commercial. "He just spray-painted this guy's cock."

"Yes."

"The guy was already out. He was down. He was cold. It was like, What new mess can I put on him, how can I hurt him more deeply now that I've already beat the shit out of him, how can I humiliate him some more. I mean, Jesus Christ," she said.

"I know. They ought to put the idiot in jail," I said. "It looks like the same guy who was beating Denny. I guess they did put him in jail, eventually."

"Jail isn't enough," Jen said. "He needs to be killed."

"They weren't sure it was him or something," I said. "Or he had a lawyer. He had a terrible life. You know how it goes."

"Did you know about this?" She waved the remote at the TV again. "I mean, before?"

"No," I said. "Never saw it, never heard of it. Spraying the guy's cock is retarded."

"No shit," she said. "It makes you want to do something. It makes you want to kill the fucker. That'd be a service to humanity, to go out there and exterminate this guy. He's fucking mental, an ape. Know what I mean?"

"You remember that show we saw where the guys had videotaped themselves mugging people, and they mugged this guy and then beat him up and then one mugger stood over the guy and pissed on his face? The guy with the video camera showed a full shot of his pal standing and pissing, then zeroed in on the victim's head so you could see the urine splashing off the guy's face. You remember that?"

"Yeah. It's the same," she said. "We ought to do this. It's worth it. He should be butchered."

"Probably, but we aren't the ones."

"We could do worse," she said. "We could train. People do that. They change. We could study, take courses."

"We're not killer material," I said. "We're never killing anybody. Movies say anybody can, but that's shit. You have to be a certain kind, have a certain background. We don't have it. Too polite. We're not doing it."

"Let's go out there, anyway," she said. "Where's the guy now—in jail?"

"Ten years, I think. He'll be out in two."

"If he was going to be out in two, he should be out by now."

"Maybe he is. I don't know. I don't think he's out. I haven't seen anything about him being out."

"Let's go see him in prison and tell him what we think," she said.

"There's a keen idea. That's bound to scare him to death, really," I said. "He's nuts and really especially bright and he painted the guy's cock, so you want to give him a piece of your mind. Good thinking."

"We could see O.J. too."

"What are you saying to him?"

"I don't know, maybe that I can't believe he did it, that I refuse."

"What happens when they prove it?" I said.

"I'm not going to believe," she said. "Besides, I didn't mean we should actually see *him,* just the key sites—the restaurant and all that. But I can sort of see it. I close my eyes and I see him there and her coming to the door and this Ronald Goldman guy coming up—"

"Yeah, yeah. O.K. Fine."

"And O.J. jumps out and does her and then this big fight with the other guy. Slasher. He's such a fuck. He lost it; he was out of his fucking mind. Or maybe it didn't happen that way. Maybe it was a drifter, a bushy-haired man. Two of them, maybe a one-armed man and a bushy-haired man. Or somebody else. Maybe one of her friends, or Goldman's. It could have been anybody. I don't want to talk about it."

She got out of my bed and into hers and clicked off her light and rolled over and faced the other direction.

"You going to bed now?" I said.

"What's it look like?" she said.

"It looks like you're going to bed now," I said.

"That's it, then."

"We can go out there if you want to."

Silence. Then she rolled back and looked at me over her shoulder. "You serious?"

"We can drive," I said. "We don't have anything else. It's July. We can go now, leave from here, leave tomorrow."

"We can't leave tomorrow," she said.

"Well, the next day."

"You're just trying to get out of spending time with my father."

"No. I like your father. But it might be good to drive out there," I said. "See some stuff."

"I'd like to stop in Shreveport to get Penny. Did I tell you about Penny?"

"Yes. Of course. College friend, angry woman, tall."

"Something like that. And there are people in Flagstaff, too. The Dog family. And a guy who runs a good board in New Mexico. I wouldn't mind meeting him."

"Can do," I said. "Let's head out as soon as you're ready."

"Let's think about it," she said. She rolled over again.

"You've got to see this," Jen said, flopping onto my bed with her laptop in hand. It was two-thirty in the morning. Thunder outside. "I posted a thing about the riots on this newsgroup, about Lopez and all that, and almost instantly I get this five-page message back from this screed guy in Las Vegas—you know the one I told you about? Anyway, he knows about Lopez and he's thinking the same thing."

"Thinking what?" I asked.

"How the guy who did it ought to be offed. So he goes on and says all these things he wants to do to this guy, and then he tells me he's from Louisiana, Dobson is. He's been living in Vegas, doesn't work anymore 'cause he panhandles his cash. He likes doing that, likes having six hundred dollars in his pocket and begging money from some Polo-shirted jerk." Jen clicked the Page-Up key a couple of times and read, " 'They think they're doing you such a favor. The winners are the worst. Fat red faces and four-color shirts, and they give you twenties like they're doing you this big favor. They need to go down, one good pop with a steel bat—love that.' "

I reached for the computer and turned it so I could read the message. "So why am I telling you?" the message said. "Who knows. You're there. You listen, read. You're not the only one. There are others. Lots. I'm just spreading the word. Trying you out. It's what I do. I write messages to people I never see. On a given day I figure to make a hundred fifty bucks jerking the toads coming out of the casinos. Cops don't much like us, so we move quick, jump casino to casino. I got a beat-up Mercedes my parents left, so that's easy. I only moved here because I got in trouble in Houma for making videos of local women as they changed in the mirrored dressing room of one of my father's shops. I wired it up with lipstick cameras, and nobody ever knew what hit them. They never knew who was looking. I was going to sell the stuff, but some local debutante caught her heel on one of the cameras while she was doing her stretches in the dressing room, yanked it out of the wall, and showed it to her father, who managed the TV station. My family settled the suits, kept things quiet, and I took a little deal with the DA about a gas station robbery, suspended sentence deal. That served the DA's purposes of convicting me and staying out of trouble with my dad, who the DA didn't want to screw around with. Probably I couldn't have sold the tapes. It was sort of a personal thing, a private collection. I wasn't even interested in the women that much. They looked kind of shabby in their panty hose with the milky stains and the holes along the seams. They didn't look like anything you'd want to go down on. It was about stealing from them, getting what I wasn't supposed to get. That was worth it."

"This guy has your e-mail address?" I asked Jen.

"Well, sure. My name, but that's all. My number," she said. "You get to the panty hose?"

I nodded at her and went on reading. "My background is petty theft and liquor store holdups and the usual drug junk. Nothing much, really. After the video deal I came out here. Got a place on Automatic Avenue, this tiny road lined in white sand and wide enough for one car going one direction at one time. Four rooms, a kitchen, a little porch on the back. If you crane your neck and it isn't spring, you can see the big-city lights from the yard. Otherwise you have to walk the half block, but then you can see them pretty well. I got this woman named Sheba I picked up at a party some college kids had—she's thirty-two and just in from California or New York or both. She's cool, full of patter, does drugs, and walks around all the time like somebody's hit her with a two-by-four. But she's got no marks except in those eyes. I showed her videos of a couple little girls. Sheba likes the girls. She thinks they're cute, sexy. She doesn't want to do them, but they turn her on, thinking about them, looking at them. There are two, thirteen or fourteen, with tiny breasts, thin little legs, white skin. They giggle when they're in the dressing room together. The camera was high in this room, so the view is from above and you get a faint trace of pubic hair when they change. They hide from each other—they're very modest when they're together. Then they're in there alone, one at a time, their bright-green braces shining, glittering under the fluorescent lights. Sheba likes to freeze-frame on a bit where one girl hits model poses in the mirror. You can tell this girl is joking, but she's serious too. The poses are full of little wishes, dreams, ambitions. She's begging to be somebody. She's living in hope she might be somebody someday. She has some gold plastic ribbon she twirls and wraps around her head as if it's a crown. She holds imaginary flowers and takes bows as she accepts the Miss Nude Little Girl award. The video shows her from the back and in the mirror from the front. This is where Sheba always stops—"

Jen tugged at her computer. "C'mon, don't worry about it," she said. "Crazies are everywhere. Maybe he'll go away."

"Live in hope," I said, shoving the computer her way.

I couldn't go back to sleep. Jen was sitting up in her bed, typing on the notebook.

"What are you doing now?" I said.

"Downloading riot stuff from the *L.A. Times*," she said. "It'll cost a fortune, but maybe I can find something out about this Lopez guy. See, I get the feeling we've been living wrong. We've kind of been hiding out, and we need to get out a little more. All this world is going on out here and we watch it on television, but these people are living it."

"Who's living it?" I said. "O.J.'s living it—is that what you mean?"

"Everybody," she said.

"I'm supposed to believe that every five minutes some guys, you know, like, steal a car and drive across America, desperate with boredom, eager to kill."

"So we got a little problem in this country with authenticity," she said. "Let us have our fun."

"And they pick up a ruggedly handsome teenage hitchhiker babe at the 7-Eleven, right? Happens all the time?"

"Cool," she said.

"They steal some drugs, kill some people, the leader loses his best friend in the gunfight, and he and the babe end up happy on a beach."

"I can't help what we all want," Jen said.

"Yeah, me neither."

"Did you know that O.J. owned a chicken franchise that was burned down in the riots? It was burned down. He had two chicken franchises in L.A., and one of them was burned down by rioters. Did you know that?"

"No, I didn't know that," I said. I was groggy and had to sort of squint to get my eyes to focus. They were kind of watery, like there were water bubbles in them.

"I found four thousand six hundred fifty-two articles in the *L.A. Times* on the riots," Jen said. "That's just 1993. Out of those articles, only nine mention Fidel Lopez, the painted Guatemalan truck-driver. A hundred and twelve mention Damian Williams, whose whole name is Damian Something 'Football' Williams. He got ten years."

"I wouldn't worry so much about the riots. I mean, you know, they were riots," I said.

"This guy went over the top."

"He rioted too much?"

"He did grotesque stuff. Particularly ugly, the things he did."

"O.K., I agree. But wasn't there a problem proving him guilty?"

"There's always a trial. There's always a problem," she said. "He was plenty guilty."

"O.K., so he was guilty," I said. "But so were the Rodney King guys."

"Of course," she said. "So?"

"Anybody else? What time is it?" I said.

"Nearly three," she said.

"How long have you been on the phone?" I said.

"Twenty minutes," she said.

"You can look up anything in the *L.A. Times*?"

"Yep," she said. "Since 1985. Or the *New York Times,* the *Philadelphia Inquirer,* the *Chicago Tribune.* It's all out here."

"Have you read any of it?"

"Just bits. I'm downloading."

"So are you going to do a special issue of *Blood & Slime*?"

"No. I don't want to just reissue stuff," she said. "Unless we start up a bunch of people to go out there and do something. I sent some stuff to that Durrell."

"That's crazy." I looked at her in the next bed. In the pale-yellow T-shirt, she looked five years younger than she was. "You sent this Lopez stuff to him?"

"Yeah. I was sending it to other people, to some regulars, and just sent it to him, too."

I flexed my feet, stretching the toes down, then back up toward my shins. "Register my exception," I said. "It's nuts. Or maybe it's O.K., I don't know. Are you going to sleep now?"

"No. I'm planning my attack," Jen said. "I want to go out there, you know? Florence and Normandie. I want to go to O.J.'s house and where Rodney King got it."

"What good's that?"

Jen leaned back against the headboard. "If we're not actually going to participate in the world, if we're not going to do anything but watch it, then we might as well be good spectators. We might as well buy the best tickets, stand in the lines, get our pictures taken in front of historic sites. I'd like to see where Nicole was resting in a pool of blood. I'd like to see Ross Cutlery—did you know that Sebastian in *Blade Runner* lived in the Bradbury Building, which is where Ross Cutlery is?"

"No, I didn't."

"Yes," she said. "We need to do something. We can't sit here and watch it on television anymore. I can't take that."

"What about the broadsides and the posters?" I said. "The stuff you're putting out on bulletin boards? Isn't that enough?"

"It's something, but not enough. There's something about being there physically. Like occupying the physical space. I think we have to go," she said.

"I told you I'm ready."

"I don't know what Dad is going to say."

"He already thinks we're crazy," I said. "He thinks you're crazy for being with me and I'm crazy for acting like I'm thirty. I mean, I think I'm crazy, too. I watch him, though, look around here, wonder why I don't have a perfectly manicured house on a perfectly manicured lawn in a perfectly manicured subdivision. He's retired, for God's sake, and I haven't even started, and he's only six years older than me. I have a feeling that he has a point."

There was a knock at the door, then the door squeaked open a little bit and Mike poked his face into the crack.

"You still awake?" he said.

"Yes," Jen said.

"I was asleep, but I woke up," I said.

"What are you two doing?" he said.

"Jen's searching the computer for information about the L.A. riots," I said.

"At this hour?" he said.

"What's wrong with this hour?" Jen said.

"Yeah," I said.

"Well, I guess nothing," he said. "I just wanted to check on you. I saw the light under the door."

"We're doing fine," Jen said.

"You doing all right, Del?" Mike said.

"I'm doing fine," I said.

"Well, you kids go on to sleep. No, don't go to sleep. Stay up and get that L.A. riot thing straightened out. When was that? I can never remember. Was that ninety-two? Ninety-three?"

"Two," Jen said. "Right after the Rodney King verdict."

"Oh, yeah. I remember it now. I watched it on TV for a couple of days. They're always having big shows out there in California, aren't they?" he said. "If it's not a riot, it's a beating; if it's not a beating, it's a fire burning a bunch of houses down, or an earthquake. They're living on the edge out there."

Jen and I said good night as Mike closed the door. Jen looked at me as if I was supposed to tell her something.

"What?" I said.

"What's all that about?" Jen said.

"Oh, you know. He talked to me—gave me that talking-to."

"So?"

"I told you already. He wants me to get out of your way and so on," I said. "He probably feels guilty."

"What else did he say to you?"

"I don't remember. I wasn't really listening," I said. "I was sort of listening. I was listening enough to respond, but I wasn't really, really listening."

"I'm going to talk to him."

"Don't talk to him. Please God, Jen, leave him alone. He's an old man, he's about fifty years older than me. Just leave him alone. He's doing fine. He hasn't hurt anything," I said.

"I think I need to talk to him," she said.

"Get the riot stuff and forget him. I'm going back to sleep. O.K.?"

"Do what you want," she said.

# four

When I came down in the morning, Jen and her father were sitting on the terrace together, drinking coffee, looking at a tiny fountain in the backyard. It was made of concrete, an angel spitting water into a disk the size of a pie plate, which overflowed into a small pool. Sort of a parody, I suppose, of fountains, or maybe just a reminiscence, a trace fondness for the great moment of fountains in history. There it was in the backyard, standing about a foot and a half tall, spitting water into a sunken pool the size of half a bathtub. It was made of concrete and lined with bricks. I tapped on the glass door and waved at Jen. Mike turned around and waved, too, and motioned for me to come out. I pointed to the kitchen and indicated that I'd be out in a minute. Then I went into the kitchen to see what there was to eat. What there was was Eggos. He had a freezer full of Eggos. Blueberry Eggos, home-style Eggos, mini Eggos, strawberry Eggos, low-fat Eggos. It looked like Mike had been shopping at Sam's. I took a couple of waffles out and popped them into the toaster. I couldn't find any syrup, so I had to go outside and ask where the syrup was.

"Refrigerator," Mike said. "On the right. Watch it—it sticks."

I went back in. My Eggos had popped up, but they weren't cooked, so I punched them down again and cranked the toaster up higher. I found the Log Cabin Lite in the refrigerator, ran the hot water over the bottle to clean it, got a plate out of the cabinet, poured myself a glass of orange juice from the carton in the refrigerator. When my Eggos popped up, they were burned around the edges. I cut that part off and poured some syrup over them. I stood in the kitchen looking out the window into the garage, at Mike's Lincoln Town Car. It was a couple of years old, maybe a 1991, maybe 1992; I didn't really know. Real squarish. It was black, with a gray leather interior. The Euro-Mafia look.

I finished my Eggos, rinsed the plate, rinsed the juice glass, left them both in the sink. They were the only dishes there, and I thought about putting them in the dishwasher but decided that would be wrong. I get nervous dealing with other people's appliances. Maybe the dishes in the washer were clean, or maybe certain dishes didn't want to go in the washer—that sort of thing.

We'd called Bud the day we arrived, so he knew where we were. He didn't know how long we were staying. I thought I ought to call and tell him something, but I didn't know how serious Jen was about California. I decided to wait. I went outside and unstacked a chair, put it next to Jen's chair, and sat down, taking the *USA Today* off her lap. The headlines were all Simpson.

"It's a thing he did in a narcissistic rage," Jen said. "It's a typical thing for people in narcissistic rages to do. Fits the pattern to a T. Everything we know about him points to this."

"I thought you were finding him innocent until proven guilty. That was yesterday, wasn't it?"

"I've grown up since then," she said. "He's guilty. I know he's guilty. I don't want him to be guilty, but he's guilty. Still, for the good of the nation, he must be acquitted. It's this color thing—America without color. That's what makes me want him to be not guilty. A beyond-color thing. All these articles are saying that O.J. is beyond color and that's why we all want him to be innocent."

"I don't want him to be innocent," Mike said.

"You don't want him to be guilty, either, do you?" Jen said.

"No," he said. "I guess I don't care whether he's innocent or guilty. Somebody's gotta be guilty."

"You mean you care about the people who were killed?" I said.

"Maybe yes, maybe no. I don't know," he said. "It's hard to really care about people who get killed. I read about people getting killed every day—it's in the paper or on television—and I don't feel anything about them," Mike said. "It's a grotesque country, a grotesque time, and all that, but as for *feeling* anything, I don't know. Not really." He swatted at a fly that was buzzing around his ear. "I guess I'm grateful it's not me."

"We're all grateful it's not you, Dad," Jen said. She turned to me and said, "Listen. He wants to go with us."

"With us?" I said.

She pointed to her father. "He wants to go with us to see about Damian Williams and Lopez. That show's coming on A&E again this morning, and I'm taping it."

"He wants to go?" I said.

Mike looked odd, embarrassed. "Well, I thought I would drive out there with you. We could go in my car, if you wanted to. I could fly back or something if I got tired, and you could take the car on."

"He wants to go to Dallas and see Dealey Plaza," Jen said. "The Texas School Book Depository."

"You want to see the Texas School Book Depository?" I said.

"I've never seen it," Mike said.

"We could go through Dallas," I said. "You want to stop there?" I was directing this question at Jen, who was fishing in her coffee for something. She didn't seem to recognize that I was asking her a question until I poked her in the arm.

"Me?" she said. "Sure. I want to go. I'm going. We're going. We're going tomorrow."

"No we aren't," I said.

"Yeah, that's what we were thinking," Mike said. "We'll just pack up and go. Pack up tonight, and just like that we're driving."

"Yeah, I think it's important that we do that," Jen said. "It's important for us to take a stand."

"A stand?" I said.

"We need to get involved, you know, in the culture. Right now, what we need to do, you and me," Jen said, "is go out to L.A. and get involved in the Damian Williams slash Lopez deal, and we need to get that straightened away. We need to demonstrate that certain behavior is not acceptable in our civilization."

"Painting Lopez?"

"You got it," she said. "Beating a guy up in a riot is expected and O.K., but painting his dick is over the line."

"Please," Mike said.

"Did they prove that?" I said.

"What, that he did it?" she said. "They sort of proved it. Some of the stuff I got last night off CompuServe said so."

"Painting the guy's genitals is more horrible than killing him," Mike said. "Theoretically, anyway. Spiritually. Something like that."

"It's more dramatic," I said.

"It's calculated. It *is* dramatic, but it's too well calculated to be only that. There's something defiant and safe and vulgar and deeply degrading, all at the same time, and that's what makes it worse," Jen said.

"It's real evil," I said.

"Yep," she said.

"Pure ugliness," Mike said.

"Nah," I said. "It's dumb. Dumbness."

"Fine," Jen said. "Whatever. But we're going tomorrow, O.K.? And Dad is going with us, at least to Dallas. We'll stop in Shreveport and see if Penny wants to go."

"Have you talked to Penny already?" I said.

"Yes. I called her," Jen said.

"She didn't say she wanted to go?" I said.

"No. She said she wanted to think about it," Jen said. "She works and has to get time off."

"What about Arlene?" I said.

"Arlene has plenty to do here without me. Anyway, I'm a mercy case for her," Mike said. "And she never was an assassination gal. I always liked the assassination, because, well, it's just interesting. It's exciting and historical. It seems historical, anyway. Know what I mean? This thing happens, and one side is busy saying it's this one loopy guy, and everybody else is saying it's CIA, a conspiracy, Castro—the whole business. It's exciting. It's like a movie."

"It was a movie," I said.

"I know that," he said.

"Kevin Costner's great performance," Jen said.

"Oh, leave Kevin alone," I said. "He's a nice guy. He did all right in that Navy movie, whatever it was. And the bodyguard movie. There's nothing wrong with him."

"Robin Hood," Jen said.

"Sure—well, who cares?" I said.

We were staring out across the backyard, which was only about fifty feet deep. We were staring across a perfectly trimmed lay of grass. It wasn't ordinary grass, either. It was golf grass. Real thing, small stuff. Not just green-colored, but fairway green, whatever that grass is called. It's very odd when you see it in a domestic setting. It looks artificial and makes you feel like you're in some futuristic world. I thought I was in a futuristic world even before I saw the grass, and now there was no doubt about it. We were on our way to L.A. to avenge the slight against Fidel Lopez. We had a mission.

"I think if we're going to do this, we ought to get us some masked outfits," I said. "Some capes and stuff."

"That's cute," Jen said. "I like to hear that out of my friend Del. Our love grows deeper every moment."

"C'mon, Jen," I said. "I agreed to go."

"I was getting nasty," she said. "I know it."

"Oh, God. The know-yourself spiral being lived out in real time in our own personal lives, right here and now," I said.

"*That* was nasty," she said.

"I don't know about you guys, but I'm going around to the recreation center to see a couple of my pals," Mike said. "See if I can catch a bridge game. See what the talk is up there. Why don't you hack each other up here in the yard for a while and then come on over and take a swim?" He got up and left the terrace, walked right out of the backyard, turned left. We heard his feet dragging across the concrete as he walked toward the recreation center.

# Five

Bud called at four in the afternoon, wanting to find out how we were doing, how I was holding up under the Mike scrutiny. I told him I was doing fine, that Mike was more interesting than I had imagined.

"I'll bet," he said.

"No, I'm serious. He's strange," I said.

"I'll bet that's true," Bud said.

I told him that we were going out to Los Angeles, that Jen had decided it was our responsibility to take a more active role in the society.

"Now, that's a good idea," Bud said. "Are you taking explosives?"

"No. I think we're just going to drive out there and look around. Actually, her father is going with us as far as Dallas. He wants to see Dealey Plaza," I said.

"I've never seen Dealey Plaza," Bud said.

"Me neither."

"Well, you want to, don't you?"

"I don't know. Not really," I said. "I've seen it on TV. I've seen it in photographs."

"Yeah, but you haven't had the real experience," Bud said.

"I can probably live without the real experience," I said. "I find as I get older, Bud, that there are many real experiences I can live without. More than I would have thought possible to live without when I was a young man."

"I remember when I was a young man," Bud said. "I was about your age once."

"How's Margaret?" I said.

"She's doing fine. She's creeping through like the rest of us. She seems to be watching a lot of television during this time of crisis."

"The Simpson moment?"

"Yeah. She's stuck on it."

"You figure he did it?"

"Golly gee, I wonder," Bud said. "It was either him or Ralph Edwards."

"It makes me feel bad," I said. "He's got eight million dollars. I don't know why he had to go and do this. I mean, passion's great and everything, but . . ."

"That's a big amen," Bud said. "That's an amen *and* an amen. That's a Give me an amen. Money can't buy happiness. So how long are you gone?"

"I don't know. I think we're leaving tomorrow or the next day. We're going to Shreveport, then Dallas. We're taking his car."

"Mike's car?"

"Right," I said. "It's a Lincoln. We're going to roll out across the prairie in the lap of luxury."

"That'll be fun," Bud said.

"Anything at school?"

"No. Everybody's off," he said. "Some people are up there stealing summer salaries, but mostly it's empty."

"You been to the casinos?"

"Three hundred at the Grand," Bud said. "In an hour. I started playing blackjack, and I was winning all over the place—won eight hundred on one hand. Then it ran south."

"Are you bored, Bud?" I said. "You seem a little bored to me."

"Margaret went to the store," Bud said. "We're having shrimp for dinner. She went to get some shrimp."

"You haven't had our coworkers to dinner or anything? Done the responsible things an up-and-coming middle-aged professor does?"

"No," Bud said. "I'm dead. You're deader. Dead and Deader is who we are. They're so timid—have you noticed that? Our coworkers? Timidity is a tarantula upon the academy. Don't get me started."

"Oh, you love them," I said. "You're just afraid they don't love you. I see right through the pose."

"I'd forgotten," he said.

"You know the Lopez thing? Have you ever heard of this Lopez guy who got his cock painted black?"

"What?" Bud said.

"In the L.A. riots. Remember the riots in Los Angeles? Supposedly the same guy who beat up What's-his-name later beat up this guy Lopez and then painted his cock black. I saw it on television. It was nasty. Jen got all excited about it because it was so horrible. Now we're headed out to ground zero," I said.

"Florence and Normandie?" Bud said.

"Right," I said. "She wants to go there and see the world as others see it. She also wants to go to jail and see Williams. She wants to find Lopez. She's got a shopping list."

"By the time you get there, everybody will be dead, probably."

"She wants to go to Nicole's house. I don't know. We're just going to take a drive, I think. We're stopping in Shreveport. She wants to see somebody in Arizona or somewhere."

"You can go to the Grand Canyon," Bud said.

"I'll get you a postcard," I said.

"Walker Percy," he said.

"O.K. I'm glad we got that out of the way."

"If it turns out to be great, give me a call and we'll come on out. We can all sort of evolve together. Buy a lot of natural-colored clothes, eat right, change our lives and complexions."

"Have you got some kind of California problem?" I said. "You got a California thing going you need to worry about? Feeling fucked-over-by-California?"

"Well, maybe. Everybody's gorgeous. They're all dolls. You want to do stuff to them, put parts of your body in parts of their bodies. That's what California kind of is, right?"

"I don't know," I said. "I haven't been to California for years. I thought it was kind of an upscale mall."

"My experience, when I was most recently in California, which was a couple of years ago, as you'll recall—"

"That would be the famous film trip?"

"Right. That's right," he said. "When I was out packaging some properties and trying to put some people together. My own experience is that you begin to ejaculate when you enter the state and you don't finish until you leave."

"Yeah, thanks, Bud. Got to run," I said. "Got a call on line two."

"Wait a minute," Bud said. "I heard this joke today."

"O.K. What's the joke?"

"It goes like this," he said. "These two ducks are floating in a bathtub."

"Two ducks in a bathtub," I said.

"Right," he said. "The first duck says to the second duck, 'Can you pass me that square soap, the Dial soap, and the soap on a rope?' And the second duck looks at him and says, 'What do you think I am? Some kind of typewriter?' "

Bud laughed a lot. I listened to him laugh.

"I don't get it," I said.

"That's not funny," he said.

"O.K.," I said. "I'll call you tomorrow or sometime. I'll call you when we get on the road."

"You're on the road tomorrow?" he said. "Let me ask you this. Has this visit taken on macabre dimensions? Is there some suggestion of a problem here? Something that I don't quite get? Are there implications?"

I thought about that for a minute. I tried to picture Bud on the other end of the phone, sitting in his bed watching TV with the sound off, or sitting at his kitchen table reading the newspaper folded out flat, page by page, very carefully. Hunching over the left-hand page, then hunching over the middle of the paper, then hunching over the right-hand page.

"I don't know," I said. "Maybe. Sure. Yes. I like her pretty much."

"Good," Bud said. "Because we like her too. Margaret likes her. Now all we have to do is sell *you*."

"I've got to go. They're getting ready to serve dinner." I craned my neck and looked at the table and spotted a bowl of cooked carrots. "We got carrots," I said.

"That's good," Bud said. "See in the dark."

Mike's dining room was small. The walls were the color of some attractive weather-worn berry. The furniture was wood that shined too much, antiques, I guessed, expensive stuff, well taken care of and glossy. It looked a little Wal-Mart, which is a problem with old furniture that's too carefully restored. It has a way of getting on your nerves—inching its way into your consciousness, forcing itself upon you, asking for more attention than you want to give.

Along with the carrots, there was rice and gravy, and peas, and a roast Arlene had cooked and Mike had carved. It was family day. Mike and Arlene seemed happy serving food, passing plates, chatting—eating like parents.

Passing me a plate with two slices of beef, a discard pile of carrots, and a little mound of rice and gravy, Jen said, "What we need to do is go out and find him and kill him. Then we need to think of other people who need to be killed and find them and kill them."

"Great idea," Mike said. "Slice and dice. Who's choosing?"

"Me," Jen said. "It's hard. I don't know whether to start with Peter Jennings, or Rush Limbaugh, or Pat Buchanan, or that monkey-faced guy that ran the Clinton campaign, or some bad actors, or Damian 'Football' Williams."

"Hunters," I said.

"Hmm?"

"People who hunt things. Last week I saw turkey-killers. They were tricking some turkeys with this plastic decoy that moved its head, or they had a string connected to its head so the head moved when they yanked on the string, and then these other turkeys came around because this was so realistic to them, I guess, and there was this one stunning turkey with a huge array of feathers, tail feathers and big ruffles, strutting around—the best-looking turkey I've ever seen—and so there's this pastoral music going, and suddenly a shot rings out and the beautiful turkey flops over and these two dirt-eaters in fatigues rush over and do that holding-up-the-turkey-by-its-neck thing. So I think hunters should be high on the list of the to-be-exterminated."

"O.K. Cool. Hunters in general. Maybe so. But I still don't know where to start. If you were going to take people out because of the damage they do, where would *you* start?"

"Anywhere. Doesn't matter," I said. "You're a young person with a whole life before you."

"Yeah," she said. "Pass the salt."

I passed her the salt.

"I don't think killing's the way to go," Mike said. "Maybe we could crush legs or something."

"We could throw paint," Arlene said. "Like they used to do with the fur coats. That was a good idea. It was really damaging, but it didn't kill anybody."

"Not enough," Jen said. "I want to kill. I want to strike at the throat of the problem."

"Way to bang it home," Mike said.

"Name the problem," Arlene said.

"Yeah, I want to know that myself," I said, waving my empty fork at Arlene. "This is good meat, by the way."

"I don't know what the problem is," Jen said. "There's always some problem. Somebody doing something that they shouldn't be doing. Somebody thinking something or saying something or wising off or having some unearned opinion or jacking around with the facts, just to serve some particular pet rock they happen to have at that moment. Some idea they just read about in the newspaper or heard about on TV or figured out from something they heard at a club the night before. It's like the whole thing's going down, with pots and pans tied to its tail, and that's why I was doing the posters, the grotesque stuff, because I figured after a while maybe everybody would see that and understand it and somehow that would decrease the selfishness and self-centeredness, would make us a little bit more inclined to help someone else or be friendly in the supermarket or hold a door or pick up a package and carry it out to the car for somebody—anything. Any little thing to make us just a little more human. Instead of the routine clubbing, shooting, paralyzing and punishing and pain-inflicting crap we get every day on the television. But I guess that stuff's too much fun. We've got Damian 'Football' Williams and David 'Football' Letterman and Peter 'Football' Jennings and Hillary 'Football' Clinton—I mean, there's no escape. That's the whole thing. It's everywhere. This imbecile is out there beating people up, smacking Denny with a rock, which is bad enough, and then he turns around and paints this poor bastard Lopez's penis. You've got that, you've got eleven-year-old murderers, you've got body-eaters, you've got the triumph of the dumb, halt, and lame, no offense intended, you've got Robert 'Football' Hoover and friends, you've got every asshole in the country going after all the easy targets, you've got kids urinating in the faces of their victims, women screwing their sons' eleven-year-old friends in suburbia, people cutting off hands and stuffing them in glove compartments, you've got Marcia 'Football' Clark and Robert 'Football' Shapiro being real proud of trying to fuck each other over, and you've got Rudy 'Football' Nureyev, with a dick the size of Baltimore and about as many annual visitors, all of whom are chatting about it (not to speak poorly of the no-longer-with-us), and you've got a president sneaking his bitches onto the plane through the refrigerator truck, you've got malfeasance and malapropism and malefactors from coast to coast, wall to wall, and you've got the Larry 'Football' King show where he decides it's important to talk about the families of Dahmer's victims wanting to auction Jeffrey's head-refrigerator for a few hundred thousand bucks, and you've got the collectors bidding up these one-of-a-kinds, and you've got people jumping on dead men's backs to get their names in the paper, and you've got extra nicotine in the cigarettes, and people spitting in the food vats, and smirking guys with TV shows going around smirking at all the wrong people, all the easy pieces, and you've got random fatheadedness everywhere, the rule of the day, turn any direction, listen to anybody eager enough to get up and speak her mind, argue on television, write a cheap opinion, hold a position, righteously, earnestly—Jesus God, it won't ever end, will it?"

"It's a wonderful life," I said.

Mike nodded. We all nodded, the three of us.

"Well, you just have to see it to believe it," Jen said.

"Not a bad list," Mike said.

"No, it's good," Arlene said.

"You're not serious, you're not tough, unless you've seen it and you can stand it, accept it," Jen said. "It's a measure of your up-to-dateness, how much grim crap you can stomach. That's what's out there. That's the idea—push the edge, press the limits, buy in on pissing in a guy's face."

"I think you're getting a little wound up here, Jen," I said. "We're just having dinner. We're making this trip, so there's no reason to get crazy about it."

"There's every reason," she said. "It isn't just the trip. That's something to do because we don't know anything else to do. What are we going to do when we get there? We've got to do something. You've got to do something or else you're just part of the shit, part of the fucking landscape. I don't want to be that anymore. I listen to the guys on television, the news guys and the specialists and the commentators and the analysts and the C-SPAN people and the interviewees and the ex-government types and the mincing little anchors and the blustering officials and the PR-nightmare senators and congresspersons and the writers from the *Wall Street Journal* and *The Nation* and the *New Republic,* not to mention Bill 'Football' Buckley, and let me tell you, these persons are not that completely bright. These people are a few fins short of a tuna. Slower than slow, some of them."

"I'll take Things That Are Wrong, for two hundred," I said.

"What's that? Is that some kind of answer or something?"

"It means things have been screwed up for a long time," I said.

"They're getting worse," she said.

"We're working on it," I said. "We're heading out. We're accepting the challenge."

"There are limits, you know what I mean?" Jen said. "There are distinct, clear limits. Some shit I will not eat and all that. There are boundaries, and these people are beyond them. They're pumping out the crap."

Arlene said, "You should get yourself a job in television, a Voice of the People thing, rebutting the commentators or something. Start small and work your way up to writer, reporter, anchor, Chicago, Atlanta, Miami, and pretty soon you'll be up there with Peter and Dan and Connie and Bernard and good night Chet."

"I don't want to wait," Jen said. "Besides, only idiots listen to those people."

"You listen," I said.

"That's different," she said. "I listen and hate. Anyway, I want to do something else. I want to run the curve, be there when the police arrive."

"That's admirable," Mike said. He was wiping his mouth with a striped napkin.

The sun was coming in the dining room window, slanting in, rippling across the bowls of food on the table, across the faces of Mike and Jen, who were across the table from me, across the wall behind them. Everything was very pretty then, and I had the feeling that I wanted to stay there for a while, just sit there. Mike and Arlene were eager to please, decent, good, friendly people. At ease.

Jen wasn't. She was exactly ill at ease, committed to newspaper horror stories—bodies discovered, heads in the street, fish that bite off fingers. Now she was adding something. She wanted to repair, to change, to hope.

"I don't think I'm going to go," Mike said. "I think you kids should go."

"Yeah, us kids," Jen said.

"You know what I mean," he said. "I think you two should go and do what you want to do. We're finished, Arlene and me." He looked across the table. Arlene held out her hand for him, stretched it flat, from fingertip to elbow, against the tabletop. He took her hand, his arm arrayed about the same way. You could tell it was a gesture they had done lots of times, it was a thing they did. It was nice to see them in that room, the way they reassured each other by this contact, the way they agreed.

"Well, we can go," I said. "I'll be happy to go. It'll be good. We'll drive out. I drove out once before. It's a lot of driving. The desert is there."

"The Painted Desert," Jen said. "I'd like to see that."

"There's a lot out there I haven't seen. Maybe we could see some things on the way out."

"Yeah, that would break up the drive," Mike said. "But I don't want you to lose this feeling you have, this intensity, the eagerness to do something."

"You think I wasn't doing anything in Biloxi?" Jen said.

"No, I think you were doing great," Mike said. "I like what you're doing—the posters, *Blood & Slime* or whatever it was. I like that you sent it to me. I don't want you to stop doing that."

"It's junk," Jen said. "Lots of people do them. They're all different, of course. There's a lot on the Internet. A lot of e-zines. They're better than mine, some of them. There's a big festival of zine people out in Oregon someplace, but as soon as you let yours become part of a move, you're slag. Might as well quit and get a job in advert. All of us with our little individualities. I hate all of us."

"You've been doing it for years, haven't you?" Arlene said.

"Yeah, but that doesn't make any difference. There were some before me. I stole the idea from a woman who was making up a magazine about herself. She was nice. She came to my school. She was, like, putting out this monthly zine called *Dorothy* or something, in which her life was chronicled. It was interesting. I thought it was worth doing."

"Sometimes Jen talks like she went to art school," I said to Mike. "There's a bit of an art school problem, if you know what I mean."

Mike just laughed and put his arm on Jen's shoulder. "There are worse things," he said.

"Uh-oh," Jen said. "Here come the lawyer jokes."

"Not what I meant," Mike said.

She got up, started picking dishes off the table.

"Well, Del's a lucky man. Now, Del, do you want to clear, wash, or nap? State your preference. You're the guest; you get to choose."

"Take a nap," Arlene said, patting my arm.

"Clear the dishes," Jen said.

"Time's a-wasting," Mike said.

I picked nap, the cushy alternative. I liked taking naps at Mike's house—in fact, at anybody's house so long as it wasn't mine. Something about the right to privacy: you get in your room, close the door, get in bed, and nobody will bother you. They'll walk by the door, maybe even listen at it, but since they've been told you're taking a nap they'll leave you alone. They'll talk to each other, carry on with their business, watch television, read books, talk on the phone, but they'll stay clear as long as you're down. It's wonderful being in the room alone with the door closed and knowing no one will bother you, that even though they're right there—they might be just on the other side of the door—they won't bother you. That doesn't happen much in ordinary life.

So I got my nap, and then started downstairs, but I ran into Jen, who was coming upstairs with some folded clothes in one hand and the handheld TV in the other.

"What have you been doing?" I said, following her back to the bedroom.

"You mean besides washing?" she said.

"I just asked."

"I saw a program on Taiwanese child prostitution and a show on the manufacture of aluminum air-conditioning ducts in Germany during the sixties."

"Are you kidding?"

"No." She dropped the TV on the bed. "There's a lot of AIDS among these child prostitutes. They pray to these penis statues, these big, colorful penis statues, and they light candles and leave sacrifices and circle the statues with beads and pray to them. It's because they get their income from the penis. They use incense, the whole thing."

"This isn't the same thing as those people who think the penis is God, is it?" I said. "That God's a penis?"

"I don't think so," she said. "These are children who have a direct economic relationship with the penis."

"I see," I said. "So did you tape the riots?"

"Yeah. On Dad's system," she said. "I have carefully studied Lopez getting his genitals varnished. It's enough to make you sick."

"Anything will make you sick if you watch it over and over."

"Not like this," she said. "This is up there. This is worse than I thought. They're going to let the guy out of jail in about a year, you know, and he's going to be out there on the street, and do you think he'll be rejuvenated or whatever they call it?"

"Rehabilitated."

"Whatever," she said. "He's just going to spray-paint somebody else's genitals."

"You're pretty cynical for a young person," I said.

"I'm young but my concerns are global," she said. "That's why I was watching these programs in the laundry room, trying to inform myself of activity on a global basis, trying to understand the world. Then I started to watch the Japanese air-train show. It's so beautiful. It's one of my favorites—I've seen it three or four times. How they made this train that rides on air. It's a wonderful show."

"I've seen it."

"There isn't any show I'd rather see. I wish I had a copy."

"Get it from Journal Graphics," I said. "Are we taking the trip?"

"We're leaving in the morning, Del. It's raining now, raining here to Dallas, raining everywhere in the South."

"I like rain. It changes everything. It's magic."

"Duh," she said. "You know what I mean?"

"Yeah, I see what you mean. What are we going to do until we leave?"

"I don't know," she said. "Go to the store. You want to go to the store?"

"To buy things?" I said. "So we can wear them, drive them, advertise them? Everything an advertisement. We are ad machines."

"Who said that?" she said. "Mary Magdalene?"

Jen laughed and started putting away her tiny square-folded shirts in the suitcase she had open on the bed.

"I guess I could do with a computer store," I said. "Or an electronics store, or an office supply store. Those are the three kinds of stores I'll go to. You want to go to any of those?"

"Sure," she said. "All of them."

We started at a local computer store, a big discounter like CompUSA but with another name. All the people in there seemed peculiar, just off normal—wrong size, wrong color, wrong shape, wrong posture.

One guy had on big black corduroy shoes—they must have been sixteens or seventeens. Loafers that looked more like model cars. Another guy was so thin and pale that he looked like a chopstick with ink on top. There were gaudy women and greasy men, too much hair combed with combs with too-wide teeth, so that you got that Robert DeNiro hair like when Robert DeNiro was playing in the remake of that Robert Mitchum movie. People were sneezing all over the place as if it were the heart of allergy season. People are always sneezing in computer stores. You can't get away from it. They're coughing, and their shirts are buttoned wrong. There are kids in the game section with hats at every strange angle you can imagine, always playing the games ear-shatteringly loud, and if you had a bat you'd start smacking them like seals.

I like computer stores, but it's impossible to ignore the disease and slime that's always present. I saw a guy with a head the size of a bucket—the kind you put mops in. His face was big and jowly and squared off. *He* wasn't all that big, but the head was mammoth. The workers wore these red shirts with their names on them, and the shirts were stained, and they wore them tucked in, with their bellies busting over, and you could see their belly buttons through the shirts because the shirt fabric was gripping the skin so hard. And people were touching things, so it was a terrifying place. If you wanted to look at anything, you had to wipe it off before you could handle it, and you had to do it so people wouldn't see you doing it and think you were overreacting or anything just because you were trying to avoid the great germ chain. The people were not pretty. Money hadn't bought them looks. They were homely, draped in plaid and khaki, hairy in the wrong ways and places. Stuff discolored the fronts of their shirts. Still, you had to like them.

Jen caught my arm as we went down an aisle full of screen savers and graphics programs, paint programs, drawing programs, morphing programs, fractal programs. "They're having a big night here at Computer Hideaway. The dead have begun to walk," she said.

"That's nice," I said. "Did you catch Mountainhead over here?"

"Yeah, I did. And that's not nice," she said. "He has some kind of disease, some kind of proportional problem. Just look away."

"Great. Then I see the Boy With the Three-Foot Slobber."

"Just follow me and keep your eye out for a video capture board. I need something I can plug the TV into when I get home so I can get some visuals. I need more visuals. Also, I want to get a little more video-oriented. I want to expand my act. I'm setting up my own home page on the World Wide Web. You know what I mean? I'm tired of being the angry young woman dressed in black jeans, black halter under an open black shirt, high-top black boots," she said.

"You don't wear any of that stuff," I said.

"In my head I do. In my head it's what I'm wearing all the time."

"You and Jimmy Carter."

"Jimmy who?"

"See, this is the problem with you being eighteen or whatever."

"Don't start in," she said. "Come on."

"Jimmy Carter. Former president. He sinned in his heart—"

"Double duh," she said. "Like I haven't been awake the last twenty years."

"Sorry."

"I knew that." She looked at me. "Do you believe me? I knew that."

"Yes, I believe you," I said.

"You're sure you believe me? Because I knew that, I'd heard all about that," she said. "I've even read it."

"Yes, I believe you," I said.

"Shit," she said, hammering a 3DO box on a shelf in front of her. "You'll believe anything. That's what's wrong with you old people—you'll believe anything. I can tell you anything and you'll believe it. Didn't you guys ever learn how to lie when you were growing up? Just say it and don't give it away. That's how you do it. I guess you don't know how to do that, do you?"

"No, I don't."

"Well, that's too bad for you, then, isn't it?"

"Well, I guess it is," I said.

"It limits you," she said.

"Did you have another nap?"

We had come back from the computer store, and I had stretched out on the bed and fallen asleep.

"I had a bad dream," I said, covering my eyes with my wrists. "There were these two dead people, and they were chasing me around, and one was my cousin, but they weren't really dead. They were supposed to be dead on television, and I was watching television, but the police didn't come to clean them up, and then they were chasing me around. I was talking to you on the telephone, but I wasn't really talking to you because I couldn't hear you. I mean, I could hear you, but I couldn't talk to you because you were talking to someone else, that guy from the Band. He was in a telephone booth and I could hear your conversation with him, and these bodies were kind of floating around, and first they were on the television, then it was three or four days since they had died and they were in my room or something, and then I kind of noticed out of the corner of my eye that one of the bodies had moved, and I knew they were alive, but I didn't want them to know that I knew they were alive, so I pretended not to look, and then they were creeping around my bed and creeping under my bedside table."

"Is that true? Is that what you dreamed, really?" she said.

"No," I said. "You're so gullible."

"It's an anxiety dream," she said. "Or maybe you probably ate too much."

"I ate too much," I said. "It was the carrots. The carrots made me dream this, this torture chamber, this scene of blood pooling, of flaps of flesh hanging over tables, of severed arteries and organs ripped from the bodies. A splashfest."

"Oh, give it up, will you," she said. "It's HBO."

"I made it up," I said. "Forgive me." I got out of bed and down on my knees by her side, tugging at her shirttail. "Please forgive me, Jen. It's a terrible thing I've done. I'm an old person. I'm doing the best I can. You are young and beautiful. You are all-knowing and all-powerful, you have the knowledge, you have the hope, you have ourselves in the palms of your hands. We are yours to do with what you will. We are empty vessels. We are over, we are over, we are over."

"You're over, all right," she said. "Get up. Quit it. Quit pulling on me. Leave me alone."

"I'm pulling in a good way."

"It's impossible for a fifty-year-old to be pulling on me in a good way," she said. "Quit it. Quit."

"I want you to have and to hold."

"Go hold your own self," she said. "I've got packing to do."

"I've got packing to do, too," I said.

"Well, get up off the floor and do it."

"I don't want to do it."

"You shouldn't nap," she said. "Afterwards you always exhibit inappropriate behaviors."

I got up off the floor and sat on the edge of my bed. "I'm wondering what might be appropriate behaviors for a man of my age and achievement."

"Incontinence," she said.

I leaned back and put a foot at the base of her spine. "You don't mean that."

"No, I guess I don't," she said. "I mean, like, no, I really don't. Incontinence would not be appropriate. There's a clean toilet right in there. Bristling with clear and colored enzymes to break your urine down into wonderful, much-needed chemicals for our area."

"In the Far East they sometimes cook with urine," I said. "Did you know that? I read that in a book. Mongolia or someplace."

"I don't think Mongolia is the Far East," she said.

"How did I turn out to be nearly fifty years old, with this chump job at a junior college, and your father is retired at fifty-three with hundreds of thousands of dollars in the bank?"

"Get over it. I've got big aims for both of us. I've got global concerns. I'm working on an international level."

"I don't take aims seriously," I said. "That's the problem. I decided what there was to aim at wasn't worth aiming at."

"That's you and your group, your generation," she said. "Me and my group, we're headed for the top. We're going through the door. We're reaching for the brass ring. We're pulling out all the stops."

"You're cooking with urine," I said.

"Amen," she said. "You got it."

"I feel terrible when I see your father," I said. "He's a nice guy and everything, but it's like we're the same age."

"Six years."

"Well, it makes me feel terrible to be around him, anyway. He seems old enough to be *my* father."

"You were the original slacker," she said. "Is that it?"

"Not," I said.

"What are you, then?" she said.

"I don't know, but not that. Never mind, anyway," I said. "I just wanted to tell you about your father and how he makes me feel."

"He makes you feel bad."

"Yes."

Jen stopped what she was doing and turned to sit on the side of her bed, facing me. The skin of her legs, of her thighs, was so smooth and unblemished and unmarked and delicate that she suddenly seemed like a thirteen-year-old. I reached across the space between the beds and put my hands on the tops of her thighs. I pulled my hands down toward her knees. The skin was cool and felt a tiny bit slick. I got down on my knees again.

# six

We got to Natchez at four the next afternoon. Jen did the driving while Mike talked about the sixties, about people he'd run into in California traveling with some band deeply engaged with indeterminacy and Cage. He couldn't play, but he could scratch and make noise, so that's what he did with the band. They played festivals and clubs in Venice and Berkeley, and audiences weren't too receptive. The band's message was a little too off-center for the time, too much aggression, too much screeching guitar, too much random shit. Mike said they had a select audience.

"You failed tribal synthesis?" I said.

"Apparently," he said. "We were making a new world and they weren't. I think we were seen as hostile to the brand-new social order. Maybe we were, I don't know. I don't remember much except this one woman who was real tall and blond."

"Go, Daddy, go," Jen said.

This talk gave me another view of Mike—a little guy who had

once been ahead of the game. On point for the revelation generation. A prophet. At least *in* the game. That was odd to think about.

The hotel was a seven-story building with plenty of rooms facing the Mississippi River, which was about four blocks away. Jen and I took a room on the top floor, and Mike took the one next to ours. These were the eighty-five-dollar cream-of-the-crop rooms, small, with high ceilings. The bedroom had an alcove beyond it, and off the alcove were French doors that opened onto a balcony where you could sit and watch the river go by. On the other side of the river was the town of Vidalia.

"Onion country," Mike said, pointing across the river. "They're all from right there if they're Vidalias."

"I think that's Georgia, Dad."

That night we drove down to the gambling boat, an old paddle wheeler that had been re-garished right up to the gills. Natchez wasn't like Biloxi, where we had fifteen or twenty casinos; Natchez had one casino, this crowded boat. We had to wait to get on. While we waited an otter swam by in the river. Everybody got real excited about this otter and started running back and forth, sort of following it upriver. One of the security guys started telling the crowd a lot of otter stories.

When our number was called and we got inside, the place was chockablock with toothy people, people who were waving their whiskey around in Styrofoam cups. People with two-day beards, women in extremely tight, satiny dresses. Lots of noise. The constant chink-a-chink-a-chink of winning slot machine plays, the occasional yelp of a successful card or roulette player. We twisted through the big room. The paddle wheeler had been gutted so they could get the maximum floor space available for slots and a few tables, and there weren't any traffic patterns that didn't involve rubbing other people. We found a change person, a two-hundred-pound woman.

"You got some good machines tonight?" Mike asked the woman.

She kept diving into her cart for rolls of dollar tokens. Then, when she looked up, she pointed off in the direction she was facing. "People doing O.K. yonder," she said. "There's a Haywire machine might do you some good."

We followed her directions and headed for a bank of progressive machines against the wall.

"Bitch," Jen said. "If she was on her back she'd have pointed at the ceiling."

"I know," Mike said. "But it doesn't hurt to try, and it makes everybody feel better, like we've all got roles to play in the game."

The machines took our money quick, so we were back changing bills into tokens within minutes. Jen and I headed up toward the other end of the boat, past a line of five-dollar slots behind a brass rail. We watched for a while. I went and changed a hundred into twenty five-dollar coins and pumped those, one after another, into one of the machines. The guy next to me had a tray full of coins and two hundred forty-eight credits on the machine, so he was doing all right. I wondered if he was a plant. He and his girlfriend occupied two stools and had a lot of attitude because they were so successful. The way they moved was disgusting, and it was worse as I put five after five into my machine and watched the wheels come up unmatched. This guy was almost swaggering, the way he had his foot cocked out on the rail one minute and the next minute was turned around with one foot on either side of the slot machine, punching the button, playing three fives at a time, losing some, but winning way too much. His girlfriend played less and was less offensive, but she won too. After I'd gone through the first hundred and gotten my second, I was pissed.

"How long you guys been here?" I said to the girl.

She looked at me like I'd smacked her with something. She leaned back and let the guy look across her chest at me. "What'd you say?" he said to me.

"I asked how long you'd been here," I said.

"We've been here awhile," he said. "Why do you want to know?"

"Just wondering," I said. "Any of these others paying off?" I waved at the other slots.

"I don't know what any of the other machines are doing," he said. "These are our machines." He tapped his machine and her machine, one after the other, with a couple of five-dollar coins he had in his hand.

"You going to play awhile?" I said.

"We may do," he said.

I dropped the last three coins I had into my machine and punched the button, standing up to leave even before the wheels stopped. "Well, if you're going soon, I'd like to know," I said.

"I don't think we're leaving," he said.

All this time the girl had been looking back and forth between him and me, not saying a word, just following the conversation. She was timid. When he told me he didn't think they were leaving, she looked at me and smiled like I was some kind of jackass.

"Swell meeting you," I said to her.

Jen and I went to the back, where they were playing quarter slots and video poker. She slipped a ten-dollar bill into one of the machines, took the change in credits, and started spinning. She did all right. She won fifty coins, then eighty coins doubled. We got drinks from the waitress and sat in our swivel chairs in front of these machines. I put a coin into my machine so nobody would bother me.

We'd been in the quarter section maybe a half hour when Mike came up carrying two buckets of dollar coins, each one full. He dropped them down on the flat part of Jen's machine.

"Big success," he said.

"You're a gambling fool," I said. "What have you got there?"

"I don't know," he said. "I won a couple hundred-dollar jackpots, one two-fifty, then I played it down some."

"You ready to cash out?" Jen said.

"I don't know," he said.

"We're down two and a half," she said.

"How'd you do that?"

"Five-dollar slots. Lose fast, lose big."

"There's this annoying guy over there, winning," I said. "He and his girlfriend need to be shot. We need to hire somebody to shoot them. We also need to hire somebody to take their money away from them when they leave."

"Great," Mike said. "You ready to go back to the hotel?"

"No. We want to stay here and lose more," I said. "We haven't lost upstairs yet. Maybe we should go upstairs."

"Del is having an attitude," Jen said.

"He's fatalistic," Mike said.

"This place stinks and sucks," I said. "And these people are virus-bearers."

"He *is* in a bad mood," Mike said.

"He's not a good loser," Jen said.

"It's not easy to lose," Mike said. He shoved one of the buckets of dollars toward me. "Why don't you try this? Maybe it'll turn your luck around."

I pushed the bucket back at him. "Nope. I'll take your daughter but not your money. Besides, I'd just dump it."

"It's all winnings, anyway," Mike said.

"Don't rub it in," Jen said.

"I didn't mean to rub it in," Mike said. "I was just—"

"I know," Jen said, eyeing me. "But in this mood, no matter what you do it's rubbing it in."

"You buy that, Del?" Mike said.

"Nope," I said. "Miss Daughter's a little sensitive."

The three of us started for the exit. Mike stopped at the cashier to have his coins counted, and Jen and I stood behind one of the blackjack tables, watching a guy with a wad of hundred-dollar bills the size of his fist play some blackjack for himself and his girlfriend, who was sitting about three-quarters in his lap. He refused to buy chips. When he won he put the chips aside and just put hundred-dollar bills down, one after another. I watched him play. He was good—he knew what to hit and what not to hit, when to double down; he played by the book. I had read the book because I had a blackjack-player career fantasy for about a week when the casinos first came to Biloxi. Then I played and lost.

Mike came up behind us, and we started to leave, then there was a lot of screaming behind us, and we turned around to see a giant African-American woman yelling because she had just hit a big jackpot on a dollar slot. A couple of dwarfs were playing blackjack together at one of the back tables. People were limping around. There was a lot of hair tonic in evidence.

Mike had to go to the bathroom, so we stopped again, near the exit, and watched the players. They were a messy lot, but all of them were eager—laughing, excited, having fun.

I was happy for them, even if they were downtrodden, underprivileged, poverty-stricken, empty-headed, too drunk, and barely dressed. I wanted them all to win. I wanted each and every one to walk away with doubled, tripled, quadrupled money, each one to take what he or she wanted from each game. I hated the casino. It counted on hate to make losers, win-at-any-cost guys, big money or small, didn't matter. I was glad I was gone, but I hoped the sad-looking people trailing in, with shirttails half out, food on their lapels, hair plastered back, eager grins on their faces, would beat this particular casino, would take it for everything it was worth. It wouldn't happen, but I could dream. The sadder-looking the player, the more I hoped he or she would win. The only ones I didn't like were the ones that came in with confidence.

In the hotel, Jen cleaned up and got into bed. I sat up in the bed next to her and finished a beer that I'd started earlier when we checked in. It was room-temperature tasty. The TV was on, with another murder special, but we weren't watching. I went out and stood on the balcony for a few minutes, in the cool late-night air, watched the lights shimmer out over the river, the lights on the bridge that crossed over to Vidalia, the lights along the shores on both sides. The hotel was the tallest building in Natchez, and there weren't any other tall buildings between us and the river, so the sky was a clear, dark dome, pinpointed with stars. All of them were visible. We were in the middle of summer, but it was a cool night. There was a breeze seven floors up. The river made a little noise, a kind of quiet hum in the background. I turned off the light in the alcove between the bedroom and the balcony and stood out there, leaning on the railing.

Jen came out and stood behind me. "Stay there," she said. "I can be out here if you're between me and the edge." So I stayed and let her wrap her arms around me, and we stood there a few minutes together, watching the river go by.

I was pissed about losing, but being out on the high balcony, staring at the rustling water, the bridge, the lights, the night, seemed to help. Occasionally there would be some movement directly below us in the parking lot, and I would look down at a bellhop coming out of the building, going to a car, carrying something inside. Mostly, though, we just faced the west, where we were going, and let ourselves be touched by the air.

Jen patted my shoulder and said she was going to look at her e-mail. She left me outside. I didn't stay long. In a few minutes I shut the doors and sat down in the alcove in the leather chair that was there and turned on the reading light. Mike called from next door to see if we were all set. Jen got the phone and told him that we were and not to call again, because she was hooking up to CompuServe.

I was thinking that I ought to act more like Mike, be like Mike. I was almost fifty, why wasn't I? Why did I have a dinky job at Dinky College, making barely enough to live on? Why was I just starting and he was already retiring? I'd always wanted to be one of the successful people—good-looking guy and his good-looking wife, their good-looking children, pulling into a parking lot in good-looking casual clothes, all carefully pressed, all carefully arranged. Their good-looking car shining like there's no tomorrow. Usually a dark color, British racing green or dark blue or even black. The whole picture just *well-to-do*. They carefully get out of the car, the kids are orderly, the mother and father are in that time-stopped world of thirty-to-fifty, still perfectly trim and handsome. They look good together. These are not young people, but not old. In their yards when you drive through subdivisions they are standing together by a flower bed. The wife always has work gloves on, even a work outfit. She's counseling with her husband about the placement of some flowers. Elsewhere some hired Hispanics are scraping the pine straw or pine cones away from the yard, or using one of those leaf blowers to clean off a serpentine brick walk. These people are too happy, too successful, too clean, too orderly. Still, I envy them.

"After the trial, Lopez said he just wanted to put this thing behind him and go on with his life," Jen says. "He's not mad at anybody, he doesn't blame anybody for what happened. He thinks it's O.K."

"He's a weenie," I said. "He's afraid of saying the wrong thing. He doesn't want to say what he really thinks. He's rising to the occasion. His lawyer told him to say that. He knows what's good for him."

"You mean he said that so they'd put him on TV?" she said.

"That's it. What good's thinking something if you can't get it on TV? We all want to be on TV, don't we?"

"I'd like to know how he got that Krylon off his balls. I'll bet he didn't want to forget it then."

"They did it at the hospital. Anyway, leave him alone. He's doing his best."

"Makes it hard for me to want to go club Damian Williams," she said. "Takes the wind out of my sails."

"I thought you were operating on principle."

"Well, yeah, I guess I am."

"So it doesn't matter what he thinks," I said. "It only matters what you think."

"Right. And I think it was repulsive," she said. "I think it was apelike."

"Careful there," I said. "You don't want to go into racist affect."

"I am not a racist," she said, doing Nixon. "But in this case the ape is black. It's not racist. If he were white, he'd be a white ape."

"You don't want to use apes."

"What do you want me to use?"

"Something else, something less stereotyped, less obviously connected, less dehumanizing."

"Oh, Jesus," she said. "You've been watching too much TV. I can say ape if I want to. It's not racist to say that the guy acted like an ape. He was an ape. He's subhuman, an ape."

"O.K. You can say ape if you want to," I said. "Don't say it too loud, and don't say it in public."

"I'm going to say it from the tallest tree," she said. "And I'm going to make sure you're standing right there under the tree."

"Thanks, Jen," I said.

"Mince, mince, mince," she said. "Aren't we the careful little somebody. You should be watching ESPN2, shouldn't you? The *deuce*."

"Now, there," I said, "is a horrible thought. Even I, in the flower of my youth, recognize that as a terrifying thought. Jock hip. It's grisly. Why don't you do an exposé? Get some stuff from the services, the bulletin boards, render an opinion, put something on the Internet. Why not start alt.sports.revolting? I mean, ESPN2 as the center of the cultural problem—it's just a little bit ahead of the curve. It'll be mainstream tomorrow."

"That's too terrifying," Jen said.

"Maybe it already is," I said. "Here I am hanging onto you for dear life, just trying to follow your group, and you're thumbing your nose at it. You're supposed to be right in the middle of the bun. Right in the middle of the bun of your generation. You're supposed to be the frankfurter in the bun of your generation."

Jen looked across the hotel room. "Thanks," she said. "I think maybe I'll shut it down for tonight." She reached over the lampshade to switch off the bedside light, and when she clicked it the room was in darkness, the only light filtering up from the streets below.

My eyes adjusted, and things became edges, corners, bits and pieces of what they were. In the dark, the room was a three-dimensional line drawing, a schematic of itself. I listened to Jen smack the pillows into shape.

Then she said, "I wish there was a way to kill without penalty. A hunting season for jerks. Or some way to shoot them into space. Something."

I opened the French doors and pulled my chair around into the door so it was partway out on the balcony. A small storm had come up, and cars were steaming by on the road alongside the river. I got a lot of Doppler as they came up on one side, crossed directly in front of me, went off in the other direction. There was rolling thunder off in the distance and the click of raindrops all around me on the balcony, on the balcony roof. Birds were chirping nearby, and doves were cooing in the distance. There were a few crickets. The cars, by the sound, were going fast. But when I looked down, they weren't fast at all. Thunder cracked way off to the right, then rolled across the western sky, crossing in front of me the same way the cars did, but the thunder was going away too, so that eventually it was just muffled drumming. When it cracked, it would echo backward, left to right. Spits of lightning went jagging across the sky, some of them bright and pretty, some hidden like lightbulbs behind black-painted lampshades. As the rain got steadier, it splattered on the balcony and kicked up on my feet, ricocheting into the room. I went back into the bathroom and got a towel to put in front of the French doors. When I put the towel down, I pulled my chair a little inside the doors. A bird screeched somewhere in the distance, then a foghorn sounded on the river, then there was a clanging sound, then just rain again. Across the river in Vidalia, there was a sprinkling of lights, a few right down along the river in a cluster and then back along the bridge, where the highway from Natchez cut across. The sound of the rain made me cold, brought up goose bumps. Down by the river, a train chugged along, slow and determined like all the nighttime freights. I listened carefully to its squeaking, the restless sway of the cars as they settled on the tracks, the way they bumped and tugged at each other. From behind me I heard Jen say, "Are you O.K.?"

"Yeah," I said. "I thought you were sleeping."

"I am," she said.

I listened to more cars and birds and rain and dogs barking in the distance. "Mike hates me," I said.

"Don't be silly," Jen said.

"He figures I'm a deadbeat," I said. "Figures I'm an Earth Shoe guy caught in the past."

"You never wore Earth Shoes, did you?"

"I don't remember," I said. "Maybe."

"I don't think so," Jen said. "You'd remember. And if you did, I'm leaving you."

"I didn't," I said. "But I envy your father. He's so sensible. He had a wife, children—you. Even your brother who got killed."

"That was a lot of fun for all of us."

"I know. But I never had anything big like that happen, so I never felt that stuff. I mean, some kids I knew got killed, or killed themselves, but they weren't much to me. A few relatives died in the ordinary course of things. Some guys I knew in high school were killed in the Army, but I didn't like them that much, anyway. In a sense, I've had an easy life, but in another way it's a punishment, an absence of grand events."

"Poor baby," Jen said.

"Maybe that's what Mike has over me. Maybe that's why he's older and settled and satisfied with his life, and I'm still living like a kid, always seeing sombreros in the trees."

"What?"

"Never mind."

I wondered if it would be more satisfying to be Jen's father than her lover. I caught myself and thought that was a strange thing to be thinking. Maybe a too-strange thing. Something that didn't bode well. It put me too far away, a little off the emotional page. Maybe I didn't think it, anyway, not really, maybe it was just something that flew through the brain there for a minute. Something academic, just following a thought path, not connected to experience. I felt something about Mike, though, and it was close to envy. He lived in a way that was silly, but a way I still wanted to live. Tidy. Complete. Finished. Withdrawn. Out of the contest. Some people get there as early as their mid-twenties. He must have been one of them. Or maybe I had an idealized sense of how simple his life was, how content he was with it, how orderly it was. Maybe it wasn't orderly at all. Maybe it just looked orderly. Maybe his life, from where he sat, was a screaming mess, as fragmented and disjointed and hopeless and dingy as mine. Just carried out on crisp sheets and with perfect chests of drawers. I figured it was just convenient for me to think that. It was a way of reducing the object of my envy, of making him no different.

"I was going to be a lawyer," I said to Jen. I didn't look, but I heard her mumble an acknowledgment. "I always wanted to be a lawyer and live a simple life, driving my Land Rover or my BMW or my Saab or my Volvo. I always wanted to do paperwork and have meetings and have an assistant and give her instructions about things I needed done. And I wanted a nice, pretty, smart wife who had a good job of her own so we could be the ideal couple. But we really wouldn't have to do much, because people would always be coming to see us. We'd live in a high-rise or an old house by the Gulf, perfectly renovated, exquisitely painted and detailed, kept spotless by a live-in Spanish woman. That's what I always wanted."

"Well, you didn't come too close, did you?" Jen said.

"No, I guess I didn't," I said. "Your father came closer than I did."

"He missed by a mile."

"I don't know much about it."

"You'll find out."

Two or three small birds went by near the balcony, swerving toward me and then away at the last minute, chirping as they went.

"There's a whole world out here at night," I said.

"Yeah, I hear it," she said. "I can see it, too, from here. It's pretty."

"Almost everything is pretty in the middle of the night."

"I want pancakes for breakfast," she said.

"Me too."

"Time to sleep," she said.

I heard her thump the mattress a couple of times, calling me. I leaned forward and scratched my chin, then got up and closed the doors, wiped off the sill with the towel that was by now soaking wet, then pulled the curtain. I undressed and got into bed.

"Are you sure you're O.K.?" she said.

"I'm fine," I said. "I'm just feeling a little long in the tooth."

"The longer the better," she said, kissing my shoulder and laying her arm across my chest. Her arm was oddly light and cool. She opened her hand and passed it gently over my chest, over my nipples, one after the other, then curved it over my side, cupping my ribs.

# seven

In the morning we crossed the river and went through Vidalia and then headed out across Louisiana through Catahoula Parish into LaSalle, across the national forest into Natchitoches and up Highway 49 to Shreveport. It was a strange drive: little highways and broken-down towns, crabby lanes overhung with trees and moss, and people who seemed a generation or two out of time. It was at once odd and comfortable—I didn't feel so far from these people who had ordinary lives going from the barbershop to the café, stopping off at the mechanic's garage to get the car muffler replaced, shopping at the screen-doored grocery. It was very green there, very wet and green and healthy. All the trees were healthy, the grass was healthy, the shrubs were healthy. Nothing was very well taken care of, but everything was enormously healthy.

"Here's what I found out last night on CompuServe," Jen said. "In the year 1241, Mongols went into Poland and took nine bags of ears, thirty thousand ears, from those people. Out of what is now Poland."

"Is that right?" Mike said.

"That's what I read last night."

"I guess Mongols will be Mongols," he said.

We stopped at a train crossing. "I'm thinking I don't have to publish my terrorzine anymore," Jen said. "I'm thinking that the world has kind of caught up with me. This morning in the paper—did you read the paper this morning?"

"No," I said.

"This morning in the paper there's this box chart with the headline 'Spousal Homicide at a Glance.' I ask you," she said.

"Ask me what?" I said.

"I hardly know what to say," she said. *"Spousal homicide at a glance?"*

"Yeah, I know what you mean," Mike said. "I read a piece in the paper about this guy who bumped into this girl in Miami, some little girl in the street, just tapped her, didn't hurt her at all, but he slams on the brakes and jumps out to see if she's O.K., and then a mob attacks him and kills him and steals his shoes and his jacket and the seats out of his car. The girl was fine."

"Of wives who are murdered," Jen said, "seventy percent are killed by their husbands, and of those, half the killers kill themselves, too."

"Life's not worth living without your loving wife, that's my feeling," I said.

"I like this Louisiana countryside," Mike said. "It makes me feel good. There's something warm about it, don't you think?"

"It's hot, you mean," Jen said.

"No, that's not what I mean," Mike said. "And it's not hot."

"It'd be hot if it hadn't rained all night."

"It's so verdant," Mike said.

"You mean, like, *green*?" she said.

"Yeah, but not just green. Sort of lush and overflowing and abundant, like with the rich soil from which this abundance comes. It's the feeling of vitality and richness and fertility. That sort of thing."

"Holy mackerel, Dad," she said.

"Watch out now," I said.

"There's a kind of sweetness to it too," Mike said. "A kind of scent that floats off the honeysuckle and the jasmine and the wet grass and the little creeks flowing rivulets of water over bright rocks and scattered leaves."

Jen hit him on his neck. She was in the back seat, I was in the front, Mike was driving. "You be careful there," she said. "You're getting a little overripe, don't you think? You're a little fertile yourself."

"I'm a fifty-three-year-old man, and if I want to get fertile I'm allowed," he said.

"I'll buy that," I said.

"O.K.," Jen said, throwing up her hands. "Pretend I didn't say anything. If you want to do me a favor, you can stop at the next particularly fertile-looking gas station. I would appreciate that."

"Will do," Mike said.

Riding the two-lane highway in the big Lincoln was a pleasure for me, too. There was something about the way we floated along through Louisiana that made me feel like things were O.K.—things were going to be O.K. Maybe it was just that things were out of my hands. I had the same sense of security I'd had taking a nap at Mike's house. Nothing was my responsibility. I was just along for the ride. What Mike said about the countryside was true. It was remarkable, rich and pretty. Notwithstanding the fact that the civilization part of it was kind of down-in-the-mouth. Ratty. But the land—the woods, the brush, the flowers—the land had done pretty well. Even the ponds looked healthy, the little streams we crossed in the middle of nowhere. We went over a fifty-foot-long steel bridge, clanked over it, and I looked at the creek below. It was handsome, right out of the advertising pages of *Field & Stream,* where you might find a couple of good friends sharing a pack of low-tar Marlboros while fishing in a little creek. It was water that was mysterious and languid and full of a kind of tempting invitation that seemed everywhere around us as we drove across Louisiana. These weren't suburbs, and these certainly weren't cities, or even towns. This was countryside. This was undeveloped, unwashed, unfrazzled countryside. You knew that if you got out in it you'd get bitten by spiders or snakes or mosquitoes or worse. But it was so handsome, so elegant and wistful in the way it cried out to you to stop and see, to walk along the banks of a stream, to lean against a tree, to climb up on a rise and look down over the meadow, to row a small boat back through the huge roots of cypresses in the swamps, that what it *wasn't* didn't matter. It was small. The scale of things was like New Hampshire, the tiny villages there, the towns, the roads, as if those places were really toys for some kind of Christmas story, something right out of a fairy tale.

The interior of Louisiana had some of that too, some of that magic of scale. The coast of Mississippi, where we lived, and Texas, where I'd lived before, were large places—open spaces, wide streets, big trees, tall sky. Not close and overgrown, crowded with foliage, not leafy limbs pressing in on you as you drove through. Not like the highways we were on, heading from Natchez to Shreveport. Not completely swallowed in greenery. No sun could get through, or if it did get through, it came in little spots, flickering over the car as we ran down the damp highway.

"So what are you two really going to do when you get to California?" Mike said.

"What do you mean, *really?*" Jen said.

"What I said."

"We're going to do something," she said.

"You're already doing something," her father said. "Guerrilla stuff—handbills and messages. You're already getting your view out."

"Nobody's listening," Jen said. "We have to do more. We have to push it, force it. Have an impact."

"You think that's possible?" he said.

"I think so," Jen said. "It had better be."

"What, because we want to?" I said. "That's the criterion? I want to, so I can?"

"It was good enough for Adam Curry," she said.

"Who's Adam Curry?" Mike said.

"You don't want to know," I said.

"He's an MTV guy," Jen said. "He started this hoopla on the Internet."

"He was already known. He was a tiny celebrity, but he'd been on MTV all the time," I said. "He had a power base."

"Lee Harvey Oswald," she said.

"Now you're talking," Mike said.

"He just stepped out of the shadows one day and did what he believed," she said.

"He was an idiot," I said.

"That's not very nice," she said.

"O.K., he was thoughtless and unkind," I said. "That's no reason to emulate him."

"I'm not emulating him," she said. "I'm embracing the idea of stepping out of the shadows. Do that and you're empowering yourself. You're demanding to be heard."

Mike said, "Can you please do it without killing the president?"

"I'm not killing the president, Dad."

"O.K.," he said. "I trust you."

We floated along the highway in the big black Lincoln. It was wonderfully open inside, with wide bench seats and all the room in the world. It was like a movie spaceship. It didn't look that way, but it was that size. Different from cars I was used to. It was like a car from the fifties, the way it wallowed like a flat-bottomed boat through the turns, the way it lumbered wherever we went, across town or down the highway, rolling left and right as it reacted to the road. It was comforting, lounging along in this old gaudy and sparkling Lincoln, with Mike at the wheel and the smell of leather all around us.

We slowed as we entered a town called Boing, where there were three mules tied up to a fence alongside the road. The town was nothing more than a handful of buildings arrayed on either side of the highway. At the far end there was a Texaco station. We stopped. I went in and got some diet Coke, Jen went to the ladies' room, Mike filled the car with gas. I bought a paper, and then we were back out on the highway.

"Here's what I know about Damian Williams," Jen said, cocking her computer in her lap and reading off the screen. "He was nineteen when the riots happened in April of 1992. He got ten years. They tried to charge him with attempted murder, but they couldn't prove that he intended anything. Fidel Lopez, the guy that got painted, was thirty-six. They spray-painted all over him, in his face and on his genitals, and then they poured some kind of liquid on him, but nobody seems to know what this extra liquid was. He got twenty-nine stitches in his head—seventeen in one ear, that somebody had tried to slice off, and twelve in his chin. Martin Sheen wrote a letter, according to the *L.A. Times*, suggesting that Williams be let off with probation."

"Martin Sheen missed on this one," I said.

"Yeah, he's part of the Painted Genitals movement," Mike said.

"Williams is from Vicksburg," Jen said. "He went to high school in Vicksburg."

"He's from Mississippi?" Mike said.

"He went to high school there," she said. "I don't know if that's where he's from. They called his high school principal or coach to come out and identify him on the videotape during the trial."

"Jesus. I didn't know that," I said.

"So is he in jail now?" Mike said. "Are you going to go see him in jail?"

"He'll probably be out in a year," she said. "We might see him. He's such a goony-looking guy on the tape, though, you don't really want to see him."

"He's not that goony," I said. "He just looks like a kid."

"He looks like he doesn't have the brains God gave a sawhorse," Jen said.

"I didn't say he looked smart," I said. "He looks like a kid who took his rioting too seriously. Besides, they're just using him so they can have somebody to punish so it looks like things work, people are accountable, and all that crap. He's the Oswald of the riots."

"Great. You're getting yellow feet already," Jen said.

I looked at her over the seat back. "Yellow feet?"

"You know what I mean," she said.

"I'm right here," I said. "I agreed to go and I'm going. The problem is real, there's good reason to go, but I'm not sure about our solution."

"So why are we going?" she said.

"It's something to do. You wanted to go. We've got the time, we can go out there, see what there is to see. We've got all this Simpson stuff," I said.

"You're interested in that?" she said.

"I don't know," I said. "It's California. I haven't been to California in a long time. Bud always goes to California, so I thought it would be O.K. to go."

"So this is like a holiday?" Jen said.

"Well, sort of," I said. "Not for you?"

"No," she said. "I'm working. I'm figuring to do something and somehow make a difference in the world."

"We're probably not going to make much difference in the world, Jen. I'm sorry. I'm not sure anybody makes much difference; even the people who seem to be making a difference in the world aren't really making a difference. Kevin Costner, speaking of him, is not making a difference as far as I can tell. See what I'm saying? Francis Ford Coppola or—what's that other guy's name, who did your father's movie?"

"Al Green?" Mike said.

"Very funny," I said. "You know, the one who makes all the movies that are highly evolved in a social-consciousness way. He made the Vietnam movie, then he made the other Vietnam movie, and then he made the Doors movie, and then he made the Kennedy movie, and then he made the other Vietnam movie, and now he's made the killers movie."

"Al Green?" Mike said again.

"Oliver Stone," I said. "He's not making any difference to anybody. Kennedy didn't make any difference to anybody. Nixon didn't make any difference. They just fill the slots, they're just pix to paste up on the wall for a couple years. You know what I mean? I guess some people probably do. Jesus made a difference, maybe somebody else I can't think of right now made a difference, maybe some of those doctors doing brain research or something, or people saving people in foreign countries, or big scientists, or stuff like that, but even that's short-term stuff. It's hard to come up with people who make a long-range difference."

"How about Al Green?" Mike said.

Jen reached out and patted his shoulder for that.

"Maybe a couple dozen people in the history of the world have made a difference, and the rest of us are just flopping around. It's like we get this little card, and the card says this is your role, and you play it, and then you die. That's it. You're finished. It doesn't matter if you're a Biloxi fisherman or the CIA director."

"That's a pretty attitude for a person to take," Jen said. "And I suppose it's quite comfortable for you, but it's not the way I look at it."

"Pardon me for being only half a citizen," I said.

"You're upset about your station in life; you talked about it. About Dad, for example," she said. "You'd rather be him, wouldn't you?"

"I wouldn't exactly rather *be* him," I said.

Mike looked at me like I was nuts. "No," he said. "You don't want to be me."

"See there? Even Mike doesn't want me to be Mike," I said. "Mike probably wants to be me."

"Right," Mike said. He shook his head as if this were all nonsense. "You don't need a reason. Just go, see what it's like. Go for the long ride. There's nothing wrong with that. Maybe you'll encounter something that will help you figure out what to do. Don't be silly about what's going to go wrong when you get there. You're not going to start a new set of riots or kill anybody or wreak havoc all over the place. You should go see the place, get to know it, see it, walk around."

"Jen got these reports off CompuServe, all the stories that ran in the newspaper out there when it happened and during the trial," I said.

"I didn't get everything," she said. "I got a lot, though."

"See, that's a start," Mike said. "That gives you some idea already."

"Mostly people are complaining about the sentence," Jen said. "Arguing details about why he was charged with what he was charged with, and why assault with a deadly weapon is a lesser charge than aggravated mayhem. Stuff like that—details. A lot of business from the defense lawyers. It's not that informative. There's not much background on Williams. A big moment in the trial was when Reginald Denny embraced Williams's mother in the courtroom, but the jury wasn't there when he did that. He did it to express to her and to the city that he had forgiven Damian Williams, that he was ready to let bygones be bygones, that he was ready to go on with his life. That's what he said. Typical California move. He has a dent in his head the size of a softball. I don't know why he would have done that otherwise. It's a horrible thing, this thing in the side of his head."

"It's kind of mushy is what you said, right?" I said. "We saw a thing on television where one of the jurors put her hand in the indentation."

"Yeah. We've got that on tape," Jen said.

"What about this forgiveness stuff?" Mike said. "Forgiving Williams—you don't think that's a good idea?"

"I think we ought to blast his sorry fat ass off the planet," Jen said. "I think that if we weren't so nice and middle class and well educated, we could probably do that. But because we're all those things, we can't. We can't even really think about it."

"That's it," I said, pointing out a dead rabbit in the road that Mike had already seen and steered left to miss. "That's the tyranny of class, of gender, of sexual preference, of unrehabilitated language. If it's not one thing, it's another, for us. We're in trouble every which way we turn. We can't move. We're sealed in. We're locked out. We're dead meat. It's our destiny to go to the grocery store, the mall, to complain about the mall, to complain about the grocery store, to buy the big black Volvo, to complain about the Volvo—"

"Nobody complains except people in the newspapers," Jen said. "And they don't really complain. It's some bogus complaint for public consumption."

"You complain," I said. "What are you talking about?"

"I'm not sure about myself," she said. "Am I complaining or am I just whining because I don't have zillions of dollars and a house on Long Island with a beautiful pool by which I could sit and read on weekends? To and from which I could ride on my twenty-three-hundred-dollar bicycle, completely geared out in my nine-hundred-dollar bicycle outfit covered with Italian slogans."

"You don't want to do any of that, do you, Jen?" I said.

"Just the slogans," she said.

"Which slogans were you thinking about?" Mike said, looking in the rearview.

"I don't know." She laughed. "I'll think of some. *Ciao bambino* or something."

We were up on the interstate again, slicing through the Louisiana countryside. Like most interstates, it was an odd bit of space, a narrow slot fenced by high trees. Occasionally there was a town off to one side, but mostly there were just trees and a green space down the middle, two, sometimes three lanes going each direction. Lots of big white trucks out there. Occasional crossovers. Little raised bridges over the highway, connecting one side to the other.

"I like highways," Jen said.

"Me too," I said.

"They're so purposeful," she said. "And you might as well be in outer space." She did an announcer voice. " 'This is a message from your Commissioner of Highways and Highway Travel. Please be aware that we have constructed everything to remind you at all times of your purpose here. We have made every effort to keep things out of your way and to facilitate your travel, and to communicate to you that you are traveling, should you forget. You are no doubt embarked upon some project of which traveling is only a small part, and while you are nowhere just now, soon you will be somewhere. You are doing a fine job of traveling. Congratulations, and thank you for your attention.' "

The road was damp, so the tires made that nice, slightly elastic sound as they rolled over the pavement. Distant trucks coming at us looked slow until they got parallel to us across the green space. Sometimes there were trees in the island between the north- and southbound lanes, making our side even more isolated from the other. This was a land where the cops wore stiff-brimmed hats. Where everyone looked at everyone else nonchalantly as cars passed one another. It was a strange kind of moving city out there. Sometimes people would wave or laugh or salute with a Coke from McDonald's or Burger King. The sky was big and rippled with dirty-clothes clouds, rain off in the distance looking like veils looping lazily in almost rag shapes from the dark-edged clouds to the flat horizon, brightened from behind with that clear yellow light.

"Penny will be more interested in the project than you are," Jen said from the back seat.

"I've never met Penny," I said.

"Neither have I," Mike said.

"Yes you have, Dad," Jen said. "You met her when I was in college. I brought her home."

"I don't remember," he said.

"She's a great big girl. She's six feet. She's got brown hair down to her butt. Now do you remember?"

Mike waved a hand. "No, but I'll take your word for it. What's she doing now?"

"She was in the police academy, but she got kicked out," Jen said.

"I think she got kicked out. Maybe she just left. Before that, she worked for a lawyer as a secretary. She's very crime-oriented; that's why I know she'll be more interested in this than you guys."

"I'm crime-oriented," Mike said. "I watch *Homicide.*"

"Maybe you and Penny can be gun molls," I said.

"Dork-o," Jen said. "I know we're not going to do anything, but don't you want to see? I want to walk Dealey Plaza with Dad. It's important that we be a part of it in some way."

"Seeing Dealey Plaza isn't going to make me a part of the assassination, the movie, the conspiracy, or any of that. It's going to make me a tourist."

# eight

Penny Gibson was six feet a hundred thirty pounds, and angular as she folded into the booth at the Chinese restaurant where we were having lunch. She was stiff-looking; her smile looked too careful. She was introduced to Mike and to me, then we all went to the menus. She said it was a fair Chinese restaurant, nothing to write home about. I ordered Three Chickens Delight, and Jen got a bowl of hot and sour soup and some braised bean curd. Mike had lemon chicken, and Penny ordered Ming's beef. We had tea and Chinese beer.

"Now do you remember her, Mike?" Jen said.

"Of course I remember her," Mike said. "You brought her home for a week at Easter. You haven't changed a bit, Penny."

"I've changed a lot," she said.

"You know what I meant," he said.

"Yeah," she said. "Thanks."

"You've been in the police academy?" he said.

"No. I was thinking about the police academy. I was thinking about it, but I didn't do it. I've got a college degree. I don't need to go be a policeman."

"Lots of policemen have college degrees," Jen said.

"They don't act like it," Penny said.

"So what *have* you been up to?" I said.

"Just the usual," Penny said. "Getting by, doing a little work, trying not to be angry, trying not to hate men." She gave me a look when she said that.

"I have a hard time with that myself," I said.

She managed a dry smile.

The restaurant had dark-green cotton tablecloths and the usual red-and-white paper place mats with the animals on them so you could figure out in which Chinese year you were born. Mike found himself on the mat.

"I think I'm a dog," he said.

"So what's the deal on the trip?" Penny said. "I want to go, but—why are we going, again?"

"Don't ask," I said.

"Damian Williams," Jen said.

"Oh, that guy. Jesus. I remember him," Penny said.

"I've got this piece of videotape I want to show you," Jen said. "Where he paints this guy Lopez's dick with spray paint."

"Great idea," Penny said.

"You can't actually see it's him," I said. "You can just see his shoes. They said it was him, and he was convicted of doing it, but we can't really see it's him."

"They identified him by his shoes," Jen said. "That doesn't seem right to me, either."

"I think it's all right," I said.

"So you want to go out and torch this guy?" Penny said.

"Boy howdy," Jen said. "But we probably won't. We're just going. We've got all this Simpson stuff now, so there's that, and we're going to Dealey Plaza with Dad."

"I'd like to go to the Cadillac ranch," Penny said. "I've only seen pictures of it."

"What's the Cadillac ranch?" Mike said.

"It's where this guy put a lot of Cadillacs in the ground twenty years ago. It's a famous thing. You'll see it on your map. It's one of those ain't-we-crazy kind of antimodernist things," she said.

"I don't like it," Jen said. "I've seen pictures of it, and I don't like it. I like that place in Arizona or Nevada where all those big weather vane things are, the big lines of them as they go across the desert. They make electricity. Big windmills, single bladed. You know the ones I'm talking about?"

"I've seen the pictures," Penny said. She turned to me, more friendly now, as if she'd just thought of something. "So are you the hero who saved little Jen from Itch, or whatever his name was—the bum with the bikini van?"

"I guess I am," I said.

"You deserve a medal for that."

"Thank you," I said.

"He was genuine scum, that one. Cheap meat," she said.

"He wasn't all that bad," Jen said.

"He was loose bowels," Penny said. "Don't kid yourself."

The waitress brought our food in two trips, and we started passing things around. The stuff didn't look too appetizing. The peppers were withered, the snow peas scorched, my three chickens all came out shining roach-brown chunks like little twisted knuckles, and the lemon chicken was pancake thin, steeped in an orange sauce. We ate it, anyway.

Afterward we followed Penny to her apartment, which wasn't too far off the highway, in a tree-shaded complex with fifty or sixty two-story town houses.

"How far is Dallas?" Mike said, as we were going inside.

"Under two hundred miles," Penny said.

"Great. We'll be there this afternoon. We can go see Dealey Plaza tomorrow," he said.

"Why don't we go tonight?" Jen said. "Dealey Plaza under the stars. That might be cool."

"Fewer tourists," I said.

"Del's worried about being a tourist," Jen said.

"He should count his blessings," Penny said.

Her apartment was clean and stark in a straightforward way. The furniture looked like it had come from a big department store—the usual couch, the usual rugs, the usual knickknacks, the Sony television, the dining table in the small dining room. It looked like nobody lived there, like a model apartment. There wasn't anything personal around, no junk. Nothing was magneted to the refrigerator. The coffee table was carefully placed, carefully cleaned, the magazines arrayed just so. I noticed that they were current magazines. One of them was the *Time* with the Simpson cover that the magazine had gotten in trouble about.

"You want to rest before we go?" Jen said to Mike.

"We could do that," he said. "Take a half hour. Take a little nap, something like that."

"Nap?" I said.

"We could do that," Mike said.

"That's great," Penny said. "I've got some last-minute stuff to do. Why don't you older guys go upstairs. There are two bedrooms up there, and somebody can have the couch. I'll be quiet."

Jen started to stay downstairs with Penny, but I signaled, asking her to come up. She turned to Penny and said, "I'll be back in a minute." We went upstairs and into Penny's bedroom, which looked like a motel room.

"Set decoration by One Stop Rentals," I said.

"Maybe so," Jen said. "Did you want something in particular, or just company?"

"I wanted to ask if you think this is a good idea. Is she going to lighten up at all?"

"I don't know," Jen said. "She's fine. What're you talking about, 'lighten up'? You just met her. How can you make some call on that?"

"She seems a little non-harmonious, doesn't she?" I said.

"I don't know," Jen said. "Why don't you take a rest, take a pill—you'll feel better."

We heard Mike groaning as he swung himself into bed in the second bedroom. The drive had taken more out of him than he'd let on.

"You want to call ahead to Dallas to get someplace to stay?" I said. "Holiday Inn or Ramada?"

"I could do that when I go down."

"You don't want to nap?"

"I'm not tired," she said. "Will you be all right?" She looked at me and patted my leg.

"Yes," I said. She smiled and left, closing the door. It shut with a satisfying click.

I rested for a few minutes, then sat on the edge of the bed and looked around. This was the master bedroom, with the master bath. I went in there and looked at the stuff on the counter and then the stuff in the cabinet, then I came out and looked in the closet, fingered a few skirts and blouses. I looked out the window, which was covered by a heavy curtain. Then I got back in bed, dropped my shoes on the floor, closed my eyes, and arranged my hands over my chest like a dead man's hands. Jen hated it when I slept that way. It drove her crazy. She would move my hands herself if she had to.

I wished I were back in Biloxi, in my own bed, listening to the rain on the balcony, listening to the cars swish by on the road out front, looking forward to a quiet night, maybe a hamburger and a movie, something plain, something not too much trouble. Maybe a couple hours of quarter slots. When I first moved to Mississippi I hated it, thought the Coast was stupid and vulgar, but now I liked it. After you're there awhile it has this weather-beaten, slowed-down aspect that's comforting, even sensible. It's hard to have large-scale pretenses when you live on the Gulf Coast. Some do, of course, but most people are admirably matter-of-fact about their condition. And the garish casinos were wonderful opportunities for failure. In five or ten years they'd be great decaying hulks, billboard-size slabs of peeling paint, fresh rust, crashed glass, sitting and rotting at water's edge. Some would be demoored and towed away, leaving beachside vacancies like the holes of giant pulled teeth. The Mississippi Gulf Coast was like Galveston, though Galveston was more charming, an old-time Texas coast town, pretty in a fifties way. But Biloxi had the right kind of failure about it, the fatalistic, nothing-to-lose feeling that made it easy to stay.

I'd cooled off about the trip. Even if we made it to Florence and Normandie, we'd just drive past a couple of times and then head out to Wendy's. You had to have more heat than we had to fix something. Jen was right about the wretchedness going on, the violent and stupid people, the crude tricks they were playing on each other all the time, the scary degree to which self-interest had become assumed and accepted, but we weren't going to be doing the repair. In Penny's bed, which smelled fresh and pleasant, antiseptic in a floral way, I knew that at least. Things weren't going to be fixed, and maybe I didn't want them fixed—I needed the mess to complain about, to point to when I wanted to devalue the system, or protect myself with a kind of alibi for my limited prosperity. And the fixer's world is always too clean and orderly, anyway, too rigid, too limited. Plus, whenever you see or hear people with a plan to "fix" things, they're always more frightening than what they propose to fix. At least we'd all worked on the mess, all had a piece of it.

# nine

The guy who handled our bags at the Ramada in Dallas was wearing a tag that said his name was Rhumbo. We had half a tense moment in the elevator when Jen asked him where he got the name and he said he'd gotten it in prison.

"You were in prison?" Jen said.

"Long time ago," he said. He was an old guy, maybe sixty-five, maybe even older, wrinkled. "I was in a state prison up in Minnesota. They called me Rhumbo."

"Why'd they do that?" Jen said.

"Well, this one guy had this book about an elephant named Rhumbo, and this was a real smart elephant who helped some kids out or something, and I guess he figured I was like an elephant the way I was always helping people out, the new guys, the rookies. I don't know, maybe it was just ear size." He wiggled his ears for us. "Either way, this guy tags me Rhumbo, and it sticks," he said.

"I like it," Jen said. "It was an affectionate deal, right? Friendly?"

"I guess so," the old guy said. "My real name is Colin, so it's a step up. You want the nameplate? I can tell them I lost it. I can tell them anything. That's something prison teaches you." He unhooked the tag from his jacket and held it out to Jen. She took it.

"Rhumbo," she said, looking at the tag. Then she held it over her chest. "Hi, I'm Rhumbo. I'll be your baby tonight."

"I've heard of Dumbo," Mike said.

"Same thing," the old guy said. "Well, nearly. I saw the Rhumbo book once. It had lots of elephant facts, like sometimes they sleep on their stomachs, and how you measure how tall an elephant is by measuring twice around the largest part of its foot. Stuff like that."

"No kidding?" Jen said.

"Yep," the guy said.

When we got to the rooms, I gave the guy a bigger tip than he deserved, and he went away grinning. He did an elephant-trunk wave from the corner by the elevators and disappeared.

When we went in, Jen dodged into the bathroom and rubbed her face with a wet washcloth, then called the desk and had them send a VCR to Penny's room.

"I'm showing her the Lopez stuff," she said to me. "Come if you want."

"Seen it," I said.

I sat down by the window and tried to unwind. It felt as if we were still out swaying on the highway. It was a quarter to nine and dark out, and the city was all lit up. Some of the buildings in Dallas had special lights around their edges. They were like Christmas lights, except all white, outlining the buildings or the main architectural features. One place had these twin spires and these circular towers and looked like it came from Buildings "R" Us. Downtown wasn't that big. We were on the loop across from it. One building I could see had these green wiggly lights on it, lights reflected in its glass, but you couldn't tell whether the lights were strange or the glass was rippled. Mike knocked on the connecting door between his room and ours. I got up and let him in. He sat down with me by the glass.

"This isn't so bad, is it?" he said. "The three of us traveling."

"Four, Mike. But it seems fine, seems good."

"I guess I feel a little awkward," he said. "It's hard for me to be Dad."

"I got the impression that you never were Dad all that much," I said. "No offense."

"I was sort of Dad, but I think I was expecting the kids to act like us all the time—adults, I mean. When they were nine I thought they should act like thirty. I wasn't tolerant. I didn't give them a lot of ground to be themselves. I didn't give them that much leeway. At least not the first one. Not the second one, either, really. Jen had more room, I guess. That's why I wasn't all that fatherly to her. I kind of gave it up by the time she came along. I let Lida take care of it." He was rubbing his thumb on the Formica table that was between us, making a squeaking sound, like he was trying to rub some spot off the tabletop, some sticky spot, rubber cement. "I'm not all that proud of this, but at the time I thought it was the best thing I could do for her—stay out of her way."

"I'm not the person to ask about it."

"I wasn't asking," he said. "You said something, and I was just saying something back, my side of the story."

"Yeah, I know," I said. "But it's not like I'm over here having an opinion about it. I don't have any opinion."

"You were married once, weren't you?" he said.

"I was married for a while."

"Didn't work out, I guess."

"No, it didn't."

"You see, that's something that's happened to me," he said. "I married Lida when I was twenty-two, and we were married twenty-one years. I was just a little tucked-in thing all that time. I'm thinking maybe I did wrong."

"Wrong how?" I said.

"Well," he said. "You're sitting there in your house in the suburbs, you go through the motions, you do everything right—pay your bills, look into the many problems you anticipate. You go to meetings, watch the TV programs you're supposed to watch, get upset about the things you're supposed to get upset about, work for a better community and town. You do all that and you end up a little fat guy with plenty of money and a Rolodex full of golf buddies who parked their brains in high school. You get fatter and redder in the face. It's depleting."

"Sounds great to me," I said. "What's so bad?"

"See there," he said. "You interest me. You're what? Almost fifty? How come you're not worried?"

"I am worried. I don't seem worried to you?"

"I mean the way you live," he said. "It's like . . . relaxed." We were both staring out the window, talking to our reflections in the glass.

"I just seem relaxed," I said. "I'm not really relaxed."

"In the way I mean, you are," he said. "Maybe you're worried, but not like people I know."

"I'm just not successful."

"That's not it," he said. "Nobody I know would take up with a twenty-five-year-old. We might think about it, we might look at the young women in our offices, secretaries and so on, but we'd never do it. It doesn't happen."

"You run with a better class of people."

"I don't think that's it."

"You can't approve of me and Jen," I said. "If I were you I wouldn't approve of me and Jen. I'd be pulling my hair trying to figure out how to break us up."

"Why would you do that?" he said.

"I don't know. Just so I wouldn't have me to deal with," I said. "Somebody my own age. It's creepy."

"What's to deal with?" he said. "There's nothing I can do. She's twenty-seven, a grown woman. If she wants a boyfriend who's fifty, that's her business."

"But you have to talk to me, see me. You've got to admit this is kind of awkward," I said.

"I said that to start with," he said. "But it turns out it's not you, it's Jen. I hope I'm not making you feel awkward."

"I feel awkward anyway," I said. "It's not new."

"When my son died, a lot of things changed for me. I hung everything up," he said. "I was stunned—out of nowhere, he was gone. It's not like losing a girlfriend or wife, it's meaner than that. Less emotional, harder. It's as if the world was telling me: You have no authority; you have no control over this situation or any situation; anything can happen to you. That's when I quit in my head. I hit autopilot, and I've been on it ever since."

"Ten years ago?" I said.

"Round about," he said. He slapped the table. "What about you? What do your parents think? They must be much older, right?"

"Eighties."

"They live in Houston?"

"Right."

"And they've never met Jen? You've never taken her over there?"

"Not yet," I said. "I don't want to shake them up. They're probably not clear on what's going on, why Jen's so young. They wouldn't say anything, but they'd kind of look and blink a lot. My mother likes Jen—they talk on the phone—but both my parents think it's odd, Jen and me."

"That's tough," Mike said. He got up and leaned against the window, looking parallel to the freeway below us, first left, then right, scratching his forehead with three fingernails. "I wonder if we ought to go over there tonight." He tapped on the glass. "Dealey Plaza."

"Are we going to eat first?" I said.

"We can eat. You want to eat?"

"Just downstairs. I don't care. Something."

"I think about when Kennedy was shot," Mike said. "When Ruby was shooting Oswald—all of that. What struck me was the music in the funeral parade, the cortege, the boots backward in the stirrups. That's what got me—the riderless horse and the boots. And Walter Cronkite saying stuff about this riderless horse, and the drums, and the music. The procession. The walk."

He pressed his forehead against the glass and stared down. The light coming up from the freeway illuminated his face in a peculiar way. Suddenly I saw in him someone else, a person he didn't show all that often. Somebody with a lot of ideas, with an active imagination, a future, a younger man, almost a child, with a child's interest, a child's enthusiasm.

This happens with people. I've seen it with the college faculty at odd moments in a bar or at a party or a softball game. In just a second, you get to see what kind of person they were once, when they were young and hopeful, when they had places to go and things to do, a time long gone, long papered over by small responsibilities, details, dead-end projects, local lives and little children, mortgages, Burger Kings, the growing pile of tiny failures and missed opportunities, things dismissed for one reason or another. I caught just a glimpse of that younger person in Mike, that person within the person, and I knew it would vanish as quickly as it had appeared. But in that few seconds when we were in the hotel room, him leaning his head against the window, me sitting in the wooden chair with the ugly fabric covering its seat and back, I felt a wonderful kinship with who he was under who he was.

"I want a chicken-fried steak, mashed potatoes with brown gravy, and peas," he said, still not moving.

"Now you're talking," I said.

"Yeah," he said. "I want to go to some little café and get a chicken-fried steak. Either that or an open-faced roast beef sandwich with mashed potatoes and peas. Either of those."

"You got a mashed-potatoes-and-peas thing going—I can climb up on that," I said.

"It won't be any good," he said. "It won't be like it was. But I want it anyway."

I shook my head, agreeing with him. "There you go. It'll be close enough."

"Things get lost," he said. "We lose stuff. We lose contact. We lose ways of thinking, ways of feeling, ways of doing things. Pretty soon our whole world is stuffed with rude people and their rude hair, and the world itself has changed. Then we're old cars out there, taking up somebody else's lane."

---

We got to Dealey Plaza around eleven. It was dark and damp, and it seemed like all the lights were orange.

"It's fucking small," Mike said. "There's the Depository, there's where the car was going. Bingo. *I* could have made that shot. I could make that shot in my sleep. In the movies and TV shows it always seems like a long way away, but it's not. What is it—a hundred yards? It's a tiny shot. Why are they making so much stew about this? Anybody could make that. It's a groundhog shot."

"Settle down, Dad," Jen said. "You couldn't make it."

"I could," he said. "With a little practice, I could make it easy. Six marksmen, my happy ass."

We stood and looked out over the plaza, then walked across the street to see the Texas School Book Depository from the downtown side, then crossed back and walked the path that Kennedy's car had taken, then climbed up the grassy knoll and went around behind the fence where the other shots were supposed to have come from. A train was going by on the overpass. We stood in the vacant lot, which was still a vacant lot, where the three tramps were found. Jen and Penny were walking around together, from one side of the plaza to the other. There was a lighted American flag in the middle of it. There were some plaques around. It didn't look like history to me. I caught up with Jen and Penny near the reflecting pool.

"He's right about how tiny it is," Jen said. "It never seemed this way on television."

"It's kind of small," I said. "Where is he?"

"He's over there behind the fence, above the grassy knoll," she said. "He's being the second gunman."

I looked across the street and saw Mike's head poking out above the wood fence that separated the grassy knoll from the parking lot. The train over there was squeaking and squealing, rocking on the tracks.

"These places are always a letdown," Penny said.

"It's still scary," Jen said. "You know that eerie feeling when you stand here—like you can go back in time, or suddenly time could switch back and you could be caught there on that day. You could be running across the grass toward the car, but the car would be already snaking off down toward that hole in that underpass over there. You know what I mean? There's this weirdness."

The big flag was popping, the wind was driving it so hard. Mike came out and stood in the colonnade on the other side of the grassy knoll. When he got back to us, he said, "This is crazy. This looks like a toy. This looks like a model of Dealey Plaza, where a toy president was killed. The real Dealey Plaza was done on television or something. This looks like it was made with those plastic blocks."

"I checked the Depository, but it wasn't open," Jen said. "Open daytime, not at night."

"I don't want to go in there anyway," Mike said.

"You can go up to Oswald's window," Jen said.

"Unless he was hanging upside down from one foot with his head in a Jell-O vat it's not worth it," Mike said. "It's not worth it. Too easy. I'm going back to the hotel."

"Let's sit here awhile," Jen said. "Just kind of soak it up. Maybe it gets better if you hang out awhile."

A busload of tourists came in behind us, maybe twenty Hawaiians in Hawaiian shirts, with cameras and funny hats. Their tour guide gathered them on the terrace alongside the reflecting pool in front of the Dealey Plaza commemorative plaque and started explaining things to them. Mike went for the street and hailed a cab.

"I'm going to the hotel," he said. "Anybody want to go with?"

"Are you O.K., Dad?" Jen said.

"Yeah, I just want to get some rest," he said.

"I'll go," Penny said. She climbed into the cab behind him, and they took off, waving.

Jen and I went back across the street to the grassy knoll and sat down, watching the traffic sail by, dipping left to right under the underpass. We watched the people walk around and point at the School Book Depository and point at the place, below where we were sitting, where the president was shot. There was a big road sign there, and I didn't know whether it was the road sign behind which the president's car momentarily disappeared in the Zapruder film or if it was some new sign. It seemed to me that it wasn't the sign or that it wasn't in the right place if it was the sign, but I wasn't sure.

"This is supposed to be a really big thing, isn't it?" Jen said.

"Yep. I believe so."

"I'm supposed to feel the weight of history here," she said.

"Right."

"Great events upon which our future turned," she said.

"Jen?" I said.

"It's not really working for me," she said. "How about you?"

"Nope." You have to believe in history, you have to think everything would have been different if Kennedy hadn't been killed. I don't, so it doesn't do much for me. I like the train, though."

"You would," she said.

"I like the way it's shimmering, and I like that steely noise the train wheels make," I said. "It sounds like a car crash in ultra slow motion."

"I wasn't even born," she said. "That's why it doesn't do anything for me. I got it in schoolbooks and stuff like that, but—"

"Maybe it's the pressure to feel something. Maybe that's the problem," I said. "It's that deal where you know you're supposed to feel something, so you can't."

"And pretty quick you resent it," she said. "Yeah, maybe that's it, because I really don't feel shit."

"You don't want him getting killed," I said. "There's the other side, which is that the guy was shot right there, and we'd prefer a world in which people weren't shot—the president or anybody. Though I have a hard time seeing why the president getting it is worse than somebody else."

"He's just one more goofball going down," she said.

"He had big ideas."

"He was just another guy with a sore dick."

We got up and started walking again. We went behind the fence where Mike had been earlier and walked around in that parking lot, then leaned up against the fence. It was kind of broken down at the corner. I wondered if it was the same fence that had been there thirty years before. We walked through the colonnade that Mike had been in and up alongside the Texas School Book Depository, then came back to where we'd started.

"This land is my land," I said. "There was a whole different deal. Kennedy took a bullet and that wised us up, so they say."

"That's crap," Jen said. "There were hundreds of thousands of you people changing it every day, stretching the limits, pushing the edges, taking a little more than you absolutely had to have, twisting the truth. Then everybody got used to it. You allowed it, accepted it. You excused it for one reason or another. You said it wasn't too bad, or it's just the way it is, or we'll get 'em next time, or whatever. You all held hands and evolved into what we are now. People get more clever. They don't get smarter."

"It probably wasn't so great then," I said.

"But did it *seem* like it was? I can't even imagine that," she said. "You guys must've been real gullible."

"You've been spending too much time with older men," I said. "We need a trial separation so you'll think kinder thoughts."

"I didn't get it from you," she said. "Don't flatter yourself." She waved out toward the Depository. "This whole place looks like it's lit with bug lamps. It's yellow. Isn't everything kind of yellowish, or is that my imagination?"

"It's kind of parchment-colored."

"It's crummy for them to charge admission to this Texas School Book Depository, it seems to me," Jen said. "There's something wrong with that—something like: kill a president so the city can make six bucks a throw on the tourists. How many tourists must they have here each year?"

"Plenty."

"That's my point," Jen said. "They even charge for kids."

"Do not," I said.

"Yes, sir. It's on the sign."

"You read it wrong," I said.

"Did not."

"I'm about finished with my big thoughts," I said. I got up from where I was sitting and brushed off the seat of my jeans. "You want to go back to the hotel and see what's on television?"

"Yeah," she said. "I guess so. Dad didn't like this, did he?"

"He left awful quick."

"Maybe leaving quick is a sign that it had some powerful impact on him."

"It could be that," I said. "Or it could be that it was so disappointing that all he wanted to do was get away."

"He's thinking of going with us on the next leg," she said.

"O.K. with me," I said. "We're getting along. We had a big talk tonight."

"About what?" she said.

"Regular stuff," I said. "Two old men."

She smiled and took my arm and then pressed her head against my shoulder. "Some of you are older than others of you," she said. "Though I must say your selection of shoes is equally noncurrent."

"I'm getting some work shoes from J. Crew," I said. "I saw them in the new catalog. They took out the metal part of the work shoe from the toe, and they took out the brass eyelets, but they still have the big, thick soles, so I'll be current."

"That was current a couple years back," she said. "This year we're going for something more modest."

"Well, there you go," I said. "How is a body supposed to keep up if you guys keep changing the rules?"

"Wear boots," she said. "They never go away."

"Too hard," I said. "They make you imposing, though, taller than you already are. I like that part. Give you a kind of automatic attitude. But they're hard to pull on and off."

We were walking back to where we'd parked the car, which was next to some architect's idea of a Kennedy memorial—thick slabs of concrete making a sort of room that stood up off the ground in an open half-block space. You were supposed to stand inside it and feel the gravity of events. Somebody had posted a concert sign on its side. We got in the car and headed for the hotel.

The streets of downtown Dallas were almost empty, so it looked like one of those end-of-the-world movies where all the people have been killed and we get long shots of the empty downtown streets. There's a wind blowing coffee cups across them, and pieces of paper are flapping in the breeze, and there are no people. It was nice enough, so we ran the windows down on Mike's car and floated through the streets for a while—going six or eight blocks in one direction and then turning, coming up the next street, going in the other direction, the wind whipping into the car, twisting our hair. It smelled that strange way empty cities smell at night, clean and metallic. Jen switched on the radio, and we turned that up and listened for a while as we rode through the streets. Percy Sledge.

When we got tired of that, we headed for the freeway that would take us back to the Ramada.

Jen had new messages from Durrell Dobson. He was upset.

"No different, Starkweather and Vietnam, the Iraqi kids we killed in Desert Storm, blowing their hands and feet off all the time, that road when they were trying to get back home and we got in with the big choppers and morphed them into thousand-year-old burn victims—like it was some other century. The trade in pictures of the dead was very profitable," his message said. "I used to think we shouldn't kill people, that no matter what, life was sacred and was to be preserved, that we had always the responsibility to maintain the high line, to see beyond the simple convictions of payback, of violence is as violence does, that we were each of us charged with this singular responsibility to see more clearly, and that the consequence of that charge was that someone always *would* see clearly, and that those of us who failed could be led out of our individual wildernesses by that person on that occasion, and another on another. And maybe I even held the hope that our country stood for that, our government meant that, but now it's impossible to maintain such a notion, and more than that, it's impossible to sit on the sidelines and watch the butchering, real and figurative, in foreign countries and in our own cities, where the blood gases squirt from open wounds, and in our ordinary bloodless lives, where secret desires rot and dismember our friends and neighbors, our families, people we encounter at grocery stores and drug counters, where everyone is a victim *and* a transgressor, a cheat, a charlatan, a con man, a rogue, a trickster, a killer. Now it is time to begin to cleanse the land, to exterminate those who violate the fundamental natural order of the humane, who see no limits save those in their own dysfunctional consciences, who seek the self above others, above all. We must flush out the bad seed and eliminate it, wash it away, remove it from among us. We must act with maximum efficiency, individually and collectively, in our neighborhoods as readily as in our international affairs. We must isolate and exterminate those in Rwanda who slaughter others, as we must in Bosnia and Bergen County, in Haiti and in Hotel, Arizona. Wherever there is unconscionable behavior, from great nations to tiny back streets, from the great cities like Los Angeles to the smallest hamlet, wherever this disease lurks we must strike, scrape out its eyes, we must become the scourge of the planet, cleaning pockets of terrorism and torture and violence and crude disregard for humanity. We can do no less in the streets of our cities. It's the least we can do for our children. It's what we must do. It's what history calls upon us to do, to act, to eliminate those parts of our race and culture that do not deserve to be called human."

"He's in high spirits tonight," I said, reading the message.

"He's been loftier," Jen said. "This is on the bloody side. I think I'll suggest that he calm down."

"Is that a good idea? Won't do much good, will it?"

"No, of course not," she said. "But he just does this for effect, anyway. It's posture. He's taking a stand for right and justice. He's probably just this little weevil guy with bug-eye glasses and clothes from The Gap."

"Let's hope so," I said.

"There are a lot of people out here in modemland who are a little off dead center," Jen said. "If you know what I mean."

"I know what you mean."

We were in our room at the Ramada. I went to the connecting doors between Mike's room and ours and pulled on the door that opened into our room. The door into Mike's was closed. I was going to knock on it but decided not to.

"I guess I'll just leave this alone," I said to Jen.

"Yeah. He's probably asleep," she said.

"Are you going to call Penny?" I said.

"I'll call her as soon as I finish this," she said, rattling the telephone cord connected to her computer.

"I guess there's no reason to call her."

I flipped on the television and went through a few stations until I got to the Weather Channel and stopped there and watched a new hurricane named Emilia, messing around with Hawaii. The video of Hawaii was quite beautiful, so I watched that. Buildings were falling down. A Holiday Inn fell down, or part of it did, the sign and the portico over the drive-in entrance. The trees were all bending vigorously, and the whole picture looked wet. It was quite lovely and relaxing, though some of the people there probably didn't think it was so much fun. For others, of course, it was wonderful. I would have liked to be there, but it was nice, too, from where I sat at the Ramada. In a minute I heard Jen's modem screech as she sent her messages off to Dobson and whoever else. She turned around and caught the tail end of the Hawaii video and asked me what it was.

"It's Hawaii," I said. "They're having a hurricane."

"Some guys have all the luck," she said.

"I don't think it's a good idea for you to be sending messages to that guy," I said.

"Oh, don't be silly," she said. "He's harmless. You should see some of the people on the Net if you think he's crazy. I could hook you up to alt.talk.bizarre or any one of the sex lists. Wait, listen . . ." She clicked around on the machine for a minute, then started reading me a message about Japanese rope harnesses as sexual aids. " 'Find the middle of the rope and make a sizable overhand knot so you have a loop big enough to fit your partner's head. Employ a rope of appropriate dimension and surface. Consider the path of the rope from the breasts, just above the vagina, taking care to border the labia with the length running then to her head and neck, and have her hold her hands behind her back—' "

"Been there," I said.

"Don't worry," she said. "He's just this weird bozo out in Las Vegas, kind of a romance rat. He thinks he's being charming and tough and witty."

"That's pretty condescending, isn't it?"

"I didn't mean it that way. I meant he's doing the best he can."

"Oh, I see. Like us," I said.

"Exactly like us. He's mad about things, and he's telling me about them," she said.

"He did the videos. He did the robberies and God knows what else."

"We don't know that. He only said that. We don't know that he really did them. We don't know that he really did this thing with the videos. Maybe he just made it up to make himself interesting."

"Everybody always wants to be so damn interesting," I said. "I'm growing fonder and fonder of people who aren't interesting."

"Age is showing," she said.

"You know what I mean. Everybody's trying to be even the slightest bit interesting. People are jumping off buildings, inventing new sports, designing houses that look like dogs. It's trouble, this 'interesting' business."

"What can they do?"

"They're working too hard," I said. "They're too nervous about being ordinary."

"Most of us are happy to be ordinary. The people you're talking about are on television."

"Maybe. But they're instructing the rest of us. It shows up in people we know. There's the guy who calls people by their last names, and there's that guy who wears all that latex to teach in, and there's the guy who's trying to be George Will."

"So you're complaining that these people are mimicking TV? They're trying to be like people they see on TV?"

"That may be it. Television defining what we *should* be."

"Durrell has a lot of opinions about that," she said. "He hates newspeople. He hates them more than you."

"I don't hate them anymore. I forgive them. I'm taking the Christ-like path."

"Thank goodness for that," she said.

"I used to hate them, but I was misunderstood. I said the left-leaning liberal running-dog media was right-wing. This was not appreciated."

"Oh, Durrell, baby," she said.

"I'm sorry," I said. "I forgot. They're doing the best they can. I forgot myself for a moment."

"I like them. They're like little puppets, like these strange puppets, with a particular location on our spectrum, on our horizon. I like shows like *Crossfire* and that silly one on Saturday with the guy from the *Wall Street Journal* and Bob Novak and that woman with the prissy little mouth and the mole. Everybody sits up so straight on those shows."

"You're a true postmodernist."

"Who isn't?" Jen said. "What choice?"

They were doing the local forecast on the Weather Channel—chance of rain. Jen's CompuServe navigator had logged her off and was waiting for her. She shut the computer down, unplugged the phone cord, and plugged it back into the telephone.

"You want me to call Penny? Do you want to go get something? What?" she said.

"No. I'm going to bed pretty soon," I said.

"I'll call her, anyway. Just to see how she is."

She dialed the phone and sat there, resting the side of her head against the handset. Apparently there was no answer. Finally she hung up.

"That's peculiar," Jen said. "I guess she's asleep."

"She must sleep like a stone," I said. "Maybe she's down at the bar, having a nightcap. Searching for an eager young man."

"I doubt that. She hates men, remember?"

"Why is that?"

"It's probably one of the ten obvious reasons," Jen said. "Why does any woman hate men? They're jerks. They're cruel and clumsy and foolish."

"I wish you had some more original reasons," I said.

"Oh, that's good." Jen shook her head and rolled her eyes and did a little doll jerk, as if she were being controlled on strings from above.

"Well, you've got to admit that the reasons aren't splendid," I said.

"They don't have to be splendid. They just have to be true."

"For her, you mean?"

"Yeah," Jen said. "I'm not going for a sweeping generalization here. At least not too sweeping. I'm just saying that when a woman doesn't like men, it's usually one of those reasons, something obvious, something plain, something ordinary."

"Tragic relations," I said.

"Yeah, that too."

I switched through the channels and stopped at CNN, where there was a program about how much money the lobbyists had spent on the Congress to affect the health-care reform. The doctors spent fourteen million to stop something, the hospitals spent eight million to stop something else, the insurance companies spent twenty-four million to stop a third thing. And all of it going into various pockets of various congresspersons and senators. There was a diagram on the screen, with key players and the amounts of reelection money they got from the lobbyists.

"It's not simple, is it?" I said to Jen.

She sighed and started to rehook her notebook to the telephone. "I guess not," she said.

"You'd have to take the whole system apart brick by brick. You'd have to start at the bottom, start all over again, in order to fix it."

"Nobody wants to do that. We're too far along. Besides, why do you want to fix it on my dime? Why didn't you fix it when it was your dime?"

"I thought you were the one out to do good and avoid evil," I said. "You wanted to go to the West Coast and visit your wrath upon the bad. Why don't you go to Washington and visit your wrath upon them?"

"Pissing in the wind," Jen said.

"I thought you guys were supposed to be less cynical than the rest of us."

"You must be thinking of some other generation. The one before us, they were less cynical, as I recall. We are more cynical. We're so cynical that our cynicism takes paint off warships, knocks airplanes out of the sky, dries up oceans."

"You bad," I said.

"Worried," she said.

On the screen there was a picture of O.J. I figured the anchor was doing a new story about the case, so I punched up the volume. An interviewer was talking about abuse and said, "There's been a lot of focus recently on the problems of spattered bouse syndrome." Then he got flustered and couldn't get it turned around at all. Eventually they cut to the videotape. I killed the volume.

"Maybe I ought to call Bud before you get wrapped up in that stuff again," I said. "What are you going to do?"

"I'm checking my newsgroups."

"Let me use the phone first. O.K.?"

Jen sighed and popped the telephone line out of the side of the notebook. She plugged it back into the telephone receiver. "I'm going to take a bath," she said. "I'll call later."

"Are there plans yet?" I said. "Like for tomorrow? What's happening tomorrow?"

"I don't think there are any plans," she said. "My guess is that we're going on."

"All of us?"

"Unless Dad changed his mind," she said. "Yep."

Bud and Margaret were watching a movie when I called. She answered the phone and wanted to know where we were, and I told her we were in a hotel in Dallas. She asked if we were going to see Dealey Plaza. I told her we'd already been.

"So what about it?" she said.

"It's small."

"What do you mean?"

"I mean it's not big," I said. "It's little. That's the collective wisdom about it."

"So did you have a bunch of historical revelations and stuff?" she said.

"No," I said. "It was like looking at an empty jar."

"You better talk to Bud," Margaret said.

Bud said, "Listen. I don't want to talk about Dallas. I'm thinking about buying some property, building a house. I was wondering if you guys wanted to go in on it with us. We could build a compound."

"You mean like the Kennedy compound?"

"Like the Kennedy compound, but smaller, cheaper, and in Mississippi."

"You mean all of us live in the same house?"

"We could build two houses," he said. "Or houses that were connected. I'm just trying to get more money into the game."

"My borrowable money," I said.

"Right," he said. "Strength in numbers."

"Have you found the property?"

"I've found the property, yeah."

"And you're building the house?"

"Yeah," he said.

"So you're going to buy this piece of property, and then you're going to build something on it whether or not I'm involved?"

"Well, I want to build a compound," Bud said. "You know, a multifamily dwelling."

"Who's going to design it?"

"I'll design it," Bud said. "It'll have big rooms, high ceilings, a lot of strange stuff. We can do weird architecture, whatever you want. Like those cardboard-box houses we used to build when we were kids."

"They were inexpensive. This seems *un*inexpensive."

"Other people do it," Bud said. "Why shouldn't *we* do it?"

"You've already got a great house," I said.

"Well, that just proves my point."

"How does that prove your point?"

"Well," he said. "I mean I can do it. I own it, I bought it, I paid for it, I helped fix it up. I can do it."

"I'll think about it."

"So what else is happening?"

"I don't know," I said. "I think we're going to Los Angeles to shake hands with President Kennedy."

"Maybe you can get that reward," Bud said.

"What reward?"

"The defense is offering half a million for discovery of new information on the killings."

"Yeah, but only if it implicates somebody else."

"That's a problem."

"People are going to be coming out of the walls."

"Yeah," Bud said. "So what else?"

"A lot of driving. Jen's trading computer messages with some insane guy in Vegas. Penny's not causing any trouble, and Mike—I don't know what Mike's doing. He's disappointed by Dealey Plaza. In fact, he left Dealey Plaza early, taking Penny with him."

"Aha."

"Is anything happening there?"

"Rain," Bud said. "The mayor back in bed with the Dixie Mafia, a new desegregation case in the schools, they landed on the moon some years ago, and there's big weather in Hawaii."

"I saw that," I said.

"Well, we're thinking about this property."

"How much?"

"I don't know," he said. "Hundred and something. It's not a particularly good area. I figure I'll put a fence around it. About a ten-foot fence."

"Don't go too short," I said.

"I get the sense you're not interested," Bud said. "I'll tell Margaret you phlegmed out, that you are no longer the good brother of yore."

"I am the good brother. I just don't think we should live together."

"In the old days, families stuck together," Bud said. "Through thick and thin, no matter what happened. Brothers took care of brothers. Think of the Earps."

"Yeah. Which one are you?"

"Guess."

"So who am I—Morgan?"

"Hey, you can be whoever you want to be," Bud said. "This is America. This is the millennium."

"We're going to Big Spring," I said. "You remember those movies with Mother and Father? During the war—he was doing something for the army, and you lived out there for a couple of years. It's that movie of Mother with the big hat. Big hat and some kind of little mountain looking out over the town. Remember that?"

"I remember," Bud said. "Where's Big Spring?"

"Between here and El Paso," I said.

Our parents spent a couple of years during the Second World War in Big Spring, while my father worked for the Army Air Corps, helping them build air bases and troop housing out there. They lived in a tiny bungalow. I wasn't quite on the scene, but Bud was there, although he didn't remember it. The films I'd seen were all very peculiar—single twisted flowers in a barren landscape that, in the eight-millimeter films, looked like something from another planet. There was one scene that I remembered particularly, which was of my mother, who would have been in her thirties then, sitting on a bench outside a park shelter, with all of Big Spring arrayed behind and below her. She was up on some kind of mountain and had on a white polka-dot dress with a colored hat. A big hat that could have been a foot across, flat, with a big brim, something like Lauren Bacall might have worn. This had always been one of the most mysterious pictures of my mother that I'd ever seen. She was like some other woman, some stranger, some aberration. The color had washed out of the film, so that it was much lighter, and everything seemed to be suffused with brightness, and the colors, like the red of her lips, the red of the hat, the white of the dress, merged into the landscape. The background was almost white, with a few twirls of shrubbery gnawing at the ground. When you saw this film you got a sense of white sand, dust blowing, a big lavender sky, and the ground falling from beneath your feet. That was because of this little mountain, this mesa outside Big Spring. It was romantic and glamorous, and it made me wonder about my parents in ways that I hadn't before. It made me think of them as characters in some forties movie, and I wondered if back then they saw themselves as characters in one of those movies, a Bogart movie or any of the film noir stuff. I wondered if movies were the same then as now relative to how people really lived—silly, overdone, art-directed like crazy, no regular house, no regular den, no dreary lives like the ones we live: everybody owns an Afghan. I wondered if that was the same in the forties, if there was as much torture of the ordinary. Sitting there talking to Bud on the telephone, I could imagine the ticking of the projector as it played the eight-millimeter film of my mother at Big Spring turning to look over her shoulder, the wind blowing her hat, and her hand reaching up to hold the brim. She had that forties look about her, that combination of freshness and danger that made the forties so much more sophisticated and intriguing than any decade since. And my mother had the look in this little home movie my father made out in the southwest Texas desert in 1944. She's the new woman in this movie, the future of women. She's entering the modern age, looking forward to a new time for women in the world.

Of course, it didn't turn out like that. It never turns out the way it's supposed to. But there's something in those home movies, and in particular this one he made in Big Spring, that defined my mother forever for me. Something about her elegance, her delicacy, her generosity and strength, something about how she presided over the time, the way she handled every problem, the way she gave our life during my childhood a kind of handsomeness that it otherwise would not have had. It's not a characteristic I would tend to apply to the lives of people I've known. It's a rare gift. Perhaps it's what all mothers do for their children when they make the world, define it, keep it at bay, interpret and explain it, protect from it. And so become little gods to their children. For me it's a woman who sits on the stone bench on a mesa in southwest Texas, holding her red hat and smiling and looking into the camera with a powerful ease. That's something she passed along to her children, something for which we are grateful.

# ten

I was the last one down for breakfast in the morning. The hotel restaurant was all light wood and light Formica and plastic flowers in fifty shades of light green. It was almost empty. Mike and Penny were sitting together at a small table near a window that looked out toward the freeway. I saw Jen in the lobby as I came out of the elevator. She waved me into the restaurant. She was getting a newspaper. Mike was slicing his fork through a tall stack of pancakes covered with pretty syrup. Penny was eating a piece of bacon off his plate. I said good morning.

"How are you?" Mike said. "Long time no see."

"I slept too much," I said. "What time is it?"

"Eleven," Mike said.

"We were up pretty late. I talked to Bud. I hear you're staying with us. Westward ho."

"I'm thinking about it," Mike said. "I could go along for a while."

"I'm glad you're going," Penny said, patting his arm. She picked up her fork and got a one-inch square of pancake off his plate. She had coffee and a roll in front of her, but she was more interested in Mike's pancakes.

"You were disappointed with Dealey Plaza?" I said.

"I guess so. I don't know," Mike said. "After so many years of messing with it and thinking about it and reading about it, getting to know all the characters in all the frames in the Zapruder film and the other films, all the still photographs and the autopsy photographs and the little girl running and Badgeman and Umbrella Man and Dark-Complexioned Man, and looking for the second bullet and imagining how the people were over the fence and the three tramps getting on that train that morning—well, you know, it's a little hard to see it in person. It's just inert."

"Maybe if we go over there today that would help," I said. "It was night. We were tired; we'd been driving."

"No," Mike said. "I don't want to go there today. I've seen enough. I'm keeping it in my head from now on. It's much more complicated there, it's richer, full of stuff and detail. Subtle. It's a puzzle that goes across time and space. You can work on it forever, keep coming back, letting it refresh, letting it show you new things, new angles—you know what I'm saying? Was she really looking back up at the Depository, or had she been called? What about the Moorman Polaroid? On and on. It's a wonderful thing."

"The trail is cold," Penny said, waving her fork at Mike but talking to me. "That's the real problem. He told me last night. You go there and it isn't the real Dealey Plaza. The real one is in the history, in the research. That out there is just a replica."

"Yeah. How many gunmen were there and all that," I said.

"That doesn't matter," he said. "That's not the point. Nobody cares if there was one or there were thirty. It's figuring it out. It's figuring any piece of life out, any act; it just happens that a lot of people have focused on this one. Anything in life would be the same, just as complex, if you tried to take it apart, tried to photograph it and analyze the photographs and check the movements of people and finally pattern it out. It's like any part of life: if you study it hard enough it vanishes, turns to dust in your fingers. The excitement is catching a glimpse of it as it goes."

Jen came back to the table with a *USA Today* and a Dallas paper. I ordered pancakes like Mike's. Penny went on eating off his plate.

"So Big Spring is next, right?" Jen said. She was talking to me.

"I want to go there, yes," I said. "We don't have to stay long. I just want to see this town that I heard about when I was a kid."

"Why did you hear about it?" Penny said.

"His parents were there during the war," Jen said.

"Is that right?" Mike said.

"Yeah," I said. "My father was working for the government there instead of going into the army."

"He has this big thing about a film of his mother that his father made," Jen said.

"It's something I remember," I said. "It doesn't have to be a major step. We can drive around, and then we can go on."

She flapped the paper, opening it to the O.J. page. "I told them about Durrell's latest," Jen said. "Dad says I shouldn't write him, that I should just leave him alone, get away from him."

"That's what I said, too." I nodded at Mike.

"Well, the two of you agree," Jen said.

By the time we'd finished breakfast and gone upstairs to get our stuff and check out of the hotel, the lovely blue sky had turned an angry gray. Thick clouds passed overhead, bleeding into each other, bringing the sky much closer than it had been, shortening the territory, making the landscape smaller.

At the gas station where we filled up the Lincoln, Jen said, "Super Deluxe Wash ahead."

"We could use it," Penny said.

I took the wheel as we headed for Abilene and Big Spring. The highway was flat and the scenery was flat, and the sky was dark and curved. It was cooler than it had been, but it looked even cooler than it was, all that shade from those thick clouds. In the back seat, Mike dialed up Arlene on the cellular phone. I scanned the dashboard with its glossy fake-wood trim and square instruments. Everything looked like a little antique clock on that dashboard. I tried not to listen to Mike's conversation.

"If we go this way we're going to miss the Cadillac ranch," I said to Jen. "Unless we turn around and go due north from Big Spring. We'd have to go back to Amarillo."

"I can live without the Cadillac ranch," Jen said.

Penny leaned forward on the back of the seat. "What's this?" she said.

"We're not going to be able to go to the Cadillac ranch unless we drive way out of our way. I mean, if we're going to Big Spring," I said.

"That's too bad," she said.

"You've seen pictures," Jen said.

"It's not the same," Penny said. "You don't get the wonder of it all."

"I don't mind driving, if you want to go," I said. "It's all right with me. We might be able to get there tonight."

"No, it's O.K.," Penny said. "I don't care." She had both of her hands over the back of the front seat, dangling them into the front seat as if she were some kind of stuffed toy. "Don't worry about me. I'll be fine."

"Aw," Jen said, and she patted Penny's hair, then drew it around her head and into the front seat.

"It's been a while since I've seen this much hair in one place," I said.

"I'm thinking of cutting it," Penny said. "But it took so long to get here that I don't want to let it go. It's a lot of trouble."

In the rearview mirror I could see Mike, the phone pressed hard against his ear, turned to his side, looking out the window trying to get what privacy he could.

When the rain hit, it was big water doughnuts on the windshield. Then it smoothed out. The landscape turned two shades darker, richer, and the air in the car cooled off even more. The big Lincoln flowed down the highway. I set the cruise control on seventy-five and sat up high and steered as if we were in a gigantic inflatable, something from the Macy's parade, maybe a magnet car.

We cruised through Abilene, the site of many gun battles I'd seen on TV shows, and on to Big Spring, which wasn't much of a town. It was kind of pretty, had one tall building and a lot of Native American residents. We drove out south of town to find this mesa where my mother's picture had been taken, and circled up that, stopping on the way at a tourist site called Prairie Dog Town. The prairie dogs were out in force when we got there, but we were the only tourists. Jen and Penny fed them some Tom's Honey Roasted Peanuts we'd bought in Big Spring, and they came running. Prairie Dog Town was a fenced piece of ground maybe thirty yards by fifty yards, which was Swiss-cheesed with softball-size holes in the ground, where these prairie dogs lived and worked. The prairie dogs had been there a long time, apparently. And they weren't confined to the town, either—there were holes dug under the fence, under the walkway that went around the fence. The fence was only two feet high. Any self-respecting prairie dog could have jumped right over it.

The rain had stopped, at least temporarily, so we all got out and crunched around the gravel that surrounded the prairie dog town, and we talked to the prairie dogs. Penny picked out one particularly plump prairie dog and named him Thumper and called him over to the fence. He came, and all the other prairie dogs followed, inch by inch. They were sort of like large, light-brown squirrels, with dog-style hair that was soft and blew in the wind. They sat up on their haunches while they ate stuff that they picked up in their hands, raccoon style. In fact, their hands bore an eerie resemblance to raccoon hands. You could hear them eating, hear the chomp, chomp, chomp when they ate the peanuts we were throwing them. If you moved suddenly, they would all dart away at the same time, almost in formation. But then they would stop and turn and stand up on their hind legs a few minutes, then come back slowly, carefully, as if expecting the worst.

"These are like little Bambis," Jen said. "You know, the way they move, the way they relate to you."

"You got the color right," I said. "Except they don't have the little white freckles."

"I don't remember Bambi having freckles," Penny said.

"They were spots," Mike said. "On his back. They weren't freckles, exactly. They were white spots."

"Do these look like chipmunks?" I said.

"I've forgotten what chipmunks look like," Penny said.

"They're bright blue," Mike said.

Penny rolled her eyes.

Jen was holding out a peanut between her fingers through the little fence. One of the prairie dogs came up and stood right next to her hand, looking at the peanut.

"Go ahead, take it," Jen said. "Take it. What's wrong with you?" She wiggled her hand a bit, and the prairie dog jumped but then retook his position. "It's a peanut," Jen said to the prairie dog. "Honey roasted. Go ahead, take it."

But the prairie dog would not take it from her hand. He just sat there up on his haunches, staring at it between her fingers. When she eventually dropped it, he picked it up, retreated, and ate it.

We drove the winding road that went to the top of the mesa and found the spot where my father's home movie had been made. The mesa was a scraggly hump of land jutting up about two hundred feet out of the desert floor and overlooking the little town of Big Spring. The foliage was mostly cactus and vines, and the ground was covered with a thin layer of Twinkie-colored sand. At the top there was an old stone building with a bench alongside it and a willow tree that I thought I remembered from the home movie. I walked around it, kicked up some dust, took a couple of snapshots with a disposable camera that we'd picked up at a 7-Eleven in Big Spring. I tried to position myself where my father would have been fifty years before, and I got Jen to sit on the bench, with the town arrayed behind her and below her, just as my mother was in the movie. I don't think I got it exactly, but I was close. It was a peculiar sensation, thinking about my mother and father up here on this mesa half a century before, with their lives all out in front of them, all unknown possibilities, hopeful, to think of them in control then, instead of the way they were now—sort of beaten down by age and change. It would not be fair to say that as I looked through the viewfinder in the camera Jen looked like my mother in the home movie, but there was something in that frame, some similarity, some reflection, some suggestion of a link between my mother in her time and us in ours, some way in which looking through that hollow finder on the cardboard camera bristled with a hint of what was to come.

When I finished taking the pictures, Jen said, "I wish I had your mother's hat."

"I wish you did, too," I said.

Then we got back in the car, collected Penny and Mike, and drove back into town, looking for someplace where we could have lunch.

There was dispute over where we should eat. I wanted to get Colonel Sanders and Penny kept telling me it was called KFC nowadays and I said so what's the difference and she said that to call it something wrong was to think of it wrong, to think of it as something that it wasn't. I said I thought of it as chicken, and I kept driving. Eventually I was outvoted, so we ended up at Gordie's Café. As it turned out, it was a good thing, because nobody had bothered to look at the map, and our route from Big Spring to the west wasn't at all clear. We could go directly north through Lubbock to Amarillo and see the Cadillac ranch, or we could go southwest and take the big highway all the way to El Paso, or we could cut diagonally into New Mexico, up through Seminole and Hobbs and Carlsbad. We had already been driving almost five hours, so the Lubbock trip was out.

"I think we go El Paso," Mike said. "It's an easy drive."

"It's still three hundred miles, isn't it?" Jen said. She grabbed the map and checked the mileage. "Besides, if we go that way we pass up Roswell."

"I thought you wanted to go to the West Coast," I said.

"Yeah," Jen said. "But on the way I want to stop in Roswell. No big hurry."

"You can go down here to Pecos on the big highway and then take that little highway north," Mike said. "Look at that. It goes through Barstow, too. If we go that way we can probably get to Carlsbad Caverns tonight."

"Are we going there?" Penny said. "I was there when I was a kid. I saw those bats fly out of that hole."

"We don't have to go there," Mike said. "I'd kind of like to go there. I haven't been there in years."

"I've *never* been there," Jen said.

The three of them looked at me. "Yeah, I've been," I said.

Jen said, "We could go to Carlsbad if Dad wants to go there. I wouldn't mind going. If we get there tonight, we can stay there and go to Roswell tomorrow."

"I want to go to Alamogordo," Penny said. "And White Sands, where they blew up the first A-bomb."

"Cool," Jen said. "But if we're going to L.A., we ought to go on Highway Ten or up here on Forty."

"I thought you said you weren't in a hurry," I said.

"Well, I am, sort of," Jen said. "I don't know. Why don't we just go to Carlsbad and figure it out from there."

"I'm for that," Mike said.

"I'm going to miss the Cadillac ranch?" Penny said.

"Looks like it," Jen said. "Can you live without? I'll get you a picture of it. I'll get you a postcard."

"There it is again," I said.

"What?" Mike said.

"Art idea," Jen said in a monotone. "The postcard becoming the thing it's a postcard of because lots of people see the postcard and few see the real thing. Plus, the thing isn't itself when it's predigested, culturally certified, an 'attraction' suitable for framing. That makes it just a verification of the postcard. On top of that there's Heisenberg."

"That's something else," I said.

"Related," Jen said.

"Beaver brains," Penny said to Mike.

We finished lunch and got back in the Lincoln. Jen was taking a turn at the wheel. I was in the front seat with her. Penny and Mike were in back. The highway was flat and quiet and very fast. We got to Pecos in short order and turned north for Carlsbad. It was getting late in the day, and evening rains were coming up, making the flat land pretty to look at. Jen started a game of "I'm going on a trip and I'm taking with me an aardvark." Aardvark was followed by baseball bat, catacomb, dromedary, earthquake, friendly dog, girlie book, horse, isosceles triangle, Juicy Fruit, and so on. There was a lot of cheating in the game.

While we played, I watched the dirt swish by and thought about Mike and how I was a little uncomfortable around him but not enough to make me wish he wasn't with us. I liked the way he was always low in his seat. He had to be thinking something about me and Jen, but I didn't have a clue what it was. Maybe it really didn't bother him. He seemed to have solved the problem of me being his age by treating Jen as if she, too, were his age, an old friend of his, perhaps, or an acquaintance from his college days. I decided I was worrying more than he was.

"Look over here," he said from the back seat. "There's a prison out there. Five miles, it says." He was pointing off toward the desert. There was absolutely nothing visible, a road that vanished into the horizon. A sign said there was a penitentiary five miles in. "Now, that's a penitentiary. Jesus, you couldn't even see the highway or anything from back in there. I mean, where is it? It's nothing. It vanishes. You vanish if you go there."

"I like these signs," Jen said. "The ones like this one here"—she pointed out a sign we were passing—"that says 'Prison Zone: Do Not Stop or Pick Up Hitchhikers.' I've seen them before."

"They'd never get out to the highway," Mike said. "They'd die of thirst on the way. They'd be out in that dirt over there."

"How's Arlene? You talked to her real long," Jen said.

"Fine," Mike said. "She sends her love."

"What's she doing?" Jen said.

"What she was doing this morning was coveting her neighbors' dog. The neighbors have a dog named Rufus. She seems to think I would like a dog."

Jen looked at me and slid her hand across the seat in my direction, as if to remind me of our conversation about Mike and tidiness and dogs.

"What? She wants you to buy a dog?" Jen said, looking at Mike in the rearview.

"Yes," Mike said. "She says that a dog would be very good for me. Would it shock you if I got a dog?"

"It would shock me, yes," Jen said. "Everything is always so neat at your house, you know, and I thought you didn't like dogs."

"Well, I'm changing," Mike said. "I'm thinking dogs are all right. They bark and wag. They sniff."

"They do everything we do," Penny said.

"They've earned that right," he said. "They've been on the planet a long time. Why can't I open up to dogs a little bit? If I want a dog, I can get a dog."

"What kind of dog would you get?" I said.

"Old English Vacuum Dog," Jen said.

"Probably something medium-size," Mike said. "A springer spaniel, maybe."

"Are you sure you want a name-brand dog?" Jen said. "Wouldn't you rather have a pound dog?"

"That might be better," I said. "You wouldn't get accused of elitism and richism."

"Been tried and convicted," he said. "Each step was a pleasure."

"Listen to him, now," Penny said. "He's taking that powerful old line."

"Thank you," Mike said, and then he went to pat Penny's cheek, or something like that, and she raised her hand as if to grab his hand, and they had this awkward thing there in the back seat, trying to make some gesture toward each other, but they were doing it out of sync and it ended up being a little swatfest.

"Settle down back there, will you?" Jen said, eyeing them in the rearview mirror.

It started raining hard just then. We were still some distance out of Carlsbad. Jen clicked the wipers on high, and we all settled back for the last part of the day's drive.

# eleven

The town was flooded. We were twenty-five miles from the caverns, and it was nearly eight o'clock. The sun was down, but there was still light buried in the thick clouds patrolling the sky. The water on the main route coming in from the highway was a metallic copper color, reflecting the sky, and it was well over the curb. We stopped at a four-way, then took a left onto a road that headed toward the caverns. We didn't go far. We pulled in at the first chain motel we found, got three rooms side by side on the second floor, carried all the bags upstairs, and then stood for a moment on the concrete balcony, talking about dinner. Jen wanted room service, and that was fine with me, but Mike and Penny wanted to go out for Chinese.

"Not me," Jen said, going into our room. "You guys go ahead. I'm resting. I'm taking a shower and watching TV."

"I guess I'll do that too," I said.

"You'll be O.K. without the car?" Mike said.

"Sure," Jen said. She gave her father a little kiss on the cheek, only about the third time I'd seen her do that, and went into our room. I followed her. Mike and Penny went to their rooms to clean up.

The motel was a recently refurbished Holiday Inn. All the furniture was new and more or less unscarred. The comforters on the beds were abnormally plump. The television was a brand-new bottom-of-the-line RCA. I popped through the channels while Jen went into the bathroom and turned on the shower, then came out and started to undress. I liked to watch her dress and undress, because she always acted like she was alone. That made it sexier, as if I was watching her strip on television, or I wasn't there at all and she was just changing, getting ready for bed or for a date—as if she were completely vulnerable. I liked how she handled the clothes when she took them off. She was neither too casual nor too precious with them. She put them down carefully but not too carefully. She folded her jeans, then folded them again. She draped her shirt over the back of a chair. She put her socks and shoes at attention at the foot of the chair. She looked good in her underpants. She looked healthy and young and a tiny bit awkward. Her skin was only lightly freckled. Her back curved in a pretty way. Her breasts were small and delicate, suggesting adolescence. Her knees had curious little wrinkles.

She slid her hands through her hair to freshen it, then stretched out for a minute on the second bed, her hands by her sides, her eyes shut. I got up and went into the bath to turn off the shower for her, and stopped to kiss her forehead when I came back, then sat down and started going soundlessly through the channels again.

"Thank you," Jen said, without opening her eyes. She reached down and pulled the flap of the comforter up on the side of the bed and over her chest and legs.

"Do you want me to wake you?" I said.

"Yes," she said. "Forty-five minutes. No more than that."

I switched to CNN and watched various muted lawyers in studios talk about the Simpson case. Earnest questions were asked by the news anchor, and earnest answers were given by the consultants. In the courtroom scenes, I spent a lot of time staring at Marcia Clark and the thing on her lip, the mole. I was glad I didn't have to listen to her shrill, self-righteous version of justice.

I must have come in late on the report, because soon after, they were on to Rwanda. The most horrifying pictures imaginable, thousands of people in a burned-out, mud-caked landscape with diseased water seeping in dark pools, the kind you see animals wallowing in, flies and bugs and people on the ground, curled up, suffering, wrapped in rags, smoke rising on the horizon, trees stripped of limbs and leaves, sagging huts, tents, people on stretchers, people being pulled by mules, ghastly, freakish, grotesquely maimed people wandering through the filth. Six one-armed boys in matching brown shorts. I wondered why we didn't forget California and go to Rwanda. People all over the country, all over the world, were thinking exactly that thought, but none of us were going to go—we were going to wonder and wait for the next news story. I rattled through the usual arguments about going or not going, and all seemed designed to make me feel more guilty or less guilty. Only the simple *go* made any sense. I took credit for recognizing that, at least until I decided it was another rationalization, a trick, fitting the guilt pattern. Then: I was being too hard on myself, I couldn't be expected to do everything, or even any particular thing, and the guilt was learned—in my case expertly, in Catholic boyhood. That was a moment of relief, until I wondered if it didn't also fit, another regression in the unending sequence of guilt and relief.

Meanwhile I wondered why my country hadn't done something about Rwanda. The massacre had been going on for months and months. I had read about it in the papers, had seen it on the news, it seemed like four or five months before. Eight months. How was it that a country, a powerful country, a country committed to decency, compassion, and kindness, routinely stood mute and inactive while tragedies unfolded? Occupied the same postures each time? First a few little stories in the press, then more stories, and pretty soon earnest concern, and then grave concern, and then elaborate grave concern while many things were thought of and many people died. And then the crisis took a turn for the worse, and there was even graver concern, and there were more deaths and more stories. And then the crisis took an additional turn for the worse, and perhaps a third, and the process was repeated until what we were fed on the nightly news was a scene of incomprehensible agony. And then the camera people did their lovely, lingering close-ups of the survivors, those new pictures matched with the hugely solemn voice-overs of the announcers.

Curiously, what was in those eyes, along with decaying hope, was an inexplicable determination to live.

I looked at the people on television and thought: Why aren't you dead? How do you manage to want *not* to die? In that hotel room in Carlsbad, I wondered what I would want in their shoes.

Then it struck me that if they were in *my* shoes, they would be sitting in a swanky Rwanda hotel watching me on their big-screen TVs as I slogged through a urine-and-feces-strewn America, and they'd be thinking how bad they felt for not helping me out, they'd be wondering why their country didn't do something. They'd consider doing something ineffective and insufficient themselves, like TV news reporting of the tragedy in America, or gathering medical supplies, or writing torrid op-ed pieces in the *Rwanda Times*—all the tricks we play on ourselves so we feel less guilty about good fortune. I figured they'd wonder about that look in my eyes and they wouldn't lift a finger.

"He's a really nice man," Penny said. "He feels he's missed something. He hasn't, as far as I can tell, but he thinks it anyway. He's so cut off from everything."

We were in the Big Room at Carlsbad Caverns, a space the size of several Astrodomes, as the literature was eager to point out, seven hundred feet underground. Jen and Mike had gone on ahead of us. Penny couldn't see too well, so she was holding onto my arm as we walked the path. It was cold in there, too cold to be comfortable.

The other cavernites were running around taking snapshots of every weird-shaped chunk of rock they could find, using their point-and-shoots to good advantage, so there were flashes everywhere. Curious formations dropped out of the ceiling, grew out of the floor. The path, lined with a foot-high pipe railing, rose and sank as it weaved through the cave.

"What'd he miss?" I said to Penny. "What does he think he missed?"

"By my reckoning it's Sting, mostly," she said. "He got married thirty years ago and lived the right life as long as he could. After the divorce he lived more of it. He's been in it all this time. And here you come along with Jen."

"So?" I said.

"You have produced doubts," she said. She grabbed my arm as we went up over a rise next to a rock formation that looked like a giant breast. The room was full of echoes. On the other side of the cave, we could see the silhouettes of people coming back along the end of the same trail we had just started on—it looped around the perimeter of the Big Room. Every word spoken in the cave rippled around the rocks. It sounded like nighttime, flooded with delicate echoes and little bits of laughter and the odd drop of water into a standing pool, the footsteps fast and slow, children running on the path, people talking in foreign languages, explaining the sights to one another, the wheezing of thirty-five-millimeter autowinders.

"So what do you want me to do?" I said. "You want me to apologize for being a failure?"

"Oh, are we a failure?" Penny said. "Is that how we think of ourselves today?"

"By certain yardsticks, of course."

"But what about the one true yardstick? The yardstick of yardsticks?"

"O.K., forget I said it."

"Does all this stuff look phony to you?" she said, waving at the extraordinary rock structures growing out of the ceiling and out of the floor. "Does it look a little bit like papier-mâché in here, or is that my imagination?"

Something had been bothering me about the cavern, and that was it. Maybe it was just because we were in the Big Room, the one easily accessible by elevator, seventy stories below the visitors' center; we hadn't walked in through the natural entrance, down through the Bat Cave, Whale's Mouth, Devil's Den, Iceberg, Green Lake, Queen's Chamber, and the other evocatively named rooms and halls of the natural path down to the Big Room. Or maybe it was that they'd overcleaned the place, what with the lamps and pathways and signs and the little multilingual handheld tape-recorded personal guides that rented at the visitors' center for four and a half dollars. Whatever it was, the cavern looked too well groomed for me, too much like a life-size model of the real cavern that might be somewhere else, hidden away, out of public view, inaccessible save to government scientists, leaving this one a cleaned-up, polished, carefully manicured, National Park Service engineer's idea of Carlsbad Caverns.

"Yeah, looks phony," I said. "But these big guys do look like walruses, don't they?" I was pointing to walrus-shaped rock formations.

"Some do," she said.

We were just then passing a place on our right called Mirror Lake. The cavern keepers had put an upside-down lighted sign just above this tiny puddle, so that when you looked into the thing the words "Mirror Lake" appeared right side up and rippling on the surface of this bit of water. The pool couldn't have been more than fifteen feet across, two or three feet deep. In the Big Room of this putative Carlsbad, it became Mirror Lake.

"This is what you mean, right?" I said, pointing this out to Penny.

"Yes," she said. "Exactly. I could do that in my bathtub."

"Mirror Tub."

"Exactly."

"Well, so much for silent chambers and timeless beauty," I said.

"I think we've been deeply injured by our time," Penny said. "I really wanted this to be wonderful. If you repeat this, I'll deny it, but this morning when I got up I was excited about coming down here. Maybe if there were a little more dirt around, if we tripped on rocks and stuff?"

"That would help," I said. "Maybe you should go down into the unexplored part. If you're young and energetic, and you are, and you pay the ten dollars or whatever it takes, you get to see an unspoiled, undioramatized version of a cavern."

"Do you suppose they've got all this dramatic lighting down there?"

"Go back two spaces," I said. "Ridicule."

"Sorry."

"After you factor out the trails and the lights and the garden-club beautification, it's still O.K., isn't it?" I said. "It really is kind of remarkable."

"Yes, of course it is," Penny said. "You didn't think I was saying it was *un*, did you?"

"Who knew?"

"I wish it were plainer. I don't think the theatrical lighting helps. In fact, it hurts. It's hard to see anything down here. Ordinary lighting would be better."

"You're the matter-of-fact kid, aren't you?" I said.

"So what if I am?" she said.

"You can't blame them. It's a precious national resource. All precious national resources are lighted this way. Have you ever seen the Washington Monument? The Lincoln Memorial?"

"We can't leave well enough alone?"

"We live to decorate," I said.

Penny sat on a stone bench in the middle of the cavern to rest. I sat down beside her. The bench was cold. A Chinese family was there with us, speaking in hushed but rapid Chinese. A plump mother, a diminutive father, and two gorgeous, lanky, silk-haired Chinese girls in their teens. The parents were eagerly discussing the scenery. One of the kids was staring at her hand, and the second was reading what appeared to be a comic book, using a flashlight the size of a Pez dispenser. A tall guy, an American, came up behind us and was talking to the people he was with, telling them all about the cavern, explaining everything, challenging the people in his party to answer questions. "When was the cavern discovered? What was its principal value then? When did it become a national park? What is the role of water in the formation of the rock structures? How many million years ago did the mesa out of which the canyon carved itself come into being?"

He'd read the manual.

Penny poked me in the ribs with her elbow. "Quit staring," she whispered. "He's going to call on us."

We got up and walked along the trail past some kind of wire ladder that dropped out of sight into a hole in the cavern floor, then past another hole, called the Jumping Off Place, then past a hole called the Bottomless Pit.

"Throw yourself in," I heard somebody say.

"This pit isn't bottomless at all," somebody else said. "Look. It's only one hundred fifty feet deep or something."

"Is not," somebody else said.

"Read the sign," somebody said.

It was much darker and colder in this part of the cave. We hurried along the trail.

"How is it you know so much about what Mike's thinking?" I said.

"He talks to me," Penny said. "Since Dallas."

"I see," I said.

"Not like that," she said.

The smart guy had come up behind us again, and he was doing a quiz on bats. "So how do they manage to hang upside down?" he asked his kids. "When they're sleeping?"

"Yeah," one of the kids said. "How do they do that?"

"Magnets," another one of the kids said.

"Don't be smart, Junior," the father said. "The answer is that when a bat hangs upside down with its feet closed onto something, its feet are in their natural condition, just as our hands are when they are open. See? When our hands are open they're relaxed, and when a bat's feet are closed *they're* relaxed. It's as if our hands were closed when they were at rest, but for the bat, relaxed is closed and open is working, like our hands would be if we were grabbing onto something. Do you see? When the bat relaxes, its feet close."

"You mean bat feet are like clothespins?" one of the kids said.

"Like clothespins," the father said. "Well, I guess so. Yes."

We stood aside on the trail and let them pass. We were looking at a small tableau of draperies of stalagmites and formations called soda straws, which made up an attractive altar-size indentation off the main path.

"Those little ones look like prairie dogs," Penny said. "See that one there?" She pointed to a little knot of rock that resembled a prairie dog standing on its hind legs. "They're just gathered around listening to *Prairie Dog's Home Companion*."

"We've got to get out of here," I said.

"What? You're not having fun?"

"I'm freezing."

"What about all these wonderful national rocks and these crystal growths and all these astonishingly beautiful and delicate objects?"

"I'm buying the video," I said. "Let's speed it up here."

And that's what we did, taking the rest of the trail at a near trot, passing up the smart guy and his kids, the Chinese family, some other people we'd seen along the way. We even passed Jen and Mike, who were walking arm in arm along the path.

"We'll be in the lunchroom," Penny said, as we went by them.

"Or topside," I said.

The lunchroom was a hollowed-out part of the cavern with a fifties-looking concrete concession stand at the bottom, the architecture reminiscent of Frank Lloyd Wright's Johnson Wax office building. We shared a quick Coke and a candy bar and then got in line at the elevator, waiting to go up.

"This is like the minus seventy-fifth floor, right?" Penny said, as we waited.

A bald guy in front of us turned around with his video camera, video'd us. Penny made some faces for him and introduced me as Jack Ruby.

"You remember Jack Ruby, don't you?" she said to the video camera.

The bald guy stopped shooting and stood up tall. "Sure. I saw the movie. Kind of a mob intermezzo." I thought this guy looked a lot like Tom Noonan.

When we got back up to the visitors center, we stopped at a trinket shop and I bought a comb with "Carlsbad Caverns" engraved in its spine. Penny bought a chrome-and-red-and-white decal. Then we went outside and sat on a stone fence in the warm and gentle sun. It was perfect up there. This little breeze was around.

At a Chinese-American restaurant in the town of Carlsbad, we sat down for lunch and tried to decide what our plan was. We'd given up on the bats flying out of the cave, because that happened only at sundown and we didn't want to wait all afternoon. We'd gone up and looked at the cave, the natural entrance to the cavern, taken some snapshots, then driven the twenty-five miles back to town.

The restaurant buffet had the usuals—sweet and sour chicken, sweet and sour pork, sweet and sour shrimp—plus roast beef and gravy, mashed potatoes, and black-eyed peas for the heavy eaters. It was a pleasant place, with high ceilings where fans swatted the air. Nobody minded our sitting and nibbling.

"We ought to have a plan," Mike said. "A route we're going to take."

"Oh, Dad," Jen said. "You always want to have a plan."

"All right, I don't want a plan," Mike said. "I've changed my mind. I don't know why I said that."

"Something came over you," Penny said.

"Right," he said.

"We're going to Roswell," Jen said. "I've always wanted to go there. They have a UFO museum."

*"X-Files,"* Penny said.

"Mmm, Sculley," I said.

"Don't start up," Jen said.

"The crash wasn't at Roswell," Mike said. "It was at Corona. Besides, the Air Force admitted they were lying and said it was this special spy balloon."

"Nobody believes that," Jen said. "That's just a new cover-up. But you've been studying, huh?"

"A little," he said. "I read the New Mexico travel magazine in my room last night."

"Also, there was a Showtime movie," Penny said.

"We get stuff off a Chicago board," Jen said. "They're persuaded. The Net has a lot of junk, too—sightings and theories and reports and counterreports. Most of it's silly."

Mike and Penny got some of the Chinese food off the buffet, and Jen brought herself a plateful of mashed potatoes and gravy.

"So we're going to Roswell?" Penny said. "What about after that? L.A. and the Case of the Painted Genitals? I thought we were going to take serious action, do something, see somebody, make our opinion known, maybe have a protest or make some big flyers like those things you make all the time, Jen. But in L.A., where it would have some impact."

"My flyers wouldn't have any impact in L.A.," Jen said. "They've got thousands. In L.A., I'm just another girl with something on her mind."

"I thought that was the idea."

"It is," Jen said. "We'll get there."

"We could shoot straight out from here," Mike said.

"I wouldn't mind that too much," Penny said.

"After Roswell and Corona, maybe I'll be ready," Jen said. "I don't know."

"I kind of want to go to White Sands," I said.

"See the movie," Penny said.

"You were the one who wanted to go," I said. "Besides, the sands are interesting. They're not sand, really; they're something else—gypsum."

"Yeah, but I've changed my tune," Penny said.

"Whatever that is," Jen said.

"Next thing, you'll want to go to that place where the rocks move by themselves," Penny said.

"Where is that, exactly?" Jen said.

Penny wobbled her eyes left and right, and refused to answer. "We're either serious or not," she said.

"We are," Jen said.

"When you think about it, we're late worrying about this guy with the painted crotch," Penny said. "That was two or three years ago. We should move on to a more recent violation. Besides, there's all this baggage that goes with it."

"What baggage?" Jen said.

"The guy's black. He's painting some white guy's dick black," Penny said. "Get it?"

"What, you think I missed that?" Jen said.

"Well, it's interpretable," Penny said. "It means something. It's a reversal of racial roles, a transformation of the white guy into a temporary black guy, and since the primary target is genitalia, then the transformation is a kind of sexual overwriting where the victim becomes what he isn't, a black person. That, of course, carries the sexual-proficiency myth, so in a sense the victim is being diminished in sociocultural terms even as he is being augmented in erotic terms, made into a performer in a way that he wasn't before, wearing the sign of the performer, which sign delivers us directly through history to the minstrel show, and the adoption of blackface, the white masquerade, and eventually, through economic dominance, to blacks performing in blackface, thus doubling themselves, denying even that identity."

Jen and I exchanged a glance that Penny didn't seem to notice, even though she was looking right at us.

"Uh-huh," Jen said. She pushed a heap of mashed potatoes over to my side of her plate.

"Well," Penny said, "because the painting is cross-race masking, the precedents of control by other means, such as lynching, for example, are suggested, and from these we 'draw' "—she did the quotes with her fingers—"the literal 'marking out' or removal of parts of victims' bodies—ears or genitals—as mementos. It isn't direct reversal because it's only seductive to paint a black person white as a mode of torture for rewriting white margins, sexual margins, say a violation of station or other perceived boundary with respect to a white woman, which was often a pretext for lynching. In this case the reversal is a taunt, the whitewashing is a preparation of the victim for sacrifice, which is a celebration of death where the ritual preparative involves detoxification of the offering."

"Yeah," Mike said. He was wolfing down golf-ball-size hunks of sweet and sour pork in pods of glistening gold-orange sauce.

"Plus, there's the tarring of whites as a secondary precedent, which is closer to this situation but cannot be unpacked except with respect to the white, who, by tarring, is reduced in status to the slave class; that might make sense here, when it's a black guy doing it to a white person, but Lopez is Guatemalan, yes? So *that* remarks on the breakdown of solidarity among the disenfranchised and the implicit deep inscription in Western culture of the dualist predisposition. And then you've got to recontextualize around the idea of Lopez being saved from death by a second black man, a religious man, who risked his own life to protect and to 'serve' this fallen semiwhite."

"That all, girl?" Jen said.

"It's a way to understand things," Penny said.

"Sure it is," I said.

"Gibberish," Jen said. "It's taming. Toss carpets on top, so when it goes it's just a jiggle in the rug."

"Maybe it helps Penny," I said.

"Disconnects the experience," Jen said. "It's white girl's overlay."

Penny stared at the ceiling fans for a minute, doing that thing we do when we want to look like we're thinking but what we're really doing is waiting a minute before giving up some ground. "Yeah, you're right. It's shit," she finally said. "Never mind. I was just practicing. He probably picked up a can and painted the guy's dick because he's a graffiti hotdog."

"That's it," Jen said.

"I thought it was good," Mike said, running his fingers over Penny's forearm. "Very collegiate. It's like looking at a movie from another planet, like you were never on this planet where this movie comes from, and so you look at it and make up all these things you see, whether or not they have anything to do with what the movie's about, know what I mean?" He was asking Penny only.

"Yeah," she said.

"It *was* interesting," I said.

"Yeah, but Jen's right," Penny said. "If we don't understand it the way it was done, we don't understand it."

"Yeah," Jen said. "Clarity. When he did it you could see where necessity vanished and malignancy remained."

"You got that in Rodney King, too," Penny said.

"Same thing," Mike said.

"Maybe," Jen said. "But there wasn't enough thought, or the right kind of thought. It was too dumb. Real lynching was worse—malignant—because it was *designed*. The King thing was just brain-dead cops."

Mike said, "I doubt if Lopez felt any worse about having his crotch painted than King did about getting cracked up by those guys."

"That makes sense, too," I said.

"Well, whatever it is, we've got to make it practical," Penny said. "Maybe we can join some movement in L.A., then go back and start our own versions at home."

"What movement?" Mike said.

"I don't know. We have to find that out," Penny said. "Find out what movements there are and which ones would be best to join, which ones make sense."

"I don't think you can go around and pick your movements," Jen said, spooning gravy into her mouth.

I reached across the table and got one of Mike's last three pork baubles. "Maybe you can. These days you have to have a movement to get anywhere, to get any publicity, to get anything done. People don't do things by themselves anymore."

"Ross Perot," Mike said. "Is that what you mean? That kind of thing?"

"Oprah," I said. "But it's a point. Maybe there's a group that's pissed about this. There are people pissed about Williams's sentence."

"On both sides," Jen said.

"You mean some people thought he got too steep a sentence?" Penny said.

"Martin Sheen," Mike said. "Didn't you tell me that, Jen?"

"Yes, I told you that," Jen said. "But give him a break."

Penny was stirring her fork through a vegetable medley on her plate, using it like a rake to get the mushrooms on one side of the plate and little cobs of corn on the other. The sauce was two-tone, clear and dark brown. When she got all the corncobs on one side of the plate, she started moving them to the other and moving the mushrooms where the corncobs had been. These were miniature corncobs, the kind that are smaller than your little finger. "We could see if we could find people of like mind," Penny said. "We could meet some people, hang out, see what happens. Try to do some good."

"That's O.K. with me," Mike said.

Our waitress, who was a plump American girl with frizzy blond hair and a bad cold, sneezed her way over to the table to see if there was anything we needed. Mike said we needed a check.

When the girl left, Penny put her fork down on her plate and said, "What I need is a hamburger from someplace that's been O.K.'d by the Centers for Disease Control. Can we do that?"

# twelve

There were two UFO museums in Roswell. The first was a tiny storefront downtown, where a little old guy who was a retired postal worker from Cleveland did his best to explain the Philadelphia Experiment—those cables wrapped around that ship, the space in the water where the ship had been, antimatter machines, all that. He had wiry hair and wore his jeans nipple-high, and he was eager to please—a volunteer, he explained, at the museum. He was reluctant to let us browse without instruction. The place was the size of a shoe shop, three rooms, the largest arranged around a long folding display board pinned with photos, texts, crummy sketches of flying saucers. In a side chamber there was a four-foot-high wooden alien with teardrop eyes and several coats of Testor's Alien Lumina Silver. We listened to the retiree tell us about the rash of sightings in 1947 and about how the Army Air Corps had clammed up about the Roswell incident. He was quick to put the kibosh on the Air Force's new bonehead spy balloon explanation of the original cover-up, too.

There were snapshots of the Brazel ranch where the Corona UFO crashed, but the property looked like nothing special, just dirt, like the rest of New Mexico.

"You see," the guy said, "in 1947 there were sightings all over this country—way up in Washington and Oregon, all the way down here, over to Alabama, up toward Minnesota, in New York State—they were everywhere. Strange lights, abductions, interactions, exchanges of fluids—I mean priests, nurses, even military officers reported stuff. For several weeks in the summer of 1947 this went on, and then it suddenly stopped."

At that, the retiree did a deliberate pause, a long pause, nodding, watching us with a shrewd smile.

"It *stopped*," he repeated. "What does that tell you? What does that say? Think about it. It says they came for a *reason*. It says they got what they wanted and they left." He slapped his hands together for emphasis. "Bam!" he said. "You have to keep up with these deals, or you miss everything. You have to think back to what happened in 1947. Who was born that year? What world historical events were precipitated by incidents that occurred then? What was invented in the year 1947? These kinds of things are the kinds of things you have to think about when you're trying to keep an eye on the big picture. Where there's smoke, there's fire—that's all we are saying."

"Amen," Jen said. "But what about that magic aluminum foil, you know? And where are the tiny purple I-beams?"

"Oh, a TV watcher, huh?" he said, shaking his head. "Well, they weren't purple, they were magenta, and where do you think? Government's got all that. Maybe Groom Lake, Area 51—you know Area 51?"

"Where some aliens were held captive, right?" she said. "But somebody discovered there really wasn't any Area 51, it was all a hoax."

He smiled and took a look at his black shoes. "Oh, there's an Area 51, all right. And a Hangar 9. There wasn't any Hangar 54, maybe that's what you're thinking about, that's more TV stuff, but there were Rainbow, Phoenix, and Montauk projects. And there's S4, MJ–12, Zeta-Reticula, and there are underground hangars at Kelly—there's a lot out here. If you're interested, check into Groom Lake, check out the Vegas airport sometime, the white jets without markings that go into the desert at night." He thumped his temple. "Don't let 'em confuse you."

Penny's eyebrows were doing Groucho moves. She pointed out toward the lobby and mouthed that she'd be waiting for us. Mike slipped off with her, leaving me and Jen to listen to the Socorro story, how the deputy had been driving along, minding his own business, kind of a pleasant evening, enjoying himself after work when he'd seen this craft in a ravine just outside of town—the full story. While he was talking I read the actual front page of the Roswell newspaper the day the Army put out the story that it had recovered a saucer. I knew the story, but seeing the paper, yellowed and brittle and hiding under glass, gave me a new sense of that time, made it seem as if the world was a toy world back then. The way the story sounded, the people it talked about and quoted, what they said, how they said it, even the people you could imagine reading the paper—they must've been like kids in adult bodies running things. That was a little eerie.

The museum was strange in the same way. It was childish, it looked like a sixth-grade science show. But there was something edgy and nagging about the pencil drawings and the snapshots with their rippled edges and the Xeroxes of typewritten accounts, something that made you uneasy—why was this enterprise still so ragtag after all these years? I stared at sketches supposedly done by the medical examiner during the autopsies of the Corona aliens, at a photo of the supposed Socorro deputy pointing at the place where he'd seen the aliens—there was a dotted marker line showing the path of the departing spacecraft—and I began to think that in spite of, or maybe because of, the farfetched and unconvincing displays, the UFO museum was entirely disturbing.

About then the retiree rubbed his hands together and looked around, as if scanning for something else to tell us. "I guess that gives you a start on it, huh?" he said. "Why not kind of meander around and get your own sense of the place now that I've introduced you? That be O.K.?"

"That's great, thanks," Jen said.

When he was gone I said, "I envy him—living here, volunteering here, explaining everything to the tourists."

"Yeah," she said. "Cool job."

"Like the details of Corona, or the Philadelphia Experiment, or Groom Lake. Wouldn't it be great to go home every night and read new stories, watch bad video copies, go through new evidence compiled and distributed by the Society for Recognition of the Adaptations of Alien Life Forms?"

"S-R-A-A-L-F," she said.

"Yeah," I said. "Or just sit out on a dusty porch in the middle of nowhere and stare at the saucer-filled sky."

"You're a wonderful person, Del," Jen said.

"Well, he's like those guys who spend twenty years building railroads in their basements, who really don't do anything but play with their trains. They live perfect lives, devoted to love."

"Oh, baby," Jen said, doing a fifties deal. "Come to me, baby." She gave me a playful and sexy hug.

I watched as the little guy stood at the front window for a minute talking to another volunteer, then he cornered three new tourists—husband and wife with child. The retiree took them on, brought them into the main room and then to one of the side spaces where he'd originally taken us. I heard him start his speech about the antimatter machine, how even *he* didn't quite understand it, but he would try to explain it to them if they could picture this massive World War II battleship wrapped in miles of thick steel cable—cable as thick as your arm!—the ship tossing in the stormy ocean waves on a bleak, wintry night, rain coming in visible sheets, and then, suddenly, without warning, in a wash of lightning the ship vanishes, leaving an indentation in the water, a footprint in the shape of its great hull.

Outside the museum, Mike and Penny said they wanted to walk through downtown for a few minutes and went off arm in arm. When they were out of earshot, Jen said, "This isn't quite the way I'd planned it."

"What do you mean?" I said.

"What's this deal with my father and Penny?"

"What deal?"

"You haven't been paying attention, Del," she said.

"Sure I have. They're just friendly and your father's not a big threat, so Penny's more friendly with him than she might otherwise be."

"It's kind of icky, him and her together, isn't it? Thinking of it?"

"Wait a minute," I said. "You and I are together."

"Yeah, but that's different," she said.

"Is not."

"Well, it's different to me. What about Arlene? And my mother?"

"Arlene's fine," I said. "Arlene's not greatly invested."

"How do you know that?"

"Birdie," I said.

We crossed Main Street and went into a little park, sat on a wooden bench under a huge scraggly tree. It was surprisingly cool in the shade. The big Lincoln was parked right in front of us, shrouded with a layer of cement-colored dust. Other cars sped by on Main Street. I noticed that the sign on the outside of the UFO museum across the street had little sparklies on it, little round shiny-colored disks that shimmered when hit by the wind.

"Besides, I thought it would be just you and me," Jen said. "On this trip."

"Wait a minute—you invited everybody, didn't you? I'm not complaining, but—"

"We could use a trip, just the two of us," she said. "Too many people, too many days. I don't know how folks keep it up all the time. It's so much work talking to other human beings. Listening to them. Being friendly. Trying so hard all the time. I was messing with Penny's hair in the car, and what I was thinking was: What're you doing, playing with her hair, for God's sake? I just grabbed it without thinking, and then I couldn't get rid of it. I had to comb at it, whatever."

"We'll be fine," I said. "Soon we'll be alone in a hotel or motel. Behind closed doors. We can be quiet."

"You think L.A. is silly, don't you?" she said. "Trying to do something, wanting to do something, thinking there's such a thing as doing something."

"Nope," I said. "Not silly, not silly to want to do something; and thinking there's such a thing, well, I don't know. We are running against the tide, though, which means 'Born to lose' tattooed on the forehead. What we should do is learn the conventional wisdom and then adopt it. Or maybe extend it a little. I mean, we're not going to kill anybody, right? If we were, we wouldn't start with Damian 'Football' Williams. So the trip is about something else. I just haven't figured out what yet."

"I've been thinking of White Sands. I don't know why. I guess it's the idea—missile range, history, all that white—just the idea of it."

"White Sands is where I want to go," I said.

"Are we going to Corona?"

"Don't know," I said. "You want to?"

"We can go Corona, Socorro, then down to Alamogordo, White Sands."

"Then what?" I said. "West?"

"Maybe," she said. "We're screwing around a lot, but there's stuff to see, it seems like."

"We need a map to figure this out," I said. "Whatever you want is O.K. with me."

"I was thinking we could do some of both," she said. "See stuff and get to California. We'll go but maybe stop a couple places first."

"That's fine. O.K. with me."

"Durrell sent me a huge zip file about assassinations," Jen said. "Everything you ever wanted to know, complete with selected gifs of the Kennedy autopsy, the head photos. He must've scanned them out of some book."

"This was last night?" I said.

"Yes," she said. "One of his many lives is as an assassination freak, I guess. There's stuff about Kennedy and Bobby Kennedy and Martin Luther King and twenty other people who've been assassinated. He was very excited about it and wanted me to read it and get right back to him. He seems like one of those guys you always hear about who got a plate in his head after some major accident."

"Connect him up with Mike. That'll fix him. Or better yet, drop from sight."

"I don't want to be rude," she said.

"You're a southern girl," I said.

"I'm a southern girl who hasn't seen so much," Jen said. "That's kind of why I was thinking about seeing a few things while we're out here. Natural things. You know what I mean? Like geological things. I liked the caverns pretty well."

"It was a little Walt Disneyed," I said.

"You have to overlook that," she said. "If you do, it's kind of amazing. Those big stalagmites, like giant ice cream cones or something. Giant dripping yogurt piles. The stuff on the walls . . . I was impressed. It's fake-looking, staged, but it's still great. If it was natural, it would be wonderful because it was natural. As it is, it's wonderful because you can still sort of imagine what it would be like if it were natural, plus it's so weird the way those people set it up—the way it was lit, and the way it was organized and arranged, and the way the paths went. It was like earth taxidermy."

"I had a hard time seeing the real thing underneath the stuffed version. I guess it was kind of O.K. Maybe we should go back for another look?"

"We're not going backward," she said. "There are lots of places up ahead I want to see. I've been watching the map—Painted Desert, Petrified Forest, Grand Canyon, Saguaro National Monument; there are some Indian pueblo things. There's a lot of natural wonder out here. Have you looked?"

"I read the guide," I said.

"So we kill two birds with one stone," she said.

"Way to plan," I said. "Driving around, seeing places, seeing how much the same everything is. It's like no matter what the country looks like, people always do the same things, build the same places, arrange the same stores, the same kinds of restaurants, same houses. Why do people always complain about that? That's a charm, seems to me. The places are different enough by themselves, they don't need our help."

# thirteen

After Roswell there was nothing but desert sand topped by little thickets of rat brush, some large stones, and miles of fence. We almost missed the turnoff to Corona, but when we got it and headed west off the highway it was as if we were suddenly in the middle of nowhere, like the prison Mike was talking about on the way to Carlsbad.

Corona was tiny and empty. We got some UFO materials at a gas station, and talked to some people about the crash site, and then headed toward where they said it was. When we got there, there wasn't any there there. It looked like the rest of the desert. We had a little sheet with a diagram, and we tried to visualize the debris field that was drawn on the sheet, but it wasn't easy.

"This feels ghostly, doesn't it?" Penny said. She was sticking pretty close to Mike.

We shuffled around in the dirt for a while, looking this way and that, and soon enough, when we couldn't find anything that looked like a flying saucer, or a remnant of a flying saucer, or a place where a saucer smacked into a hill, or a missed fragment of the silver flight suit of one of the aliens thrown from the craft, we got into the car and drove back the way we'd come.

"Socorro next?" I said. I was driving this leg.

"Forget it," Jen said. "Let's shoot south. I'm torched on the saucermania."

"What about you guys?" I asked, spotting Penny in the rearview. "O.K. we just go for White Sands?"

"That's fine," Penny said. Then she turned to Mike, who I couldn't quite catch in the mirror, and asked him. He waved his agreement.

"We roll, then," I said, and pointed us south on Highway 54.

A couple hours later, we cut into the mountains so that Mike could see Ruidoso, the racetrack, then took an older mountain highway that led us into a toy-size resort town called Cloudcroft. It was getting late. The town part of the town was a tourist hive with dinky wood buildings and a semi–Old West motif: T-shirt shops and candy shops and ice cream shops. Jen asked the woman at the T-shirt shop where we could stay, and the woman said there was a hotel on top of the mountain, so we took a twisting road that went up the hillside and emptied into a parking lot that surrounded a huge old three-story hotel with a turreted roof and a glass-fronted restaurant. It was called The Lodge, and apparently it was famous in the forties. Movie stars stayed there when vacationing in New Mexico. It had a lovely view, with layers of treetops going down the mountain and, in the distance, another row of mountains, with the sun just disappearing behind them. The sky was rippling pink, yellow, and green as the sun set. Jen and I had a room at the front of the hotel on the third floor, while Mike and Penny had a room with two double beds on the second floor. When we were carrying the bags up the stairs, there was some question whether maybe Jen and Penny ought to bunk together. They talked about it, each offering to do it, but neither seemed to want to, so we took our bedroom and they took theirs.

The room was plain. It was charming in an old-fashioned way. The furniture was antique but not precious, nice because it was unassuming.

"We haven't had much time together on this trip," Jen said.

We were sitting together on the bed. The television across the room was off. Out the window, the last bit of sunlight mixed it up with the lights from the parking lot. We had the window open, and it had just started to rain the lightest rain imaginable. It was as if this rain was slightly embarrassed about being there—so quiet you could barely hear it, drops like fine sugar. We sat on the bed until the room turned completely dark, lit only by reflected light from the parking area below.

"This is something in the world," Jen said. "This is doing something. I never thought we'd be here in a million years. Look, this is a place with chintz curtains. Chintz," she said, pointing at the curtains.

"I see them," I said.

"There's a rocking chair over here," she said. "This isn't our kind of place. We don't go for quaint, or charming, or characterful, or burnished. We go for Holiday Inn. But we're here and we like it, right?"

"Yeah, I know," I said. "It's an amazing thing."

The rain patted down on the roof outside our dormer window, restful music as we lounged on the bed in the dark.

"I'm not moving," Jen said.

"Me neither," I said.

"You don't think Penny is sleeping with Dad, do you? I should call Arlene. She probably feels left out. Do you think she feels left out?"

"I told you, no. We asked her to come, didn't we? Besides, Penny told me there wasn't anything happening. You can't worry about it. You can't control it. Even if there were something happening, it wouldn't be up to you to worry about it."

"We've got to get rid of her," Jen said.

"What do you mean?" I said.

"We need to send her back. Put her on a plane. Why doesn't she have the sense to get her own room?"

"Maybe she can't afford it," I said. "Maybe your father is feeling his oats a little, having her stay in there with him. Even if they don't do anything, it's a big step. You don't want to take that away, do you?"

Jen rested her head against my chest. "No. Not if they aren't doing anything."

"There you go," I said.

"But I can't know they're not doing anything," Jen said. "I have to take Penny's word for it."

"You don't trust her?"

"Jesus, are you crazy?"

"This place even smells good," I said. "It smells old and wooden."

"It is," she said.

I listened to Jen's breathing, slow and methodical. I listened to the water running in the gutters, the wind in the tops of the trees, and the squeak of an attic fan somewhere outside our room. I ran my hand over the chenille bedspread, leaned back against the carved headboard, and allowed myself to like being in a hundred-year-old hotel. A little bit of thunder rolled through the evening sky, far off. Jen fell asleep in my arms. I closed my eyes.

After dinner the four of us wandered around the hotel. There were only thirty-four rooms, and the halls were wide and had high ceilings. The place had a kind of western grace. The paneling was dark and scarred, very old, the doors were all bevel-glazed, the runners in the halls were ancient, and the floor creaked. There was a gigantic moosehead-and-neck combo over the fireplace in the large library that had been converted into a guest area. The hotel wasn't elegant so much as old, well worn, as if it had earned some respect. Maybe it had been elegant at one time, at least a certain kind of elegant, but now it was charming because of its age, because you could read the ideas that went into its design and see in those ideas characteristics of another era—ease, naïveté, gentleness, an old notion of comfort.

We went for a stroll on the grounds, and Jen caught up with Penny and took her off ahead. Mike and I stayed behind.

"You like this place?" Mike said.

"Yes," I said. "How about you?"

"It's very comfortable."

"You don't seem comfortable," I said.

"No?"

"Jen is worried about you."

"She is?" Mike said. "About Penny?"

"Yes."

"She asked about Penny this morning," he said. "You think it's a bad idea for us to stay in the same room?"

"I don't know," I said. "What's going on in there?"

"Nothing," Mike said. "We're watching television, talking, sleeping."

"Hey, that's what we're doing, too. Nothing wrong with that. It's fine."

"We're good as gold," he said. "Funny the way Jen talks to me and the way Penny does. This morning I was Dad for the first time in a while, walking through the cavern with Jen. It was like long ago when she was a child and we did things together. She knew more about the cavern than I did, but I was still the father. It was a wonderful feeling. It's something I've noticed since you guys came over. I've felt it more than before, from my side and from hers. It's unsettling, but I've missed it a long time. We got so separated after she went to school. It was as if she'd run away, out of my life. I kind of got used to living without her, without hearing from her or talking to her, just sending her checks occasionally. That would be before your time, of course. Now that she's back, I'm glad. You account for some of that, too, Del. For her being back. I have you to thank for that. That's the way I think about it."

"Well, thanks," I said. "That's very pleasing to hear."

"No, I mean it."

"I know you mean it, Mike."

We walked around the back of the building to the golf course, where the desk person had said bears were sighted the night before. It was way too chilly for summer out there.

"So where's your ex-wife now?" Mike said.

"She lives in Oregon," I said. "She married a painter, an artist. He's not too successful, but I don't think that matters to them."

"You still talk to her?" Mike said.

"Sure," I said. "Now and again. It's a little harder than it used to be."

"The divorce?"

We were standing together on the first tee, looking down a fairway lit by the moon. It was like an enormous trough, its sides made of tall, dark trees.

"Yeah. I wished it wasn't happening, but it was and it wouldn't stop, I couldn't stop it. It was nobody's choice; we just came apart. What I remember most is how helpless I felt, like a spectator, like it was happening to somebody else but I was stuck there, feeling everything."

"I know that story," Mike said.

"The whole world changes when you're not watching. You're moving along, doing your business, taking care of what you have to take care of, and suddenly you turn around and it's not the way it was the last time you looked. Sometimes you can handle that because it's just a small change, but sometimes the change is so big that there's no hope. It's like you tried to grab somebody's hand and missed and you're just falling into the new way things are. She's falling too, but in a different direction. Maybe she's not falling and it's only you that's falling. Whatever it is, you don't have any control over it. The whole world looks different—the grass on the ground looks different, things smell different. Then you panic and you're hopeless and you go to the grocery store and you miss her so horribly that you start crying in the canned vegetable aisle. You can't stand to go to the grocery store anymore, so you go out to eat. That's no good because you and she went to all the places together, so you can't go there anymore. And then you go out with some other woman and she smells wrong. You put your arm around her, hug her, smell her hair, or she sleeps with you in your bed and you smell her on the pillow in the morning and it's all wrong. And the worst part is you have no way to fix it. You can try to put it back the way it was, but it won't go. Then you suddenly realize you're a lot older than you were just two days before. Your attitudes are all different; what you can put up with and what you're interested in, what you're willing to do, what you'd like, are all different."

Mike did some imaginary golfing while I talked.

"Maybe you don't even try to put it back together. I'm trying to remember," I said. "I think you don't try. What happens is you have a nothing life, alone all the time, lonely, but you don't want to be with somebody enough to go back to her even if you could, because going back would mean living in a way that'd be sort of a lie now that you've changed."

Mike was staring at me, his eyes gentle. It was as if I'd hypnotized him. I tapped his shoulder and pointed back up toward the hotel, then started walking in that direction.

Jen was using the notebook to get her e-mail and check her newsgroups on the Internet. She had new material from Durrell Dobson—a long piece about Vince Foster that started with evidence of semen in his shorts and blond human head hairs, not his own, found on his shoes and socks, his belt, his pants, and his T-shirt. Durrell went into detail about how Vince Foster's head had been identified as being correctly photographed by the park police and by the so-called confidential witness, and how, because of the blood flow on his face, running from his nose to his ear, where he was found couldn't have been where he was shot. Durrell ended up saying, "I don't care anymore. I just don't care. Something's got to be done. These people are crazy. These people are killers. They're running the country. Did you know that Fiske was involved with the company that sold Whitewater property for McDoogle? It's never-ending. There's no way we can continue like this. Something has to be done. You're right about Damian Williams. You're right about the Philadelphia Five. People have to be executed, removed from the gene pool. Now is the time. We need to learn the lessons of history and pursue our goals and objectives with a single-minded purpose heretofore unknown. Jennifer, we need to meet. Can we meet in Las Vegas? Can we meet somewhere as you head west? It is becoming clear that our destinies are linked. It is time. Let us follow the lead of Sergeant Adrian Mannilla, who said, after he'd chopped off the head of a fellow soldier who had slept with his wife, 'That is what happens to you when you commit adultery.' This is our model. When the police came to get Mannilla, he was sitting on his wife's bed, looking at her head, which was propped up on the nightstand. We have a future, Jennifer," Durrell Dobson wrote. "There is a clear path ahead of us. We are going to bring face-branding to the forefront as a means of permanently marking those who we do not wish to exterminate. We are open to new methods, new research, new avenues of inquiry. We seek only truth. We stop at nothing."

I swiveled the computer back around so she could see it, and said, "He's got that Hitler thing, doesn't he?"

"He does," Jen said. "I think this is a new beginning for him. He's reaching out to touch someone."

"Blessed be God," I said.

"Blessed be His holy name." She gave me a distinctly limp-fingered swat.

"You've been writing him back every time?"

"I have," Jen said. "I have been trying to show him that he is perhaps slightly overwrought. I have been trying to shepherd him gently into the nineteenth century, to walk with him into the light."

"It ain't working. He wants to meet in Las Vegas and commence blowing up the world," I said, tapping the top of the notebook's flipped-up screen. "Wants to have a little powwow."

"I don't think it's happening," Jen said.

I looked around the room, looked out the window, which was still open a little, and I said to Jen, "There's no air-conditioning."

She looked up from the computer. "You're kidding."

"There's no air-conditioning," I said again. "What a wonderful thing."

"I'm going to tell him we're taking another route," Jen said. "Like Tucson, Phoenix, down there."

"That *is* the way we're going, isn't it?"

"Maybe," Jen said. "Unless we cut up north to see the Grand Canyon. But there's no real need to do that, I guess."

"We can think about it later," I said. "The way I figure it, we're going to Phoenix anyway; at least that's what it seemed like when I was looking at the map."

"Phoenix is pretty high up."

"Uh-huh." I was thinking about my wife and the stuff I'd been talking to Mike about. I hadn't thought about her in a while and hadn't thought at all about the time when we separated. I remembered it now as a hard time, scalding and bleak. Everything had been unforgiving. Every conversation, every acquaintance, everything. A trick of the mind, of course, but no less true for that. And then there was us, how we changed. That was no trick; that was real. I was a different person than I had been. I didn't want or hope the same things. I didn't have the same ideas. I didn't believe the same things. Everything in my life was different, and I suddenly realized it. It wasn't better or more complicated or richer or more interesting—it was just irretrievably different. Things that were important weren't; things that weren't were. Soon I forgot what I used to think, so comparisons were hard. I was a reverse chameleon, shedding my inner self while my skin remained intact. I was replaced, my self snatched, and I had done the snatching. Things we'd spent ten years putting together—the marriage, our way of getting along, our plans—were down around our feet. It wasn't her fault. It wasn't even about her. It was about me. Me being somebody else, somebody that I wasn't before, somebody who didn't love Karen the way the person who used to inhabit my body had loved her. The new guy had to move along, smartly. He was colder and tighter and tougher, and he knew that the sweetness that had been real for the previous tenant would thereafter be a formality performed but largely unexperienced, unfelt. The reason? There was no reason. The deadly grass. I remember looking at the grass and being depressed by it—the grass in the backyard behind our apartment in Houston—being depressed by its blankness, the color of it, the way it just sat there on the ground, the way the sun hit it, the way the shadows crawled across it. When the grass depressed me, I knew I was in trouble; that's when the snatching began.

"What are you doing?" Jen said.

"Thinking about my sins," I said.

"We don't have enough time," she said.

"Ha ha," I said.

"I got all this great rosary stuff, if you want it. I got it from alt.religion something a couple days ago."

"What rosary stuff?" I was on my back on the bed, looking at the ceiling, studying the whorls of the sea-green paintbrush tracks.

Jen clicked some keys, getting a file she was looking for up onto her screen. "It's just this list, a free Catholic mailing list of all the different rosaries, or all the rosaries this person who put it together could find. Listen to this," she said, reading from the screen. " 'Certain rosaries are listed without mysteries. This simply means that the rosary exists, but I have been unable to ascertain its mysteries.' Then she lists rosaries she's found, including the Little Beads of Our Lady of Consolation, the Little Crown of the Blessed Virgin, the Little Rosary of the Seven Sorrows of Mary. And then there's all this other stuff in here, about what prayers you are supposed to pray in each rosary, and so on. There's even one with a leader and a response, a litany deal where the response is always, 'Have mercy on us,' and the leader starts off saying, 'God the Father in Heaven; God the Son, Redeemer of the world; God the Holy Ghost,' and then he goes on to say, 'Jesus, Son of Abraham; Jesus, Son of David; Jesus, Son of Mary and Joseph; Jesus Christ who is above all; Jesus, Son of the living God; Jesus, Light of the world; Jesus, the Word made flesh; Jesus, Son of the Most High; Jesus, King of Israel; Jesus, King of kings; Jesus, King of nations; Jesus, King of Righteousness; Jesus, Prince of all life; Jesus, Shepherd and Guardian of our souls; Jesus, Lamb of God; Jesus, Savior of the world,' and so on," Jen said. She looked at me. "And then it goes to that 'Lamb of God, who taketh away the sins of the world, have mercy on us' stuff."

"It gives me the heebie-jeebies," I said.

"My favorite is the Rosary of the Little Crown of the Twelve Stars of the Blessed Virgin Mary," Jen said. "Or maybe the Little Flower Rosary. It even tells you how to make a rosary out of rose petals and water and salt and oil paint. It says if you prefer the traditional black rosary, cook the rose petals with a rusty nail."

"That was in alt.religion?"

"Uh-huh," she said. "You want me to read you some more of it?"

"I want you to read me more prayers," I said. "That Lamb of God business is so wonderful, even now. I can't tell you how great it is to hear it again. I smell the incense."

"Yeah, me too."

"They didn't have incense when you were growing up," I said.

"I know, but I went to a radical church when I was at college. I had a boyfriend who was a Catholic, and he was fighting for the restoration of the Latin liturgy."

"They never did that, did they?"

"Don't think so."

"So what did you find out from Penny?"

"Same thing you told me," Jen said. "Good, clean fun. It's all harmless."

"You feel better?" I said.

"No. I don't like her," Jen said. "It's not this thing with my father. It's something else. She's some other kind of person now, and I don't know her very well, and I don't like what I know."

"She seems nice enough to me."

"She would. You're a man."

"I thought she hated men."

"Oh, sure," Jen said. "Like she's the one person on the planet who's that simple."

"There are others," I said.

"I think I'll repackage some of this Vince Foster stuff with some of the rosary business and put it out on the boards," Jen said. "It seems like I need something else, but I can't think of what it is."

I had fetched the map from the floor beside the bed and was studying it. "We could stay here a couple of days," I said. "We could go down to White Sands tomorrow and Alamogordo, then come back up here tomorrow night and then go to Socorro the next day. After that, we can go on into Arizona on this less celebrated highway here."

"Is it two-lane?" Jen said.

She turned around and I gave her the map so she could see what I was looking at. "I don't know," I said. "It looks like it. It goes through these mountains here. It goes through Magdalena, Datil, Pie Town, Quemado, Red Hill, and Springerville. It's got our name all over it."

"I want to go just to see Pie Town," she said. "It crosses the Continental Divide right there, just before you get to Pie Town. But look here," she said, pointing down to where we were in the mountains. "We could come down from Cloudcroft to White Sands, down to Las Cruces and then back up to Truth or Consequences and Elephant View. Then Socorro and across. Or we could go down to White Sands and then back up to Socorro and then down to Las Cruces and up through Silver City where those cliff dwellings are and then back to Springerville. That's right through the heart of the mountains there."

"You missed Pie Town."

"Good point," she said. "But look where we end up when we're in Springerville—right next to the Painted Desert. Well, maybe not right next to it, but pretty close."

"We could take a little detour," I said.

"It wouldn't be that much of a detour," she said.

"I won't rat on you."

She got up on all fours and reached across me to catch the light from the lamp of one of the bedside tables. She clicked it off.

"Do you ever just wish we were lawyers or something?" she said. "Doctors. Eye doctors, maybe? Gynecologists? Had a nice house by a lake and had matching cars and everything? And we, like, went to work every day and came home and had a cocktail party and dinner for a few close friends, also doctors, and then every once in a while we'd take a vacation for a couple of weeks to a place like this or the islands or something?" She curled next to me in the bed in the dark of our room. A little moonlight was visible out the open window.

"You mean a more orderly life?" I said.

"I mean really orderly," she said. "And every day when we came home from work, we'd know we'd done something good for our fellow human beings. Every day would be guilt-free. Every day full of things we could be proud of. And we'd be powerful and we'd be helping those people who were less powerful than we were, so we'd feel good about that. After all, they would come to us because they needed our help, and we'd give them our help freely."

"Freely?" I said.

"You know what I mean. We'd get paid to help people."

"I think you have an idealized view of what doctors do."

"Maybe so," she said. "But they *could* do that, couldn't they? We could do that if *we* were doctors. And if we were lawyers we could spend all our time trying to get to the truth. Same thing if we were reporters on big metropolitan newspapers."

"Or detectives," I said.

"We could clean up the force from inside," she said. "Or we could work for the government. We could work for the CIA or the FBI. We could ferret out traitors and work for the spread of democracy. We could go back to Greenpeace or the ACLU or some rescue organization. We could save greyhounds. That could be our job."

"A journey of a thousand miles."

"I know. That's the disappointing part."

She got off the bed and went into the bathroom and started the water in the shower. She came out, undressing.

"Maybe we should just go back to Biloxi," she said. "Hunker down. Take it one day at a time. Do what we can."

"Now, there's an idea," I said.

"At least it's within our grasp." She folded her clothes carefully and put them on the chair by the television.

I heard some people walk by in front of our door, and the floor squeaked. They were talking in whispers, laughing. They sounded like young people.

Jen went into the bathroom to take her shower, and I got up to close the window and curtains, then got back on the bed and turned on the television. The phone rang. It was Mike, calling to talk to Jen. I told him she was in the shower and that she would be out right away. I asked him if he wanted me to have her call him. He said no. Then there was this pause on the line, and neither one of us said anything. I expected him to say good-bye and hang up, but he didn't.

"Is everything O.K.?" I said.

Another, shorter pause, then he said, "Well, maybe not."

I flicked through some channels. "What's the problem?"

"I don't know," he said. "I was thinking maybe you could sleep down here."

"You want to swap rooms?"

"No, I mean you could sleep down here with me and Penny could sleep up there with Jen."

"Oh," I said.

"I know it's a nuisance," Mike said. "But things have sort of veered off course. I think it might be better if Penny slept up there. I tried to get another room, but they don't have any."

"Well, fine," I said. "I'll come down directly."

"I'm sorry about this, Del."

"Not a problem," I said. "Where's Penny now?"

"She went for a walk."

"O.K.," I said. "I'll be down in a few minutes."

I hung up and sat on the edge of the bed for a second before I started for the bathroom. I tapped on the door, but Jen couldn't hear me because the shower was running, so I went in. She jumped when I pulled back the curtain.

"Careful," I said, reaching to steady her.

"What?" She was rinsing her hair. Suds were rolling down her face and were on her shoulders. She squinted at me.

"Your father called," I said. "He wants me to come down there and sleep."

She did a quick rinse and shut off the shower.

"He wants you to come there and sleep?" she repeated.

"Yeah. And Penny's coming up here."

"Trouble," she said. "Great."

"He tried to get another room, but there weren't any."

I heard a knock on the door to our room. "That must be Penny," I said.

It wasn't. It was Mike, bringing Penny's luggage. He gave me the second key to his room and asked for the second key to ours. I gave it to him.

"It's a big room down there, Del," he said. "Two double beds, the whole thing. I really appreciate this."

Jen stepped out of the bathroom with a towel wrapped around her. "Are you O.K., Dad?" she said. He looked a little shaken to me.

"I'm fine, sweetheart," he said. "I'm sorry about this."

"It's nothing," she said.

"It's just for tonight." He turned to me and said, "You want me to take your bag down, since I'm going?"

"No, I'll bring it," I said.

He left, and Jen looked at me and shook her head. "I don't know what's going on. Did he tell you anything?" she said.

"No," I said.

One of the beds in Mike's room was untouched. The other was mussed, the bedspread pulled down and the pillows stacked against the headboard. Mike wasn't there. I put my suitcase on a chair, switched into some shorts and a T-shirt that I could sleep in, and got into the fresh bed. I snapped on the television and went through the channels. Nothing.

I called Jen. "Is Penny there yet?" I said.

"No," Jen said. "Is Mike there?"

"No."

"Are you O.K.? Is this O.K. with you?"

"It's a little lump in my landscape," I said.

"Amen," she said. I heard a knock on her door through the telephone. "I've got to go. Somebody's here."

"Call me if you need anything," I said. I started going through the channels again and stopped on one where three or four people were exercising by sliding back and forth on what looked like a piece of slick plastic on the floor. It was an exercise device I'd seen skaters practice on. It looked like fun, more fun than most of the exercises you see on television. It looked a little bit magical, the way they were sliding. I wondered if you could get them wider than the ones they were using, like ten or fifteen feet wide, so you could slide a good long way before getting to the other side.

Mike's room was bigger than ours but furnished similarly. There was an old high dresser in a corner and a pair of long-ago covered chairs in the open space near the door. Some of Mike's clothes were hanging neatly in the closet. There was a pint of Jack Daniel's on the bedside table, along with two drugstore-style glasses, half full of ice and water and bourbon. I looked at the other bed, to see if it looked as if some kind of crisis had taken place there. It didn't look that messed up.

Mike came in and waved, closed the door, put the chain on the lock. He was sweating. He had on running shorts and a T-shirt, sweat socks, running shoes.

"Where'd you go?" I said.

"Town," he said. "It's not that far. Everything straightened away here?"

"I think so," I said. "I think Penny's upstairs, and I'm right here watching these people with this slide thing on television." I pointed to the television to show him the exercise device.

"Oh, yeah," he said. "I've seen that." He sat down in one of the two upholstered chairs and started unlacing his shoes. "I guess you figure I'm some kind of dumbball."

"Nope," I said.

"We got a little crossed up, and we thought it would be a better idea if we just took it easy. You know what I mean?"

"It's fine," I said, holding up both hands like stop signs so he'd know he didn't have to tell me any more.

"She's a beautiful girl," he said.

"I know," I said, nodding, squinting at him, raising my eyebrows in agreement.

He got up and started across the room and put his running shoes and socks in a special bag he had, which looked like it was made for exercise equipment; it had a little door in the bottom, which he zipped open and slid his shoes into.

"I'm going to take a shower," he said.

"Good deal," I said.

He took a set of what looked like pajamas out of his suitcase and went into the bathroom and closed the door. I was uncomfortable alone in that room with him. I wished he'd gotten another room, and I thought about calling the desk to ask if they hadn't overlooked some empty room. Then I thought that was silly and I should just settle down. I called Jen back, but she didn't want to talk to me.

"Everything's fine up here," she said.

"Here too," I said. "Mike just came in from his run."

"Good," Jen said. "I'll see you in the morning."

"I don't like this," I said.

"I can understand that."

"Penny's right there?"

"You got it."

"I miss you," I said.

"Ditto," she said.

I switched the TV to the Weather Channel and slid the remote onto the bedside table near Mike's bed. It smelled funny in the room. It must have smelled funny all along, but I hadn't realized it. Maybe it only smelled funny after Mike came back in. It wasn't a terrible smell, just a little bit sour and stale. I rolled over on my side, facing away from Mike's bed, and rested that way for a few minutes and then felt strange about him coming out and finding me that way, so I turned over on my back and pulled the covers down to the pocket of my T-shirt. I didn't like the way the bedspread and sheet settled on my body, so I raised one knee, but then my foot kept slipping down on the fitted sheet. I had to fold my leg sideways so I could use my right heel to rest my left foot against. I had both arms out from under the covers.

When Mike came out, he hustled the glasses off the bedside table and put the Jack Daniel's back in his suitcase. Then he wiped the bedside table with a bath cloth and took the remote control and clicked the television off.

"You're finished with that, right?" he said, waving the remote toward the television.

"Yeah," I said.

His pajamas were white with blue stripes and piping. "I want to crack this window here, O.K.?" he said. "Just to get the air circulating."

"Fine." With my eyes closed, I listened to him move around the room, open the window, come back and climb into bed, turn off the light. When I heard the light switch, I opened my eyes. "Good night, Mike."

It seemed like a long silence, and then he said, "Did you and your wife have affairs before you split up?"

"Yes," I said, into the darkness. "Not too many, but some."

"I didn't," he said. "I don't think Lida did, either. Oh, I was tempted. There were lots of women in the office, at a couple of conventions, but none of them seemed particularly interested in me, so it was easy enough not to be interested in them. I don't know what

I would have done if somebody had been interested. Same thing, I guess. Did you have trouble getting back together afterward?"

I could hear a little breeze outside the window and the pip pip pip of stray drops of rain from the eaves above. I pushed myself up so I was sitting in the bed, leaning against the headboard, trying to think about the last time I'd had an affair when I was with Karen and how we'd settled it.

Finally I said, "I don't remember. I remember one time when she had an affair with a guy who ran some store in the mall. I remember asking her if she was having an affair, and her telling me that she was. I was in the bedroom and she was in the bathroom. We were shouting back and forth over the sound of the water. But that wasn't as bad as the first time."

"When was that?"

"Early," I said. "I thought I would never recover from that, and in a way maybe I didn't. She told me later that she'd been paying me back for being interested in some woman, some friend of ours. She was playing hardball and I was playing soft." I tried to remember back to that time in my marriage to Karen, and I could almost picture us. I could remember the apartment we lived in and the furniture we had, the way it was arranged in the apartment, the cars we had, where we worked, where we watched television, what the kitchen was like, what you saw when you looked out the apartment windows, the kinds of things we did and the places we went for fun, but I couldn't remember how any of it felt, what it felt like.

"I just remember it was crippling," I said. "For months. We almost didn't get back together. We had to rebuild everything, start over. The other ones weren't so bad as that. I think it was the newness of it. We'd only been together a couple of years, and it was a surprise. It was like I had been counting on this one thing, and then suddenly I couldn't count on it any longer. At least I didn't think I could, and neither did she. We had to relearn each other after that. It took a year."

Mike made some guttural noise to indicate that he had heard me.

Then it was silent in the room. I was still trying to think about Karen and our life together, twelve years of marriage. I couldn't remember any of it. Maybe I could remember parts of it, but I couldn't feel much. And when I felt little bits of things it was scary, like it was so sweet and lovely that I didn't dare remember it, because it made me feel guilty for not wanting it now, for moving on, for changing. One way or another, it was some other person who'd lived that life.

"So how do you feel about it now?" Mike said. "Do you regret having affairs or what?"

I thought for just a second about that, and then I smiled there in the dark as I realized what I thought. "I wish I'd had more. I wish every time a woman had smiled at me in that odd way that says possibility that I'd reacted quickly. I regret not sleeping with the women I could have slept with. I thought I was doing the right thing, trying to do the right thing. Now I wonder if I wasn't just scared about what might happen, worried about what was at risk, thinking about the little picture rather than the big one."

"That's what you think?" Mike said.

"That's what I think now," I said. "With the luxury of hindsight and the safety of not having to go out and do it tomorrow. Now, when it's easy to think that, that's what I think. When it was hard, I wasn't so sure."

I listened to the ticking of the antique clock on the dresser. Then I heard some birds fluttering their wings outside the window. It had gotten quite cool in the room. I pulled the cover up to my chin and folded my hands over my chest. I could hear Mike breathing in the bed next to me. He was breathing through his nose, slowly, making a whole range of very high-pitched, delicate, whistling noises as he inhaled. And I could hear stuff going on in his stomach. When I looked over there, I could make out only a partial silhouette. Mike seemed to be sitting in bed with his head cocked back against the headboard.

Finally he said, "This is a strange time for me. I feel as though I've gone through some closet into some world I didn't know existed, some place where lots of things are different, where I'm not nearly as old as I am, and at the same time I'm there looking at myself being this way, and I'm looking at myself in that world, and I'm thinking I look like a fool. I've always wondered how people get into these things. I never thought it was possible or that it would ever happen to a person who was sensible and paying attention. But here I am calling you up and asking you to sleep here." He snorted, and I lost his silhouette as he wrapped his hand over his face. I could hear his hand moving over the stubble of his beard.

# Fourteen

White Sands was astonishing. A huge blanket of thirty-foot crystal dunes kicked by winds and shadowed by clouds. We got to the park at ten-thirty in the morning. It was cool even though the sun was bright. The sand was already warm to the touch, but if you stuck your hand down into it, it was quite cold. From the top of the dunes, the landscape was unearthly. As far as the eye could see in any direction, there were ridges of pure bright light. These were bordered on the east and the west by smudgy mountains in the distance. The winds over the dunes were constant, and they peppered us with the gypsum sand. What desert plants there were, were spiked and tall, and everything was moving—the surface of the dunes, the dunes themselves, driven by the winds, the high clouds. The huge ridges were seamless, tight-creased along their tops, delicate in spite of their size. We had driven eight miles from the visitors' center into a dune field, to a site called Heart of the Sands. There weren't many other tourists there, though a film company was setting up shop. Jen and I climbed to the top of a glassy slope near where we parked and walked some distance away from where the car was nestled between hills on the hard flat of the road. We had to turn our backs to the southwest wind in order to protect our faces. We stood together on top of one dune and looked north to the missile range.

"This is it," she said. "The most amazing thing I've ever seen in my entire life. This makes the whole trip. It's perfect—I will stay forever."

I heard jets overhead, shielded my eyes with my hand as I searched. I caught them coming out of the east, from Holloman Air Force Base, I guessed, which we'd passed on the way down. Holloman was the supposed site of a famous UFO encounter, the one that *Close Encounters* was based on. The two jets flying overhead were stealths. I'd never seen one, but they looked just like their pictures. They banked together and headed north, yet the sounds they made didn't connect to the way they moved—it was as if there were other jets up there somewhere, making all the noise, and these two were running silent.

Jen stilted down the side of the dune and crossed the flats back to the car to get the camera. I waited where I was. She took a couple of snapshots as she walked back up, and at the top she stood alongside me and held the camera out as far away from her as she could and snapped us with the dunes in the background. She snapped another couple of pictures of that shot. We were at the top of our dune for a while and then crossed to the next one and went over that, and on the other side were some fifties-looking pavilions made of corrugated metal sheeting that was anchored into a slab, then curved from a narrow base at the back into a broad roof supported by painted pipe columns on the front edge. These roofs were like giant chocolate shavings painted in faded desert colors, and they covered picnic tables that were bolted into the ten-foot-square concrete slabs. There must have been thirty of these sheds in this stadium-size hard sandy flat between the dunes, and they seemed too far apart; it was surreal the way this picnic area snuggled down into the high dunes. A couple of cars were parked at pavilions on the far side of the flat. It was completely out of the past. I'd never seen anything that looked so perfect, and I held my breath, afraid something would spoil it. It was a photograph out of a forty-year-old *Life* magazine in an attic somewhere, a newsreel seen at the Alabama Theater on a Saturday morning, a snapshot in a yellowed newspaper, leisure time nineteen fifty-four, completely foreign and unknown. An antique Oldsmobile crawled by, its tires crackling on the sand-covered, tightly packed ground of the flat. A large man with a ruddy complexion, wearing a straw hat and a short-sleeved shirt, was driving the slow-moving car. He had a wife and two children with him. They circled the clearing, weaving in and out between the cabanas like a race car warming up for a restart. The Oldsmobile was copper-colored, shining in the sunlight as it circled.

Jen and I climbed back to the top of the dune and sat down together. A small, white-backed lizard waddled and hopped across the hot gypsum, moving away from us. The jets made another pass, this time heading due south, black triangles passing directly above us, but with engines screeching way off north. We lay down and hugged for a minute and then rolled a few feet, trying to get started going down the dune. It didn't work, though, so we stopped.

"I don't like sleeping without you," Jen said, whispering in my ear so she wouldn't have to shout over the sound of the wind.

"You smell better than your father," I said.

"Is he O.K.?"

"He has a crisis."

"Duh," she said.

"He asked me a lot of questions about affairs."

"What did you tell him?" Jen said.

"I told him the truth," I said.

"Which truth?"

"About how much fun it is, count your blessings, all of that. He asked about Karen and about people I'd had affairs with, how they were. How I felt."

"You told him all that?"

"As much as I could remember."

The towns in New Mexico seemed to be built along highways. They were like strip shopping centers. Every place we'd been through, every place we'd stopped, was that way. Alamogordo, where we had lunch, wasn't different. We stopped at the Broken Wing Café, which had a lot of Air Force memorabilia on the walls and big booths with mini-jukeboxes. The seats were covered in that swirly green plastic that was always used for café booths and counter stools. The woman who served us was named Pepe, and she looked a little bit Irish, but she didn't have much of an accent. She asked what we wanted and then pointed at the wall, to a list of things they were serving. It was a big list, with a section for beef, a section for hamburgers, a section for chicken. They had chicken-fried steak in the chicken section, so that's what I ordered. Mike wanted a hamburger. Jen and Penny ordered salads. The Broken Wing was right on the highway, so we watched cars go by while we waited for our food. We watched planes coming out of Holloman Air Force Base.

Alamogordo was about two blocks wide, one block on either side of the highway, and it had a lot of small manufacturing places with 'Welding' in their names.

"We're going to zip through Socorro," Jen said. "Then I think we're going to go up this old highway into Arizona. Is that O.K. with you guys?" She had the travel atlas, and she was showing Mike and Penny where we planned to go. They both nodded.

"So eventually you get up and catch Forty across?" Penny said.

"That's the idea," Jen said.

"Maybe we could stop in Vegas," Mike said. "Do a little gambling."

"You just did gambling," Jen said. "In Natchez."

"That was years ago," Mike said. "I can't even remember if I won or lost."

"Jen's Compupal is in Las Vegas, so I don't think we want to go there," I said.

"Oh, right," Mike said.

"He plans to meet us in Los Angeles, anyway," Jen said.

"He can't meet us if we don't tell him where we are," I said.

"But he might think that's rude," Jen said.

The waitress came back to the table and told Mike they were out of hamburgers.

"You're out of hamburgers?" Mike said.

"How about a nice flounder?" Pepe said. "We've got a fresh whole flounder we could give you."

"We're in the middle of New Mexico," Mike said. "Where'd you get a fresh flounder?"

"Well, it's not fresh fresh," Pepe said.

"How can you be out of hamburgers?" Jen said.

"We didn't get any in," Pepe said.

"Oh," Jen said, nodding at me.

There was an Air Force couple with their children at the next table. The guy was all bristly and red and puffed up, in fatigue pants and a brown T-shirt. His wife was wearing pedal pushers and a sleeveless blouse. The children had mud on their faces. The guy leaned back and caught Pepe by the sleeve of her uniform.

"You're out of hamburgers?" he said.

"Yes," she said.

He hunched back over his table and talked to the wife for a minute, then all four of them got up and trooped out of the restaurant.

"I'll have the same as him," Mike said, pointing at me.

"You going to want the cream gravy with that?" she said.

He nodded.

"You ever see a UFO, Pepe?" Jen said.

"Sure," she said. "Hundreds of times. They're all over the place out here. With these boys over here at the base, you can't tell, though, really. They've got some weird stuff going on over there. They had something out there in the sixties, but I don't really remember it because I was just a kid. In eighty-seven there was a big uproar. But I see stuff all the time. I'm walking home, and I'll see stuff in the sky. Nothing ever really up close, but—" She turned around and looked at the cook, who was staring out of the little slit in the back wall behind the counter. "Give me another chicken-fried," she said to him, then turned back to us. "You folks UFO hunters?"

"Not really," Jen said.

"We get a fair number out here," Pepe said.

She was wearing a uniform with a very short skirt and a white collar and lapels. It looked as if the uniform was once Pepto-Bismol pink, but by now it was faded and almost light-emitting.

"But the ones you saw—were those really UFOs or were they something else?" Jen said.

"They were plenty real, that's what they were. None of them got close enough, though. I didn't see alien life forms or any of that sort of thing, but I've seen things going around in the sky that don't look like they ought to be there, things that aren't doing what they're supposed to be doing. I guess that don't mean nothing, but it's curious."

"I've always wanted to see one," Jen said. "A lot of times I just sit out there and wait. We live down on the coast in Mississippi, and I'll just sit outside there in a car or on the beach and watch the sky at night. Nothing."

"I think you have to be looking the other way," Pepe said. "It's one of those things that only happens when you're not looking for it to happen. If you're looking for UFOs, they go someplace else." She laughed and excused herself to wait on a table on the other side of the room.

"Don't look now," Mike said.

"What?" Jen said.

"Oh, nothing," Mike said. He was working hard to seem jovial. I guessed he didn't feel jovial. There was a new stiffness between Penny and him—she didn't play with his food when it came. He didn't look at her. I figured it was going to be a tough car day.

Pepe came back to check us, then was off again to see to her other customers. A couple of trips later, she stopped again. "So how's everything going?" she said. "That chicken-fried steak O.K.?" She had her hand on Mike's shoulder. He nodded. He had a mouthful of chicken-fried steak.

"It's good," I said.

"How about you young girls?" she said.

Jen waved at herself and Penny. "We're doing fine."

"Well, now, I was back there with the cook a minute ago," Pepe said. "He was asking me, and I thought I would come ask you guys exactly what's going on here. Are you guys fathers and daughters or what?"

"Both of those," I said.

"He's my father," Jen said, pointing to Mike.

"I'm her friend," Penny said, pointing to Jen.

"Well, I guess that just leaves you," Pepe said, looking at me.

"Seems like it's always that way," I said.

"Cook says he's seen UFOs, too," Pepe said. "He didn't call them UFOs, but he said he'd seen things—lights in the sky, that sort of thing. Last night, he says. About four a.m. And he knows somebody who knows that deputy up at Socorro who saw the UFO land out there. That's the father of a friend of his. Cook says that's not the strangest thing that happens around here."

"Oh, yeah?" Mike said. "What is the strangest?"

"Mutilations," Pepe said. "Animal. And abductions. Those are the scariest. Cook's been around these parts for a long time, and he says he's seen just about everything. With all this military around here and all that scientific stuff, he says it doesn't get any weirder than this. He says UFOs can't even bust into the top ten around here."

"You and cook got some kind of relationship going?" Jen said.

Pepe did an odd wiry smile. "Up jumps the devil," she said. Then she slid off to see what the three young soldiers who had just come in and taken a booth by the window were going to have for lunch.

We finished eating and paid the bill and said good-bye to Pepe and packed back into the car. Mike was driving, and Penny was in the front seat.

We got on the highway, but as we neared the edge of town there was a supermarket, and in the parking lot five or six eighteen-wheelers were parked at odd angles to each other, with big billboards painted on their sides. One said it had a thirty-thousand-pound whale inside, one said it had the world's largest steer, one said it had the world's smallest horse, another one said something about a gigantic snake. Mike pulled right into the parking lot and stopped.

"This is too good to pass up," he said.

"Oh, go ahead. Pass it up," Penny said.

"The whale's frozen," Jen said.

"What?" Mike said.

"Frozen," she said.

"How do you know that?" I said.

"I've seen it before," she said. "They've had it down in Biloxi. You've never seen it? Down at the Edgewater Mall?"

"No, I've never seen it," I said.

"It's been there. A frozen whale. It fills that whole truck, but it's frozen. It's kind of soggy on the bottom."

"And they drive around the country with this whale, this frozen whale?" Mike said.

"Well, maybe it's not all the way frozen; maybe it's just refrigerated," she said.

"I want to see it," Mike said. He got out of the car. I got out, too. Jen and Penny stayed in.

We got tickets at the booth and started with the whale. It wasn't quite frozen, it was just deflated inside the back end of this cold eighteen-wheeler. It kind of spread out on the floor of the truck, and toward the back, where they didn't have enough room to get the whole whale in, they'd apparently shortened it and cut a bunch out. There was a piece of burlap over the hole, and a sign that said: "Here we removed ten thousand pounds of blubber in order to get this great whale into the truck."

"I can't believe they're dragging this whale around," Mike said.

"It's a big world," I said.

We filed out behind some children and went to the other trucks—the one with the giant boa constrictor, the one with the world's smallest horse, and the one with the world's largest steer. The steer was sitting down, but he was big—twelve or thirteen feet long. The horse was tiny, as advertised. The guy in the ticket booth had snake tattoos all over his arms and glasses held together with toothpicks and tape. He kept his eye on us as we went from truck to truck to look at the exhibits. The last thing they had on show was a live two-headed sheep in a phony hay-strewn corral in one of the smaller trucks. This sheep was looking right out through the Plexiglas at Mike and me. It was pretty clear that the second head had just been treated and preserved and sewn onto the body of the real living sheep, but it was still pretty eerie. Whenever the sheep turned its head, the other head followed. The second head's eyes were pointing forward and a little bit toward the main head, so when the sheep turned around, it looked as if the second head was looking where the first head was looking. This was a pretty old sheep, and apparently he had been at this awhile, and he didn't seem to take too much notice of this extra head attached to his neck. Although it did seem problematic when he tried to get his face into the bucket his food was poured into. He kept banging this other face into the rim of the bucket.

There was a big, hand-lettered sign on the wall behind the Plexiglas, detailing the supposed life story of this sheep, born in an Indian village high in the mountains, discovered at dawn, believed by the Indians to have magical powers in the area of procreation. It went on to say how the sacred sheep had happened to come into the hands of the present owners upon the death of a great chief.

We moved out through the flapping canvas that covered the exit from this last truck and cut across the parking lot to the car.

"How was it?" Jen said.

"The whale smelled bad," Mike said. "The horse and steer were O.K., and the two-headed sheep was a stunner."

"They have a two-headed sheep?" Jen said.

"Technically, yes," I said.

"Oh, I see," she said.

Mike said, "When I was much younger, I used to go to sideshows all the time, and they would have the freaks in there, and there was this one woman who had a baby whose head was supposed to be inside her stomach or something. The body was outside, but the head was inside her stomach. You had to go into the tent to see this, and then, when you saw it, of course it was some kind of device, some kind of doll with its head cut off and its neck attached to her stomach somehow. She had a dress on, with veils over this thing. After you got inside she pulled up the veils so you could see the doll jutting out of her stomach."

"Some of those things are real," I said. "There are people with parts of other people coming out of them in different places."

"Hey now," Jen said. "Now we're talking."

We stopped at a Texaco station to get some Cokes, then got on the highway headed for Socorro. Jen got out her computer and cranked it up so she could look at her e-mail and some AP stories she had captured off CompuServe the night before. Thirty or forty miles up the road, Mike took a quick right off the highway at a sign that pointed to Three Rivers Petroglyphs Recreation Area. This was right on the edge of the Mescalero Apache Indian reservation.

"We're not going to get anywhere if we keep stopping all the time," Penny said.

"I just want to see these petroglyphs," Mike said.

Jen handed me the computer and got out so she could see them, too. Penny stayed in the car with me. Mike and Jen climbed up the side of this hill and kept bending over, looking at rocks. We couldn't see anything from down in the parking lot.

The mountains we'd stayed in the night before were just beyond this site. There was some weather coming up, some thunder, and the sky was uniformly gray. I looked at the file of wire service stories Jen had open on the computer, occasionally reading bits and pieces out loud to Penny, who mostly just grunted her comments.

The first story was about turtles dying on the Texas coast. The next was about a forty-year-old woman being convicted for stealing her daughter's twelve-year-old boyfriend—she'd been going around on an electronic tether during the trial, then was found guilty of some sex crimes with this boy, whom she'd given a "love coupon" book, handmade, in which each coupon represented a specific graphically described sex act that he could redeem from her. There was also a story about a policeman who got ninety days for killing some woman who had driven irresponsibly in front of his patrol car, slamming on the brakes and beeping the horn and steering left and right too quickly while he was driving behind her with his siren on and his lights blinking; when he finally caught her and forced her to pull over, he said, he thought he saw a gun, so he went up there and shot her. There was also a story about the world's heaviest woman, who had apparently died; a story from London about the Human Fertilization and Embryology Authority giving the go-ahead to use of fetal eggs and ovarian tissue from live donors and dead women in research; another story about a woman with amnesia who discovered she was from Washington State when the nurse sang the "Fifty Nifty United States" song to her and she responded positively when the nurse got to Washington. There was a piece about a guy who was convicted of murdering his wife and abusing her corpse by putting it in a punching bag, hanging it from the rafters in his garage, and then walking around and smacking it with an ax handle for days on end; and a story about a Japanese boy who died in a triple-parked car while his mother played pinball in a roadside pinball place; a story about a Shetland pony with horribly disturbed hooves, curving upward sixteen to eighteen inches like a leprechaun's shoes; a story about two men who forced a woman to have oral sex with them in the back of a police van; and a report about a guy in Arizona who committed a "spontaneous act of barbarism" when he forced his wife to get into a bathtub full of still-living fish.

When I got to that last one, Penny said, "Don't read me any more, O.K.? Nobody wants to hear those stories. They're too horrible."

"They're all I ever hear," I said. "This is just the tip of the iceberg here, these are ones she got last night. Or maybe this is a file she just keeps adding things to. All I have to do is punch Page-Up or Page-Down."

"Why don't you punch the Off key?" Penny said. "I could never understand why Jen was interested in that stuff."

"She's marking the edges of her territory."

"It's car wrecks," Penny said.

"Yes," I said.

It was as easy as it was true. For some reason I felt the need to defend Jen, so I said, "There's something about the open way she does it, though. She doesn't try to kid anyone. She really likes grotesque stuff. She's like a kid that way. She looks and she recoils, and her revulsion is pure and true, a real feeling."

"You don't have to go that far to get a real feeling," Penny said.

"I think she knows that."

"That feeling is no more real than the feeling you get when you want to buy a new mixer at the department store."

"It's bigger," I said. "It's more sweeping, has range."

"Yeah, but it's not more real," Penny said.

"No," I said.

She didn't say anything else, and in a minute I got out of the car and crunched around in the gravel parking lot. The rain was almost on us. Thunder was ratcheting in the distance, and dark clouds were moving over the little mountains, and there were odd breezes jerking around, coming at me from all directions, starting and stopping suddenly. I could feel the presence of the storm that was about to hit.

Jen and Mike were coming down the path from the mountain, back to the parking lot. Suddenly a jackrabbit ran across in front of them. Jen took off and ran after it into the low brush. She darted this way and that for a few seconds and then stopped, laughing, bent over with her hands on her knees and breathing hard.

"She's a real rabbit catcher," Mike said to me when they got all the way back.

"You should have seen it," Jen said.

"I did see it," I said. "It was a rabbit."

"It was great. It was eating something, and then it was running," she said.

"That's a rabbit for you," Mike said.

"We'd better get on the road before this weather arrives," I said.

"We could stay here and wait for it," Jen said. "You could go up and see the drawings on the rocks. They're just gorgeous. They're stunning. Pictures of little men with their arms pointing in different directions and animals like salamanders and drawings of the sun and clouds and waves and stripes. Pictures that make up this beautiful language. Even if you don't know anything about the people that made them, you can imagine what kind of people they were. You can see how sweet they were from the drawings, how lovely the world was in their dreams."

# Fifteen

Socorro was a ratty little town that dangled off the highway the way a broken leg hangs off a dog that's been hit by a car. It was mostly dirt, sand, red grass, and squat cactus peppered with little brown houses that might as well have been ovens.

We'd had to see Socorro because of the alien craft that landed there in 1964, and the little guy in Roswell had been so hot on it.

"First we find the site," Jen said, "then we go after Lonnie Zamora and Sergeant Chavez. Everybody O.K. with that?"

"They sound like a couple of real dweebers," Penny said. "What's their deal, anyway?"

"Zamora saw the spaceship and Chavez came in later and saw the traces—burning bushes and all that," Jen said. "It's a big deal because the Air Force didn't write it off."

"Typical," Penny said.

We found the spot out of town where the deputy had seen the UFO. That was pretty easy. The UFO had supposedly landed there in this gully, and these little men were standing around it, and then when Zamora got out of his car or something the men got back in the ship and blasted off. The town had the spot marked with a big sign. But when we tried to find Zamora himself, that wasn't so easy. Everybody we talked to had a different idea of where he lived. In fact, some people had different ideas of who he was, which made tracking him difficult. What we did was cruise up and down the dusty, chuck-hole-filled roads, sliding in and out of stringy subdivisions. We knocked on a few doors and finally ran into some people having a chicken picnic in the dirty sand that was their front yard. They invited us to join them, but we declined, though it looked to me like Penny was interested.

"We're trying to find the guy who saw the UFO," Jen said to an older, skinny man with a rubber-like complexion and a bum leg that seemed to point toward the other leg whenever he tried to walk. The Charlton Heston thing.

"Everybody's seen them," the guy said. "They're all over the place. You only have to turn around and you see one."

"Have you seen any?" Jen said.

"Well, I haven't," he said. "Not me, personally. But everybody else I know has."

"I hear that," Penny said. "Lot of young bright men seeing UFOs every day."

"We're looking for Lonnie Zamora," Jen said. "Or Chavez, the state cop. You know them?"

"There's a cop lives around the corner there," the guy said waving off to one side. "But he's new, just got here in town last year. He's from Anchorage, I think. May be an Inuit, or have some Inuit blood. That's what I heard, anyway."

"Yeah, yeah—Eskimo to us mortals," Penny whispered.

The guy was standing knock-kneed in his front yard holding a quarter chicken by the end of the drumstick. One bite of chicken about halfway down the leg was already gone. He was sort of shaking this chicken at us as a kind of invitation. His wife and their kids, all of whom seemed extraordinarily tiny, much tinier than they ought to have been, almost like circus tiny—the wife was *maybe* four and a half feet tall, the kids were smaller—were back by the folding table on top of which was a fat pitcher of blue Hawaiian Punch. I figured it had to be Hawaiian Punch or Kool-Aid because it was blue, but these folks looked like the Hawaiian Punch crowd. The kids were slurping this stuff out of giant lock-top plastic glasses that had elaborate roller-coaster straws coming out of them.

On the card table there was a boombox plugged into an orange extension cord that slid back across the dirt, up over the porch rail, and into the front door that was cocked open a little. They had old-fashioned ballroom music swinging out of the boombox, dance music, and both the elders—him tall and skinny and her small as a medium-size dog up on its hind legs—were swaying a little in time with the tunes, threatening to dance in the driveway. We waved as Mike dropped the car back into gear and let us roll away.

"That poor woman got stuck and stuck hard," Penny said, shaking her head.

Apparently the town council had tried to set up a tourist deal in Socorro like the one in Roswell, but it hadn't worked out. They had a Spaceship Cleaners, a Fourth Dimension Café, and, on the way out of town, a homemade fast-food place called Out of This World, but that was about it for UFO-marketing. O-O-T-W, as its neon said, looked like a Dairy Queen that'd been caught between a couple of giant pieplates and then rolled in car aerials and whip antennas covered with SuperStik. The parking lot was spray-painted a remarkable golf-grass green. We stopped in the drive-through and Penny got their specialty, a Littlegreenmanburger. She told Jen she didn't know whether to eat it or smack it so hard it blistered.

It was close to dark when we pulled out of the green lot. Mike was ready to pack it in for the evening, find a local hotel, but Jen wanted to head on toward Arizona.

"I can drive," Penny said. "Just as soon as I finish this burger."

"If we stay here in a hotel we can try to find the guy tomorrow," Mike said. "I mean get the story firsthand."

"He ain't ready for me," Jen said.

"You figure he ought to be standing out here on the highway, waiting for you?" Mike said.

"Dad," Jen said. "We're hitting the road."

So Mike and Penny switched places, and we headed back down Highway 25 to where we could get to the cutoff that went to Pie Town and parts west. Although it was dark, we could still see the mountains on either side of us, tall, solid hulks crisscrossing the road. There was a big stream running down one side of the highway, silver, reflecting lights from the little cabins alongside it. Pretty soon we were higher into the mountains, and the roads were smaller and the stream was gone and there weren't any houses, just a big black hump squeezing the highway. I realized we hadn't done much night driving on the trip, and I was thinking that was too bad, because things seemed more comfortable in the car at night. The inside seemed a lot bigger. There was territory there between the riders in the Town Car, and it was cooler and quieter, and the road wasn't making so much noise, and the noise it did make was more soothing at night than in the daytime. Watching out the front window at the white lines edging the road and the yellow line in its center, I had a more profound sense of being on a seam than I did in the day, an edge between two places, a track, lit by headlights and not much else. The big Lincoln seemed to shoot itself forward into the darkness. What lights there were outside the windshield seemed to be glittering. Headlights jiggled as they came toward us, and the reflectors embedded in the highway threw our lights back in our eyes. Even the houses up in the hills seemed to be shining like storybook houses. It was Christmas out there, in the middle of summer.

The road was mostly two-lane blacktop, but there were sections of divided highway, too. These sections didn't seem to make sense, because there wasn't any pattern to their appearance or disappearance.

We'd drive awhile, and then suddenly there'd be a mile of divided highway, then back to blacktop. We passed a hut that was renting trailers, and our lights caught the taillights of all the trailers at once, making them look like a herd of small animals there in the ditch alongside the highway.

Jen pulled out her computer and said, "I'm going to read your tarot now."

"Oh, yeah?" I said. "Why don't we watch TV instead?"

"Nothing on up here in the mountains."

"Where is the little TV, anyway? I want to see what happened to O.J."

"O.J. who?" Penny said.

"Forget him," Jen said. "Plus, I got this new tarot program off a BBS. It's pretty nice—it does everything. It has the Celtic cross and two or three other spreads, and it explains everything. When you get the Death card, I can explain the hell out of it."

"The Death card can be good," I said. "It just means change in your life, right?"

"Yeah, if you say so," Jen said.

She got the computer started and ran the tarot program and asked me to shuffle the cards by punching a couple of keys.

"You can stop whenever you want to," she said.

"How do I know the cards are changing under there?" I said.

"You trust me," she said.

So I stopped shuffling, and then she said, "O.K. Now you have to pick out your cards." The laptop had a track-ball, which made picking out the cards a little difficult, but I got it done. "Are you ready?"

"I guess so," I said.

She moved the cursor to a button that said "Reveal" and clicked it once. The first card in the center of the cross rolled over. Death. I shook my head.

"That's great," Jen said. "Now, that's a really great card to get in that position. It's all about starting a new part of your life, putting the things of your past behind you and going forward, reaching out to conquer new challenges, stepping out of old, bad habits, leaving your worn clothes behind. It's a wonderful sign, really. It's about the best card you could possibly ever get in that position."

"Jen," I said.

"O.K. O.K. So there is some little downside to it," she said. "But it could be a lot worse. See, like, position is everything. Like, if it were up here in the fourth house, then that would be a problem. I'd tell you that too, I'd just come right out and tell you, but here, at the center of everything, it's a very, very good sign." She clicked on a couple of buttons to bring out the explanation of the Death card. "See here," she said, pointing at the screen. "It says right here that 'the Death card represents the clearing of the old to usher in the new and, therefore, should be welcomed as a positive, cleansing, transformative force in our lives.' "

"Let's do it again," I said.

"What do you mean, do it again? You can't just do it again," she said.

"Let's shuffle and do it again."

"Are you sure?" she said. "We'll lose this whole spread."

"That's the idea," I said.

So she clicked on the shuffled deck, and we went through the whole process again, dealing another set of ten cards. This time when she clicked on "Reveal," the first card that came up was the Devil.

"Progress," I said.

She brought up the text on the Devil card and read parts of it out loud to me. " 'The Devil represents hidden forces of negativity that constrain us and deceive us into thinking we're imprisoned by external forces,' " she said. " 'There's a devil in each of us. It's like an inner force. He's an embodiment of our fears, addictions, and harmful impulses.' " She pointed at the screen. "These two people chained at his feet are 'entranced with the paralyzing fear of his illusory power and therefore stand there and look numb.' But see, the chains hang loosely, so they can break free of their hypnotic attachment if they really want to, if they have the will," she said, clicking back to the main spread.

"This is not good," I said. "This is worse than last time."

"Well, maybe," she said. "But there's a very real sense in which it's better than the last one, a cleaner beginning, a solid ground situation against which to work."

"Why don't you go ahead and turn over the next card?" I said.

She clicked on the button to turn over the second card, and the second card was Death.

I said, "Death can be one of the most fruitful and positive cards in the deck."

"This is not a good spread," she said. "This is not good news. I think maybe we want to move away from this spread."

The third card was the Hierophant. "Stop," I said. "Turn it off."

"No," she said. "Let's just take a peek at what's here." She turned over the rest of the cards. I had the Emperor in a position of the recent past, the Moon and the Crown, the Wheel of Fortune in the position of the future, and the other four cards were the Chariot, the Hanged Man, Judgment, and the Magician.

"This isn't really so bad," Jen said. "It looked a little iffy there at the beginning, but as it plays out, it's not so bad. I've seen worse than this. I did one for Gary Gilmore that was a lot worse than this."

"Please," I said. "Tell me tomorrow."

"I'll save this and we can look at it again," she said. "O.K.?"

"That'll be fine," I said.

"You don't believe in this stuff, anyway," she said.

"I believe in everything," I said. "A little bit in everything."

Jen shut the computer down and slipped it back into the bag she had in the footwell on her side of the car.

"Penny," she said. "Where are we?"

"Pie Town thirty-one," Penny said.

"Is that all?" Jen said. "What are you doing? Seventy? Eighty?"

"Something like that," Penny said.

Mike stirred, and I realized that he'd been asleep, with his head pressed against the window glass. Penny waved a hand to hush Jen up, and then Jen turned sideways in the seat, resting her head against the window on her side of the car and running her feet across my lap into the door on my side.

"We stop there, O.K.?" she said.

Penny waved again.

Jen said to me, "I want to wake up tomorrow in Pie Town. Just the idea is great. Maybe the idea is more thrilling than actually doing it, even. But I want to do it."

"It's doable," I said.

"You bet," Jen said. "I'm beginning to like this traveling stuff, this touring around and seeing stuff."

"I can tell that."

"Well, don't you like it?"

"Yes, I like it. I told you I liked it."

"I think it's worthy," Jen said.

Up in the front seat, Penny sneezed a couple of times and then looked up into the rearview to see if we were watching her. I tried to look away quick, but I think she caught me.

Mike sighed, his head still against the window. "Why is everybody making so much noise?" he said.

"Maybe you should call ahead to Pie Town and see if we can get a hotel there," Jen said.

"Why don't you?" Mike said, tossing the cellular phone over the back of the seat.

"Can't," she said.

"How come?" Mike said.

"I'd have to call Information, and I'd have to call somebody in town and ask if there are any hotels. There's not going to be a Holiday Inn in Pie Town."

"So why were you asking me?" he said.

"Wake you up," she said.

"There's bound to be something," I said.

"We'll just get it when we get there," Jen said. "It's not going to hurt if I don't call."

"Let me have the phone, then," I said. "I want to call Bud."

"Here we go," Jen said.

"I don't have to call him if you don't want me to," I said.

"No, go ahead," she said.

"Go ahead," Mike said from the front seat.

"Maybe he's seen some UFOs," I said to Jen.

"Is that the nicest thing you could possibly think of to say?" Jen said.

"I'm sorry," I said.

"You go ahead and talk to Mr. Bud, and I'll join our fellow travelers up front and see what's happening." Jen leaned forward over the back of the front seat and put an arm around Penny and an arm around Mike. "So what's up, guys?" she said.

I dialed our number at home thinking I'd check for messages first, but the transmission got crossed up or something and I ended up connected to a guy on another cellular who was driving across country up in Arizona. He was trying to call his mother, he told me. I told him we were driving through New Mexico, that we'd been to Roswell and to the UFO museum, and that we were headed for a spot called Pie Town. He told me he'd seen a UFO once, up in Idaho where his mother lived. He told me he always called his mother at odd times and that he had a sixth sense about how she was doing, and lots of times when he called it turned out to be precisely the right time, just when she needed him. That was the kind of thing that made him wonder, he told me.

# sixteen

It was nine-thirty when we got into Pie Town, which was so small we drove all the way through and rolled out the other side before we realized what we'd done. Then we turned around. Jen had been right about the motels—there wasn't a Holiday Inn or anything like it. The town was about three-quarters of a mile long and straddled the highway, and it didn't look very prosperous. There was a blinking orange traffic light at the main street, and when we cut off the highway, we were instantly in the town square, where a giant pie sculpture was set in the middle of a fountain. Water was flowing out of the simulated vents in the sculpture's simulated crust.

"We'd better find a phone booth with a yellow pages," Jen said.

We looked around but couldn't find a phone booth, so we went back to the highway and drove all the way through town again. The buildings along each side were old, dusty, run down, falling apart. There was a laundry, a closed gas station, a handful of adobe houses with open porches, a few older wooden houses. The one luxury the town had was large trees that towered over all the buildings, good for shade in the daytime and wind catching at night.

On the second trip through town we found a little dive called the Cabana Motel at one end. Some of the rooms were lit up, and the office was at one end of the property, with a badly damaged neon sign. There was a shell parking lot in front of a series of little buildings with bright white roofs that were spaced out along a tiny creek running diagonally through the property. These were the cabanas, we figured. Mike and I got out and went into the office, where a guy who looked Indian asked if he could help us. We said we needed some rooms, and he said he had some rooms and how many did we want? Mike looked at me.

"Three," I said.

"Three," Mike said to the guy.

He had a free-form kidney-shaped desk, with a pale-green Formica top and a lamp made from a hunk of driftwood on one end. It was a movable desk, like a portable bar, only bigger. There were a couple of dogs in the office, small, ratty, and mean-looking. At one end of the room was a glass-top case with handicrafts inside—bamboo flutes and ceramic bowls and beads of all kinds and some little bits of silver jewelry.

We got our rooms and went back to the car and then crunched across the shell and crossed the little creek to the cabanas. We had 3, 4, and 5. A big woman in a print dress was in 2. She was sitting out on the steps into her room.

"How's it hanging?" she said to me as I unlocked the door to number 3.

"Pretty tired," I said.

"Just go in there and splash some water on your face," she said. "It'll perk you right up."

Jen came into the room behind me, with her eyebrows raised. "What's the deal here?" she whispered.

"Some friendly woman," I said. "Shut the door, will you?"

Our room was barely big enough for a double bed and a couple of dinner-plate-size bedside tables. The bathroom had a plastic shower stall with a galvanized pipe hanging over the top, where the shower head should have been. I splashed some water on my face, just like the fat woman suggested. It felt good. I used one of the two towels we had to dry off.

After we got settled, the four of us went to get something to eat at a gas station and all-night restaurant on the highway. Jen picked up a new travel guide for Arizona and New Mexico from the rack, and we went back to the motel. Mike and Penny decided to sit outside for a while, take the air. Jen and I went inside and locked the door. There was an old television, but it got only one or two channels, and both of those were frosty. I tried the handheld, but there was nothing doing, so I rested in the bed while Jen paged through her new travel book. After a while I got up and looked out the window and saw that Mike and Penny had moved to the little bridge over the creek. The moon had come out into the middle of the sky. It was nearly full. There were some wisps of cloud around it. The moon showered the parking lot, made it a pretty basin of light.

"I think it's on again," I said, climbing back into the bed.

"I could have told you that," Jen said without looking up. "You know, we missed a lot coming this way. We could have gone up to Santa Fe and Taos and up there."

"We still could."

"No. It's backwards," she said. "I'm thinking we shoot straight up to Gallup and then over to the Petrified Forest and the Painted Desert."

"Inching west," I said.

"Don't remind me."

I got up and went to the bathroom, then stopped back by the window.

"What are they doing now?" Jen said.

"They're still on the bridge," I said.

Some kind of night bugs were flying around over by the office.

Crickets or something were howling. I saw Mike look up in the direction of our cabin, and then I saw him wave. I dropped the venetian blind I had been lifting with my forefinger.

"He caught me," I said.

"Serves you right," Jen said. "You know, there's a lot of interesting stuff in this book. New Mexico is full of stuff, so is Arizona, so is Utah. There are a lot of Indian ruins around here and up in the top of New Mexico and the bottom of Colorado. You should see these pictures—they're gorgeous." She turned the book she was looking at around so I could see a few pictures. They *were* gorgeous.

"I have a feeling that what is out of sight is out of mind," I said. "Lopez and Damian Williams and Los Angeles and all that."

"It's still there," she said. "But I didn't realize how much stuff there was out here to see."

"It's just tourist junk," I said.

"Just because everybody looks at it doesn't change what it is."

"That's not very modern of you."

"Unless they've Carlsbad Caverned it to death," Jen said. "And even then, you can see through what they've done to it if you try."

"First-order experience."

"Do you think we ought to go out there and check on them?" she said.

"I think we ought to leave them alone," I said.

"I have been thinking of killing a few people. Just an introduction, I've been thinking. A few people carefully chosen, highly visible, whose deaths might be noticed. I was thinking of starting with politicians and television personalities, because these two represent sources of evil that are unparalleled in the contemporary world. It can even be argued that the television personalities are the greater evil, that the politicians simply follow the rings in their noses. But it is time, it seems to me, Jennifer, to act. I am ready to kill and maim and damage and wound and dismember and eviscerate, to do what is necessary to bring about the change that is required. Are my plans too grand? I wonder that as well. I think to myself maybe something smaller. A local grocer who habitually cheats his patrons. A woman at a laundry who mistreats her clothes folders. A kid who thoughtlessly bullies another. I've thought of starting locally, of starting small, but it's risky. I might get caught too soon, before I've had the opportunity to do any real damage. No, I think I must take the larger stage. I must be a scorpion on a bedroom wall in Washington, D.C. I must strike everywhere at once and must not be too proud of my method."

We were looking at one of the new messages from Durrell. Jen had hooked up in the Cabana Motel and fetched her e-mail. She read the message and then showed it to me.

"Why are you still sending mail to this guy?" I said.

"Well, I haven't, not in the last couple of days," she said. "But once they've got you, you're an audience. They never let go."

"Why don't you just change your e-mail address, your name and address?"

"I suppose I could do that," she said. "But then everybody else who wanted to send me e-mail wouldn't know where to get me."

"They'd know after you sent them something."

"It's too much trouble," she said. "Besides, I think he's just doing this bad boy stuff for fun. People do that all the time. It's one of those things where talk is freed of consequence, where it's real but not real at the same time. He's one of those guys who jabbers about getting even but never does."

"He's a man of a thousand injuries," I said.

"Like the rest of us," Jen said.

I started looking at the computer again, paging up and down. "What else is on here?" I said.

"There are a couple more Durrell screeds. There's a long thing on guns he sent, and I've got a story about a four-hundred-twenty-pound man on death row in Minnesota who can't be hanged because it would be cruel and unusual punishment to rip his head off his neck with a rope, which is what his lawyers say will happen if the state tries to hang him."

"So what are they going to do?"

"I don't know. Hit him with a speeding car, maybe," she said. "It's the new, life-affirming mode of capital punishment. Integrates capital punishment into the culture in a fresh way."

"You know, Jen," I said, "sometimes I think you're just a little too something for your age. You know what I mean?"

"I watched a lot of MTV," she said. "In the early years. I hung around with older men. I was bad to the bone."

I smiled and nodded and read some more of Durrell's energetic prose. Durrell figured we were in a bind because on the one hand we wanted to give everyone equal opportunity, we wanted to be generous in thought and deed, and on the other hand, some of our fellows seemed to be taking advantage of this, going for the personal benefit even while proclaiming adherence to the high ideals. Those weren't exactly Durrell's words, but that was the substance of tirade two. His resolution was that he would not be constrained by his own goodheartedness, his own goodwill toward men and women, but instead he would slit throats and gouge out eyes, cut off tongues with scissors, put penises in waffle irons, break Coke bottles inside vaginas. All sorts of things.

Jen went to take a shower, and I shut off the computer, putting it into its sleep mode, and then went out for a walk around the grounds.

Mike and Penny were no longer on the bridge. The fat lady was shut inside her room. I couldn't tell by the lights whether the guy was in the office or not. It was pretty dim out there. I stood on the bridge for a minute, the little stream trickling underneath me. I crossed to the shell parking lot and walked out to the highway. There I turned around and looked over the Cabana Motel. We were in the Cabana because there were no ordinary motels in town, but to be staying there made me feel happy, because the place was so odd. The office and the parking lot were in a little clearing surrounded by large trees. The cabins looked like puffy cinnamon buns, with their icing-white roofs. The stream flickered slightly in the moonlight. I looked both ways and crossed the highway to an abandoned cinder-block building with a plate-glass window in the front wall and a bench beneath that. I looked in the window but couldn't see anything except for a couple of bicycles leaning up against the window, so I sat down on the bench, facing the highway and the motel. Cars came by occasionally, usually at a fairly good clip. Some had people in them reading maps that were unfolded like giant birds in the front seats of the cars. More often I just saw the silhouettes of the drivers and passengers buzzing through Pie Town on their way to somewhere else. I wanted to imagine that I knew what these people felt, what it felt like to be them in their cars, going where they were going. But I didn't know. I didn't have the slightest idea. It was easy to imagine them grimly pursuing their goals through the night, but that was too easy and made me think it was probably not what they were doing. But they weren't happy families either, necessarily. Some were businessmen, salesmen on the road. Some could have been criminals. Some would be people people going home late after a dinner party at a friend's house. There were carloads of white people and carloads of black people and carloads of Indian people. There were new cars and old cars. There were trucks and vans. There were sports cars and clunky family sedans. There were many dusty pickups, a couple of eighteen-wheelers, an RV or two, U-Hauls, boat trailers, motorcycles—all manner of wheeled creatures.

When I wasn't watching the passersby, I was studying the motel, studying our room, Mike's room, Penny's room. Lights were on in all three. At a certain moment, Mike came out of his room, went to our door and knocked, waited there until Jen opened the door, and then talked to her for a minute, kissed her good night, and returned to his room. Then the manager came out of his office and stood on the steps outside the door and stretched. He wandered around in the shell parking lot, looking up at the sky, then he picked up a shell and sailed it across the lot into the trees on the other side. Then he saw me. I don't think he recognized me, don't think he knew who I was, but he turned around and headed back for the office.

There weren't any real blocks per se in Pie Town, there were just driveways and dirt roads heading off perpendicular to the highway, so it was a guess how many blocks it would have been from one end of town to the other—a half dozen, maybe. There was a shoulder on either side of the highway, and after a while I got off the bench and decided to walk. I headed back toward the eastern edge of town. It was about midnight, and nobody was out. There were a few dogs around, but they seemed friendly. Small black dogs wagging their tails, some beat-up brown dogs. There was a wonderful old gas station, which was shut down, but it must have been the standard model for 1955 or something. There were a couple of wood-siding houses, weather-beaten, sort of ramshackle, each with a light or two in its windows. There were old barbed-wire fences and rusting cars in small fields and the trees with their leaves flapping with each breeze. A couple of houses on the other side of the highway had cows behind them. I saw one pale gray horse. I got to the far edge of town, crossed the highway, walked back on that shoulder. I felt happy out in the middle of New Mexico, walking along the side of the highway. Even though I didn't go very far, it was wonderfully refreshing. When I got back to the motel, I didn't want to go inside, so I went straight past it, passing the café, which was closed, a grocery store and a gas station that were closed, a feed store, and a couple of little adobe houses back off the road. I stopped at the edge of town and sat down on a folding chair on a platform that I thought must be the bus stop, and I watched the road, the hills, the sky, the stars shining. After a while I was scanning the whole sky, going left to right, raising my gaze each time I went across, looking for I don't know what—some strange lights, some strange movement, ordinary lights, scanning the night sky for a visitor, an interplanetary traveler, an alien being, a UFO. Sitting there, I imagined Durrell at his computer, clicking out his program for fighting fire with fire. His education, I thought, was just beginning.

---

The motel was a little less inviting in daylight. Still, with the shadows cast by the tall trees, and the stream running like a children's plaything across the property, and the dusty shell parking lot, it was a place I was glad I had spent the night. We got our stuff together and got out to the car a little after ten. Jen went to the office to get our receipt and gave me her set of keys, so I started the car to get the air-conditioning going. An old guy in khakis with suspenders, a T-shirt, and a baseball cap went by, walking a duck on a leash.

" 'Morning," he said to me.

I waved at him.

"That you, Andy?" he said, raising his hand over his eyes to shade them so he could see me better. He had stopped right in front of me at the edge of the highway.

"Nope, not Andy," I said. "Must be somebody else."

"You sure favor him," the old man said. He gave a yank on his duck and looked at me even more carefully, leaning forward slightly. "You ain't the Gainor boy?"

I shook my head, held up both of my hands, raised my eyebrows.

"Huh," the old man said. "That beats it. I'm just an old man out walking his bird, I guess. You from around here?"

"No," I said. "We're from Mississippi."

"Oh," he said, doing a big understanding nod. "Well, no wonder."

"Uh-huh."

"Well, that explains it." He corrected the way his hat was sitting on his head and gave the leash a little tug. "Take it easy there, Spot," he said. "We'll be going directly." He turned back to me. "You stay here last night? I mean in the motel here?"

"Yes, sir," I said.

"I've never even been in that motel," he said. "All the years it's been here, not once. We had some bad trouble in that motel one year. That was a long time ago. That would be in room four. You weren't in room four, were you?"

"No, sir," I said.

"That's good," he said. "Because room four got a hell of a working over. We had some boys in from out of town and some trouble developed between them and, well, it was an awful mess."

"When was this?"

"Oh, fifteen, sixteen years ago," he said. "Way before your time. We haven't had any trouble there in years. In fact, a young friend of my daughter's lives over there in number two. That would be Misty. That Misty lives over there. She's a big girl, but nice."

"I think I spoke to Misty last night," I said.

"I wouldn't doubt it," he said. "I wouldn't put it past her. She likes to sit out there and talk to whoever comes by. She used to keep a lot of turtles in there, but they all died one winter. Nobody knew why. I think they must have gotten some kind of turtle poisoning."

The duck started making a half-quack, half-gag sound. The old guy tugged on its leash, which snapped the duck's neck back and almost knocked it off its feet.

"You don't have a snack for Spot, do you?" the old man said.

Jen was coming toward us across the parking lot.

"I've got some peanuts in the car," I said. "Will he eat peanuts?"

"Oh, sure," the old guy said. "He'll eat anything. He'll eat shoe nails."

Jen leaned over to pet the duck while I went to get the peanuts out of the car.

"Careful there," the old man said. "He'll give you a bite."

"You won't give me a bite, will you?" Jen said, talking to the duck, combing her fingers back over its head.

"I guess not," I said, handing her the peanuts.

She poured the peanuts into her palm and fed the duck. The old man kept snapping at the duck's leash as if he wasn't pleased at how well the duck was getting along with Jen.

"He tells me there was some trouble in cabin four," I said to Jen. "Some years ago."

"Yeah, it was like a slaughterhouse," the old guy said. "Worst killing in the town's history."

"Is that where Mike was, or Penny?" Jen said.

"Penny, I think," I said.

"It was a bloodbath," the old guy said. "The way the killers took off the victims' heads, hands, and feet and put them in a pile in the corner. They had to gut the place because of the stains and the smell. The people had paid by the week, so it was about a week before anyone found the bodies."

Jen stood up and cleaned her hands by slapping them together.

"So how come they call this place Pie Town, anyway?" she said. "I asked the motel manager, but he didn't know."

"Aw, he's just a youngster," the old man said. "The story goes that many years ago some settlers were staked out here, and they got crosswise with some Navajos. One day the Navajos had them surrounded and were about to kill them off, when one of the women brought out a couple of pies, which she offered to the Navajos as a peace offering. The Navajos liked those so much they asked for more and eventually spared the people and what was later to become Pie Town. I don't know whether that's true, now."

"Sounds true to me," I said.

"Why didn't they just kill the settlers and take the pies?" Jen said.

"Well, you see, if they'd killed the settlers, that would have been the end of the pies. But the way it was, the settlers kept making the pies and giving them to the Navajos, so it came to be known as Pie Town."

"Oh," Jen said.

"Yup. It was known far and wide," the old guy said.

"Well, we've got to pack it up," I said.

"Yeah, I've got to get along, too," he said.

Just about then, Mike and Penny came out of cabin 5, carrying their luggage.

"Whoops," I said.

"Those your friends?" the old guy said.

"Yes," I said. "We're all traveling together."

"You know, you and he are about the same age, and this girl here and that girl over there are about the same age," he said.

"Yes, that's right," I said.

"Hmm," the old guy said.

I opened the trunk again, and Mike and Penny put their bags in. Penny crouched down to say hello to the duck, and Mike started off for the office.

"We already got it," Jen said.

"Oh, yeah?" he said.

A couple of eighteen-wheelers rolled by faster than they should have, kicking up whirls of dust and little rocks, shaking the ground.

"Let's move out before the dust starts growing on us," Mike said.

He got into the car, behind the wheel, and the rest of us climbed in, too. We all said good-bye to the man and the duck. The old man started shuffling across the parking lot toward the office. We were on the road headed out of town when Jen saw something off to the right that looked like a flea market.

"Look," she said. "It says 'Live Rattlesnakes.' Come on, stop."

"Jen, you don't really want to stop, do you?" Mike said.

"Yeah, we've barely started," Penny said.

"C'mon, pull over. It'll just take a minute. I want to see these rattlesnakes," Jen said.

We pulled off the road into an auto junkyard in front of a battered tin barn. Three or four adults and a couple of kids were gathered around a waist-high fence that was built up against the building. As soon as we opened the car doors we could hear the sizzling of the rattlesnakes. The tourists who were already there had long plastic sticks they were poking down into the fenced area.

There were eight or ten rattlesnakes, curled up in this dirt-floored pit about two feet deep inside the fence. There was water and some stuff that looked like cat food in there, and tree branches the snakes could slither on, but that was it. The rest was these people with sticks that had balloons tied to them. They were putting the balloons right in the snakes' faces, smacking the snakes on the nose, trying to get them to strike the balloons. The rattles were going full tilt, and every once in a while one of the snakes would get pissed off and crack the balloon that was being poked at it. Then everyone shrieked. Just inside the door, a fat guy with a lot of facial hair and a cowboy hat was reading some magazine about knives and guns. He looked like he had a corner on the local bacteria market. You had to pay him twenty-five cents to get a balloon, then you had to blow it up yourself and put it on the end of one of the sticks. The snakes looked tired of this. The people doing the stuff with the balloons were regular-looking mothers and fathers, sons and daughters.

"This is not good," Jen said.

"No kidding," Mike said.

A burly guy whose son was slapping a smallish snake over the head with his balloon gave us a dirty look. "They're just snakes," he said.

"We're just bananas," Mike said.

I wondered if that was smart, talking to the burly guy like that. I figured he wouldn't get what Mike meant, he might think Mike was saying he was crazy, and that'd cause more problems. But it didn't happen. The guy shrugged and put a meat-loaf-size hand on his son's shoulder, turned back to the fun.

We watched for a few minutes and then got in the car and pulled out onto the highway, headed north.

A little distance out of town, Jen said, "Now, Durrell would say we should've stuffed that entrepreneur and all his customers, especially the fathead guy, into the hole and let them snakes bite bite bite. Then we should've set all the snakes free and flamed the place, burned it to the ground."

I tapped the side of my head. "Yeah, but that's Durrell. Mike said what had to be said."

"Maybe it wasn't enough," Jen said.

"You were the one who wanted to stop," I said. "We didn't have to stop. They didn't make us. We drove right in there and got out and started looking."

"Yeah, well, that would've been going on whether we stopped or not."

"You gotta start somewhere," I said.

# seventeen

Penny was reading the map. We decided to go west to Quemado, then north up to Gallup, then west again into Arizona on Highway 40. In the back seat, Jen pulled a map of recreation and heritage spots out of the New Mexico magazine she'd been carrying around. She started pointing out the places we'd already missed—the Gila Cliff Dwellings, Bear Canyon Reservoir, Sleepy Grass, Silver Lake. We'd missed City of Rocks State Park.

"We're missing too much," Jen said. "We need to organize."

"I thought we were going to Los Angeles to shake hands with President Football," Mike said, looking at her in the rearview mirror.

"That was before," she said. "We just saw this thing on TV and it was horrible, and I thought, well, let's do something, and then it wears off. Some other horrible thing is on TV or something is out here in the middle of the street. I mean, what are we going to do when we get there? Stay in a motel, eat hamburgers, gawk at O.J.'s house. We have to get realistic. We're not going to any prison to see

Damian 'Football' Williams. We're not talking to Fidel Lopez about his painted crotch—that'd be great, wouldn't it? I can see me saying, 'Well, Fidel, about this painted crotch thing? How'd you ditch the paint? How'd you feel, like, inside? What about the deep structure of this painted dick? Did you feel reduced as a human being, as a man?' What am I going to say?"

"What? You don't care about that?" Penny said. "How are we going to fix anything?"

"Don't know," Jen said.

"Jesus," Penny said.

Jen was pointing out spots on the map she wanted to see. "Beautiful Woman Mountain," she said, ticking a spot in northeastern New Mexico. "Aztec Ruins National Monument. They aren't Aztec. They're Anasazi, the same ones as in Colorado at Mesa Verde. Here, let me show you Mesa Verde. This is just over the Colorado border." She pulled out a guide and showed me a picture of ruins built into a cliff. "Wouldn't you like to see this? It's where the Anasazi lived. It says, 'A remarkably preserved prehistoric Cliff Palace, inhabited 200 B.C. to 1300 A.D.' "

The Cliff Palace was cut into the rock, round rooms and towers, walls with irregular openings. Adobe brick. I read about Mesa Verde National Park, about the Anasazi and what they ate and how many different kinds of Anasazi there were at Mesa Verde at different times, what they did, and how they disappeared just as their culture seemed to become most complex and interesting.

"So what do you think?" Jen said.

"Cultures do that," I said.

"No, I mean about going."

"We should at least go to L.A. first," Penny said. "I don't like starting and not finishing something. We were going to act instead of let things happen to us."

"You talking about *Time* magazine's version of things or the way we actually live?" Jen said. "Generation X and Baby Boomers, or what we actually do?"

"Is there such a big difference?" Penny said.

"They simplify, but they've got the basic drift."

"Sorry. You missed Media 101. Having the drift right is the essence of missing the point altogether. You think you can generalize about it. It's like what happened to Del and Dad—the sixties. The public-consumption version, the historical version, is nothing like what really went on. Isn't that so, Del?"

"True," I said.

"What about you, Dad?" Jen said.

"Yeah, I guess that's close," Mike said.

"Thirty years later the public version has *become* the truth, the history. Nobody remembers or cares what it was actually like."

We were making good time through the foothills. We were on the Navajo Indian reservation, headed for Black Rock. After that we were going to cut diagonally into Arizona near a town called Lupton. I was looking at this on the map.

I said to Jen, "So do you want to drive up here and mess around, or do you want to go to California?"

"Cali," Penny said.

"I don't know," Jen said. "I don't think it makes any difference what we do, I guess. Let's go to the Captain Tom Reservoir up here." She tapped the top of the map where the Captain Tom Reservoir was. "What do you suppose goes on up there?"

"They have a lot of state parks here," I said, looking at her state park book. "White Sands, Carlsbad, Petroglyph National Monument, Bandelier, Pecos. And Arizona has its share too. What's this Canyon de Chelly?"

"It's *d'shay,*" Jen said.

I turned to the page about the National Monument. More masonry houses in the sides of huge canyons. It was like where the cowboy movies of the fifties were shot, six-hundred-foot flat canyon walls to a narrow band of farmland.

I showed Jen the pictures. She yanked the book out of my hands and flopped it over the front seat so Penny could see.

"That's amazing," Penny said. She handed the book back to me.

"We can go there," Jen said. "It's not as far as Mesa Verde. About half as far."

"We can go by way of Window Rock and Fort Defiance and all that," I said. "Go up and across."

"Then shoot right back down to the Painted Desert," Jen said. "It's just a little detour. What is that? About eighty miles up there and back? Eighty miles each way?"

"What it looks like," I said. I put my finger on the scale of miles and then measured how far it might be to make the trip. "That's about it. Maybe a little more."

"It's O.K. by me," Mike said. "You guys got it all figured out?"

"It's not going to hurt anything," Jen said.

"So I guess it's decided," Penny said. She tapped Mike on the shoulder. "What you want to do is get up here to Forty, cut a left down to Lupton, then turn right on . . . what highway is that?"

"That's Twelve," I said.

"Take a right on Twelve," Penny said.

I handed the map back over the front seat, and she folded it into a small square so it was easier for her to navigate.

We were going through pretty country. Although the road was a junk highway, it was an easy drive. I put my head back and tried to stretch my legs and let the rush of the highway and the wind and the thump of the road make me sleepy. I let my eyes shut for a few minutes and then suddenly stirred awake to see what was going on in the car. It seemed like Penny was talking to Mike a lot, whispering to him, leaning over. Jen was messing with the handheld TV, trying to get some picture that would stay still for a few minutes. After an hour or so, Penny found a road on which we could cut across to Highway 40, so Mike took that and ran into the interstate, and we cut down toward Lupton.

There was a crazy red stone mesa just past the border into Arizona, a two-hundred-foot-high red rock mountain that crowded the highway with sheer cliffs. At its base was a gaudy tourist strip with a huge tepee on the roof of the Tee Pee Café, a stateline store with its facade in the shape of Arizona, and a long, low building called Yellow Horse Souvenirs, with a big sign advertising a live buffalo inside. Up on the first cliff, about seventy feet above these stores, there were larger-than-life models of cows, deer, buffalo, eagles, bear. All the buildings had animals on top of them. Yellow Horse Souvenirs had a prancing mustard-colored palomino right in the middle of its roof, along with a couple of similar-colored baby horses and some black-and-white steers, plus a sign saying that all their authentic Indian jewelry was for sale at sixty percent off. There were hundreds of newspaper-size American flags and Arizona flags flying, plus some flags I didn't recognize, the usual Indian drawings, assorted telephone poles, hand-painted signs, Port-O-Matics, broken-down trucks, sleeping guys, stray dogs, and used lumber. Next to the big yellow horse on its hind legs above this store, there was what seemed to be a ship's mast strung with thick black wires. A ten-foot-tall unpainted Indian stood in front of Yellow Horse, and a sign that said "All Items Must Go." Above the Arizona Welcome Station there were more Indians. They were shaped just like the toy Indians I'd had as a kid—wide-open legs for the one supposed to be on horseback, others with bows raised in triumph, some kneeling with arrows drawn, ready to shoot—the same Indians I'd had, but they were six or seven feet tall, standing there with their lances, their bows and arrows, in among the brightly painted signs and the fluttering flags, and the huge, hand-painted Indian art. "See Live Buffalo," it said. "Ice Cream Churn," it said. "Cigs $5.99 per carton, Marlboros $11.99," it said.

Mike drove off the highway, and we got out of the car and stretched our legs, looked at some of the Indian jewelry that was on sale. We went through the stores one by one, and eventually I bought an antler ballpoint pen with "Arizona" burned into the side of the bone. Jen bought some tiny beaded dolls, and Penny bought a hamburger. Mike got another disposable Kodak camera and took some snaps, and then we got back into the car and headed north, passing the Indian Galleria and Ice Cream Shoppe on the way. The landscape was stunning—huge outcrops of rock on either side of the road, cut by long open vistas of prairie, with mountains rising out on the flanks. The cliffs alongside the highway were the most beautiful I'd seen—tall, stately. In one stretch there were giant formations jutting up out of the ground just this side of the mountains like huge incisors, or molars—a row of fifteen of these things three hundred yards off the highway, gray, building-size, pointed like ancient teeth.

Later we got to Window Rock, which was the name of a town and its big geological feature. The town was the capital of the Navajo Nation and the site for a lot of the Indian Affairs bureaucracy. Window Rock was a huge slab of a mountain from which an almost perfectly round section was missing, a giant rock knothole maybe fifty feet in diameter, with a natural bridge over the top. Next to Window Rock was another tall rock formation, which looked like a boot, and another that looked like a pyramid. These were rock hills, outcrops a hundred, sometimes two hundred feet tall, pure stone, no shrubbery, no dirt, nothing but red and gray rock. At their feet were the parking lots and the official buildings of the Navajo Nation and the Bureau of Indian Affairs.

We headed north again. The roadside rock formations were spectacular, almost all jagged, standing up hundreds of feet, sometimes right next to the highway, sometimes two hundred yards away. Great cliff faces like you see only in movies. Slabs irregularly cut with jagged lines where sections had dropped off. Freestanding obelisks. Tall, narrow trees like spruces occasionally in among the tin-shed communities at the feet of these cliffs. In front of us, in the distance, there was a long, horizontal, squared-off mesa with a gray line of jagged rock along the top. Eventually, when we passed that, there was a flatter valley, with trees and a river, and beyond that a single, castle-like rock outcrop on top of a densely forested mountain.

We were almost parallel to Canyon de Chelly when we turned off the highway and drove down to the north ridge of Canyon del

Muerto, which was the northern part of the national monument. We stopped to look at the ruins built into a cut in the rock face of one of the cliffs. The canyon was breathtaking—vast and open, nearly a thousand feet deep at that point and a quarter mile across. You could've herded blimps in there. You could see a mile or more back up into the canyon. Trucks and horses were barely specks on the canyon floor. There was nothing to compare it with, so nothing prepared you for what it was like to stand on the edge of the canyon and see sunlight playing on rocks jutting out of the cliff faces. Stripes of rock tilted and shimmered in the midday light. Way down, a hundred feet up from the canyon floor, seven or eight hundred feet below where we were, there were small masonry structures in a crease in the canyon wall, the ruins of the small houses of the Anasazi. They were baby small in the geography of the canyon, like a toy a child would build, bricks the size of bits of pencil lead. We climbed around on the ridge overlooking the canyon. We didn't talk much, just shouted "Look at that!" and "Did you see?" because we were all struck by the place. Jen and I sat down on a huge boulder and stared out into the canyon for a few minutes, while Penny and Mike moved on a little way to find a site of their own.

"This is good," Jen said.

I nodded and made some noise meaning I agreed.

After some time just sitting and staring, we got up off our boulder, brushed our clothes, and walked back up to the parking area, where a couple of Indian women were selling beads. We bought nothing.

When Mike and Penny got back, we drove along the rim of the canyon, pausing at some of the other overlooks, at Massacre Cave, Standing Cow Ruin, Antelope House, and then we stopped at the monument headquarters, which was called Thunderbird Lodge and Campgrounds, for a map of the southern rim of the canyon. Penny was watching a quiz show on the little TV when we stopped at the White House overlook. Jen wanted to walk all the way down to the canyon floor to get a close look at the ruins there, and to be *inside* the canyon, but Mike and I both said we couldn't make it on account of age, and Penny didn't want to go. So we got in the car and made stops at Spider Rock and Monument Canyon. These were as breathtaking as the first views we'd seen; nothing to do but stand and stare. Like White Sands, Canyon de Chelly redefined the world, made it more wonderful than we thought—it was like seeing sky for the first time. Standing on the ridge overlooking the canyon, I had that sense of wonder at the color, the space, the scale, the farmland on the canyon floor, the great power of sheared rock—the Red Sea, parted in stone.

"We're thinking about going home," Mike said.

We had finished the drive back down to the highway from Canyon de Chelly in record time. The highway was mostly empty, and there wasn't much there until we got to Petrified Forest National Park. We were driving through the park when Mike made his announcement.

"Me and Penny were talking about it last night," he said. "We were thinking we would fly home, and maybe you guys could take the car on."

"You're leaving?" Jen said.

"We were thinking we'd go on to Flagstaff and fly out of there," Mike said. "We could probably make Flagstaff tonight."

"Isn't this kind of sudden?"

"We've talked about it a couple of nights," Penny said.

"You're going to fly to Shreveport and he's going to fly to Baton Rouge?" Jen said.

"Well, we thought we'd both go to Baton Rouge for a while," Mike said. "And then she'd go back up to Shreveport. Maybe I'll take her."

Jen looked at me as if I ought to have something to say about this. Something to persuade Mike and Penny to stay.

"Why don't you guys just stay with us?" I said. "We'll travel around and decide what to do after a while."

"Everybody's already decided," Penny said.

"Is that what you're pissed about?" Jen said.

"I'm not pissed," Penny said. "I'm just ready to go."

"She sounds pissed," Jen said to me.

"I don't think so," Mike said. "You're not upset, are you, Penny?"

"Not really," she said. "I'm just ready. Don't you want to go?"

"Yeah, kind of," he said.

Something in their voices said they had no misgivings, just wanted to be a little less public than they were forced to be with us.

"Sounds like they want to go home," I said to Jen.

The part of the Painted Desert that was in the park was a disappointment. It looked like a sandpit with some colored dirt mixed in. In the distance, north of where we were, you could just catch the glinting of yellows and oranges and pinks of the real part of the Painted Desert, the part that stretched as far as the eye could see. It was out there and open but out of reach. The part we were driving through was unspectacular, small red hills with ashy deposits and then stripes of different colors of dirt.

At an overlook I said, "It doesn't look one hundred percent painted to me." Then some kind of fight broke out in a van that was parked next to us. Two teenage girls were screaming at each other, and their mother was screaming at both of them. Meanwhile the father was out with his video camera, panning from one end of the horizon to the other.

"It looks like the moon, doesn't it?" Jen said. "It's more painted, but the surface is the same—kind of low."

"It doesn't look completely like the moon," I said.

"Yeah, I guess you're right," she said.

"We were spoiled by the canyon," Penny said. "It was so take-your-breath-away that everything else looks kind of dull."

"But I like this, too," Jen said. "It's calm." She was standing in front of the park commission plaque that explained about the two distinct geological periods represented in the hills we were looking at. She read part of that to me.

"Yeah, but it's not fabulous," Penny said.

"Maybe it'll get better," Jen said.

We crossed the highway down into the Petrified Forest, and the landscape was more interesting down there, not because of the petrified stuff, but because the desert was more colorful and we were more in it, more part of it than we had been at the overlooks north of the highway. Now the rocky, irregular moonscape was all around us. We drove through it, got out, and walked in the sandy soil. We walked between the house-size hills with their faded, prewashed J. Crew blues and grays and reds.

"See, it's getting better," Jen said. "Look at these things. They're like tepee rocks or pyramid rocks. They must be seventy or eighty feet tall."

Many of the pointed hills were isolated, sitting apart from each other. We stopped at Newspaper Rock, where rocks the size of buses were covered with petroglyph graffiti—hunters, animals, birds—and then at a place called Blue Mesa, where an info plaque described how the ingredients of the rock became sticky when it was wet, and then it cracked and shrank when it dried, and how, when the clay eroded under the petrified logs, the logs rolled down the hillsides.

"This stuff looks like elephant skin," Jen said. "Right here on this hill."

"It *is* pretty cool," Penny said. "Maybe I was wrong."

"There are a lot of flies around here," Mike said, swiping a hand past his head.

We got back into the car and completed the circle around Blue Mesa, stopping at one more place to look at the stripes in the sides of some hills. Jen, who was reading the guide, said these were different minerals—iron, manganese, and other things in the clay. Then we went down through a section called the Flat Tops to the Rainbow Forest, where we all got out to look at the petrified wood. There was a lot of it, and it was petrified. Some of it was sort of pretty, but most of it looked like something from Wal-Mart. We had a big deal as to whether or not we should steal some. There were signs all over the place saying it was a federal crime to steal even the tiniest piece of petrified wood, but Jen and Penny insisted on sneaking toaster-size pieces into the car. They were walking funny and holding stuff behind them and sliding their feet sideways trying to get to the car.

"You look real natural," Mike said as Penny tripped over a stone and dropped the piece she was carrying.

Jen got a small piece, about half a toaster size, and punched it under the seat. When we drove out the back gate, the guard asked us if we had picked up any petrified wood, and we said we hadn't.

We took some dinky highway back up to the interstate at Holbrook, and just before we got into town, Mike said, "Why don't we stop here for a snack and then go on to Flagstaff?"

"How far is it?" Jen said.

"It's eighty miles from here," Penny said. "It's all on Forty, so it'll go fast."

"What time is it now?" Jen said.

"It's seven," Mike said.

Jen looked at me, and I shrugged. She said, "O.K., that sounds fine."

Holbrook was another one of the Arizona tourist towns, all decked out in Pow-Wow Trading Posts, Indian jewelry shops, and a place called the Petrified Rock Garden, which was selling bits of petrified wood and fifteen-foot inflatable dinosaurs. Everything was done in bright colors and fake Indian designs, right down to Scotty & Sons Auto Parts. Outside the Navajo County Museum, some Indians were in full-dress regalia, complete with feathered headwear down to the grass, their brightly colored orange-and-red-and-yellow outfits covered with beads and other decorations. They had a considerable audience of tourists up in a short bleacher. Some of the older buildings in town had big murals on them—Indians chasing horses across the desert, Indians camped out on the plains, Indians in war paint. A place called Julian's Roadrunner had a giant mural of an old town, with a square presided over by a gigantic jackrabbit that was three or four times the size of the people who were milling about. The people in the mural seemed to think this was as natural as apple pie. We circled a few blocks and passed a second place that seemed to specialize in dinosaurs, only these weren't inflatable. They looked like papier-mâché. Geodes were on sale for eighty cents each—Indian Rock Shop, it was called—and on the roof of the place next door it said "See Prehistoric Dinosaur Bones." Another open-air shop, which might have been a gas station once, was advertising a dinosaur on petrified wood for ninety-nine cents.

We couldn't decide if we wanted to eat at Joe and Aggie's Café or the Café Romeo. These two places were across the street from each other, next to the Adobe Inn. Finally we chose Joe and Aggie's. It was a linoleum-floored room, very dark, with a bar at one end and a few linoleum-topped aluminum tables around. The eaters were locals; they looked us up and down when we went in. We got sandwiches and sat at a table near the door, listening to the cars swish by outside.

"You sure this is what you want to do?" I said to Mike. "Leave, I mean. Everything's going O.K. We can just travel around some more. We don't have to do anything in particular. We can go to California if you want."

"Yeah," Jen said. "I'm sure there's stuff out there."

"Thanks," Mike said. "But we're getting tired."

"You're both going to Baton Rouge?" Jen said to Penny.

"Yeah," she said, maybe defensively. "It's easier to fly to one place. Then he can take me back up, or maybe I'll get a flight—either way."

"We may just hang out in Baton Rouge," Mike said. "Dinner, movies, I don't know—normal stuff."

"And leave us alone out here?" Jen said.

Mike waved his hand. "You can handle it. So what will you do?"

Jen looked at me, and we sort of shrugged. "We don't know,"

she said. "Probably we'll think about it and figure something out. Right, Del?"

"Sure," I said. I couldn't tell what she was getting at, whether she meant that or had some secret message.

We finished our food and drove out of town past the Wigwam Motel, which was next to Tribal Treasures, another jewelry shop. The motel was made up of individual units shaped like big white tepees and decorated with Indian drawings in clay color and black.

"This is a famous place," Mike said. "I've seen pictures of it. It's a landmark."

The motel wasn't very crowded. There were six cars for the twenty or twenty-five units they had. Mike took a snap out the window with the Kodak as we passed.

The drive into Flagstaff was quick and pretty. We were headed right into the sunset—oranges and yellows, pale greens, clouds lit from behind as they shuttled across the low sky. At one point, when the sun had just gone down, the horizon was all lit up like there was some huge chemical fire there—bright orange, almost white at the center, radiating out from a long, slender lozenge near the horizon, gradually turning golden, then gray and green as it got up into the clouds. Soon all of the landscape was dark, pockmarked by house lights and car lights and celery-colored street lights towering in the darkness. Everything above the horizon was a fiery orange, bleeding into a docile slate. As we drove on, the fire vanished from the orange, leaving it pale, pearlescent, even lovelier. That was when we first saw the silhouetted mountains of Flagstaff.

# eighteen

I watched news in the hotel room while Jen took her shower. The news was the usual debate in Congress, people distorting each other's views, arguments among the pundits, expert opinions solicited from highly qualified experts, assorted murders, arsons, rapes, carjackings, execution-style slayings, tortures, hostage situations, fast-food killers, mall voyeurs, forest fires, and new deaths in Rwanda, Serb attacks in Bosnia, trouble with Cuba and Haiti, worry about the Middle East and Russia, trouble in Finland, problems with pornography, the Manson anniversary, the anniversary of Mary Jo Kopechne's death, TV essays on black-on-black crime, stories about killings in grade schools, gun control arguments, political payoffs in Congress, big-name legislators coming back in spite of obvious misdeeds, presidential appointees being investigated for one reason or another, the administration stonewalling its latest crisis, Michael Jackson in Yugoslavia with Elvis Presley's daughter, and of course O.J., the great American lesson in how things work, legally speaking, dozens of lawyers drawn into prominence nightly, and somewhere along the way a set of quintuplets, a boy born with no arms but miraculously healthy otherwise, the tragic story of an athlete who committed suicide after a failure on a particularly important play in a game on a weekend. As the faces flashed across the TV screen I recognized most of them, the characters in our collective game of television news—a bigger Sim City, a better Dungeons and Dragons, a never-ending, multipart, to-be-continued docudrama about the way we live now. Marcia Clark's skirt was very short, I noticed. Michael Jackson was whiter than I was, I noticed. The Presley girl did not seem too damn happy, I noticed. Michael Kinsley was going to be on the Leno show. The fires were still raging in the West, and somebody was murdered in a bathroom, holding a cigarette, and Billy Crystal's new movie hadn't done so well, and there had been another train wreck, and three different people mentioned Ding Dongs. The cross-eyed woman on CNN, whose eyes were not only crossed but seemed lit from inside, producing a very disturbing robot-at-the-helm aspect, had been shifted from her daytime dead-end career right into prime time. Triumph! That Arkansas poultry producer was at it again. Then, more western fire—very pretty to look at, as were the old airplanes dumping the veils of red powder down into the smoke. The weatherwomen were showing a little bit of lace, I noticed. And of course, that was just the beginning of things, that was just flicking through channels while waiting for Jen to get out of the shower. A dose of real time. I was sorry there wasn't a flood somewhere, because I wanted to see those people in the boats floating around with only the roofs of their houses showing. I wanted to see them rescue the kittens or the dogs. I wanted to see the guy who found a snake in his chimney. It was too bad there wasn't a passenger plane wreck, one where the plane goes off the end of the runway into the water, into a bay somewhere. A wreck where nobody was killed, nobody really hurt too badly, but perhaps some pilot error was involved, where there were suspicions, where there was mystery and intrigue, where there were flickering and bright police lights, firemen in bright-yellow slickers, people being dragged out of the water, and a giant plane in the background, cracked dramatically in half, with flares burning everywhere, police tape strung from tree to tree. There were many things I didn't see on my little trip through television-land, but I knew I would see them soon enough, tomorrow or the day after. The problem with cockfights would be discussed. Half a body would be discovered somewhere. Money would turn up in a bus station. A folksy senator would be revealed as a lecher and a harasser.

Somehow they would get a story about oral sex on the news, and something about tough but goodhearted cops who had helped a black kid in Los Angeles. Like all Americans, I was looking forward to every minute of it. I wanted to hear it all. I couldn't wait. Weren't we having a national flea emergency? Were those lobsters tainted by upstream pollutants or not? And what about all those people who saw that image of the Blessed Virgin appear on the side of that silo in Germany? Was that possible? Could it be true?

When Jen came out of the bathroom, she looked worried. She was standing in our room drying her hair with a towel, wearing nothing. She was upset about Mike and Penny. "I feel terrible about this. It's like he came all this far and now he's leaving. If he'd left at Dallas it would have been fine, but now . . ."

"I think he just wants to be alone with Penny," I said.

"Are you serious?" Jen said.

"What it looks like."

"They're going to . . . you know?"

"He's a free man."

"He's been a free man for years," she said. "That doesn't mean he has to jump my friends."

"He could do worse," I said.

"I guess she's not really a friend anymore. She's too . . ." Jen waved her arms around, folded the towel a couple of times, then unfolded it. "She's too something. I don't know what."

"She'll be your stepmother if they get married," I said.

"Oh, Jesus," Jen said. "You don't think . . ."

"You never can tell."

"Oh, Holy Jesus," Jen said. "Now I really don't know what to do."

"Why don't you send a message to Durrell, telling him we're not going to Los Angeles," I said. "Then we'll take a look at the map."

"I could do that," Jen said. "I could tell him that tonight, and we could do map stuff. That'd be O.K. That might even be more than O.K."

I was relaxing in the tub, the water almost up to the rim, the shower curtain pulled halfway across the curtain rod to keep the light out of my eyes, when Jen walked in and told me we had big news from Durrell.

"He's got his targets," Jen said, sweeping aside the shower curtain and sitting down on the edge of the tub. She had the computer with her and was reading off the screen.

"Listen to this. 'I am eager to begin what I hope will be a long and productive career as a righter of wrongs, a rectifier. I have been making a list of potential victims on the national and the local levels. I am eager to share my thoughts with you, to compare notes, and to get your opinions. I had thought for a while of bombing or some other means of mass destruction, but I am so much fonder of the personal, the intimate contact, fonder of the idea of killing one person at a time, with each death allowed its opportunity for impact. This means, of course, that each killing will have to take place at medium to long range. Thus the handgun materials that I sent you some time ago are not useful. I have also decided to do some random attacks as a means of confusing law enforcement. I may even do them in pairs. I am worried that you and others might find my lists idiosyncratic, but I am reluctant to provide those lists here, lest they fall into the wrong hands. I am, of course, using a pseudonym and a UNLV account (I apologize for not having told you this before) but it is still possible that I might be traced. I have changed my place of residence twice in the last two weeks in preparation for upcoming activities. It also seems to me that if I am not greedy, if I do not insist on killing every day or even every week or even every two weeks, my prospects for tenure improve. And so I intend to take little trips, little vacations between my assignments, and as I am very near the first of those, and as you are presumably approaching Los Angeles in service of your own particular grail, I am hoping that we might meet there.' " Jen stopped reading and shut down the notebook. "And then he goes on to say how he expects to be on the Net tonight after midnight if I want to contact him."

"He didn't send you the list?" I said.

"No list," she said. "But he's in Vegas, so it's probably Wayne Newton."

"Why would he kill Wayne Newton?" I said.

"I don't know," Jen said. "Maybe the hair. Maybe he thinks Wayne is big and ugly and greasy and stupid. Maybe he thinks Wayne is a corrupting influence."

"Don't be silly. Wayne's fine. He's been doing parodies of himself and all that—he's one of the guys nowadays."

"Hmm. Aren't we generous," she said.

"There's a looseness about Durrell's strategy that's scary, seems to me."

"You mean that he has one, or the kill-the-harmless problem?" Jen said.

"Right," I said. "Both."

"I worried about the second thing earlier, when I was making a list of who I wanted to kill," she said. "A lot of times you think, well, I'll kill this person or this person, and then when you think about it for a minute, you know the people you've picked are sort of harmless, finally. And if they're not *exactly* harmless, maybe they're just doing what they get paid for, or what they can think of, or what you might expect them to do, or what other people expect them to do, or some version of some right thing that has gone wrong somewhere along the way, and you can't really expect them to do much better than that."

"So you have to go for government kill," I said. "Or network, or corporate—studio chiefs, lawyers, loudmouths on TV. Is that the deal?"

"That's it," Jen said.

"You can't kill Rushdie for being a self-absorbed nit milking his dinky assassination threat, and you can't kill the monkey boys who run him around the world, right?"

"Monkey boys are our friends," she said. "Besides, Sal has been superseded by that Bangladeshi woman, whatever her name is. He's trying to jump into her light, but it isn't going to happen. He's off."

"What about Garcetti and Marcia Clark?"

"Necklaced. Both of them. Shapiro, too—he's such a wheezer. See, that's the problem. You start naming people who don't really really deserve it, maybe, and you're lining up shots for people because they've got bad manners."

"Essence of anarchy," I said.

"Yeah, yeah," she said. "You're a major tough guy."

"I'm talking theoretically," I said. "I'm not killing anybody, except maybe the way that guy on TV does, pinching their heads. Remember that guy? I could pinch heads day in and day out."

"I remember him. He was Canadian," she said.

"So you didn't tell Durrell yet that we're not going to L.A.?"

"I didn't have a chance," she said. "I got on, got my mail, and here's this letter. I brought the letter in to read to you."

"At my most vulnerable moment."

"Go, Speed Racer," she said, dropping her hand and filleting the bathwater with her fingers.

We were on the sixth floor of a high-rise Holiday Inn. Our room was cleaner than most. It was downright cozy—two double beds and a very good color television and a view out the window of streaming lights on the highway and the tall mountain beyond, silhouetted against the sky.

"Look at this," I said to Jen, who was wrapped up in towels on one of the beds. "It looks like that *Close Encounters* place a little bit. You remember that?"

"That's Devil's Tower," she said. "I don't know where it is, though."

"It must be around here someplace," I said. "It's like all that stuff we saw today, isn't it?"

"I guess," she said. "I don't know."

I closed the curtain and came back to the bed. "Where's the computer?" I said.

"It's in the bathroom, where we left it," she said. "On the vanity."

"Oh."

"What are you going to do?"

"I thought I'd make my list of people to kill," I said. "Maybe I'll write your letter to Durrell."

"I can write my own letter," she said. She was crosswise on the bed, on her back, her head hanging over the edge of the mattress, looking at me upside down. There was a little red scratch on her neck, and both her nipples looked like they'd been scrubbed behind the ears.

"No kidding," I said.

"Sure," she said. "How about this: 'My dearest Durrell, Thank you very much for your e-mail of this date, which I will always cherish. Its eloquence is unmatched, as usual. Once again you have plunged your hand deep into the open and bleeding wound in the still-heaving chest of our time and withdrawn from there and brought into the light for all to see the heart-thumping heart of the problem, etc. etc.' Will that do?"

"You won't be able to remember it."

"O.K. So I'll just say, 'Fuck you. We're not going to L.A.' "

"Get a grip," I said. "Get real. Wise up. Take a powder."

"I'll tell him we're off to ride the high country. I'll tell him he's a faucet for bile. I could tell him anything. I could say get a statue of the Blessed Virgin and put some red votive candles in front of it, and you'll never do any better than that."

"All these things would anger him, would they not?"

"There is that possibility."

I picked up the telephone. "Whatever," I said. "I'm calling Bud, to tell him where we are. Are we going to eat or what?"

"We just ate in Tourist Town back there," she said. "Lew and Margie's or whatever."

"That was hours ago," I said.

Jen got off the bed and stepped into a pair of shorts and pulled a T-shirt over her head. "I'm going down to see what they have in their travel rack," she said. "I'll be back in a minute." She took the key and left, letting the door latch slowly after her. I dialed Bud's number.

When he came on, I told him we were in Flagstaff and that Mike and Penny were leaving us and that we weren't going to Los Angeles anymore.

"So what are you going to do?" he said.

"I think we're going to drive around and see the sights," I said. "They get to you after a while. Your life changes. You become a different person. It's fun to see them. You wake up every day thinking of the things you're going to see. Even when they're disappointing, they're better than what you usually do. They lift you up and make you feel like everything's possible, everything's worthwhile. It's that feeling you had in grade school when you went to get supplies at the end of summer, before school started—the wonderful new tablet, some fresh pencils, the lunch box, the heartbreaking thermos you took home and drank out of right away, just because you had it. So I figure that's what we're going to do."

"That thermos deal sounds cool," Bud said.

"You could do worse," I said. I was flipping through the channels while talking to Bud, landing on a lot of news, weather, and sports. I made video eye contact with all the people who'd made news that day. I imagined they were all at home asking their spouses and live-in lovers and companions how they'd done.

"Are you going to the Grand Canyon?"

"I don't know. I suppose. It's not far from here—fifty or sixty miles."

"Are they leaving in the morning?"

"I don't know," I said.

"It's not a good idea for you to see the Grand Canyon in your present state of mind," Bud said. "I'm afraid you might see through the movie *and* the postcard, and become one with the canyon."

"I already did that," I said. "Today at Canyon de Chelly."

"That's great; exactly what we need in the family," Bud said. "Nature man."

"You're being callous, Bud."

"Envious," he said. "But what about the movies? You'll never get in if you don't go to California."

"It's not me that wants in. It's you."

"Yeah, but you could make some connections—you know, superior social skills and all that. Jen could generate some interest. She could be hot, hot, hot. They love the young."

"We love the young too, Bud."

"Right, right," he said. "But they love the young and have a lot of money."

"The young don't want money," I said.

"I'm not talking about what *they* want," he said. "Oh, never mind. How long are you going to be traveling? I'm getting lonely here. Margaret's lonely. We don't have anything to do. We just sit around all day waiting for you guys to get back. O.K., we don't do that, but it's close."

"I don't know how long," I said. "They go tomorrow and then we drive around and then we come back."

"You interested in a log house?" he said.

"On the beach? That's not right, is it? A log house on the beach?"

"I guess not. I was just wondering. So keep us posted, will you?"

I said I would, and then we hung up. On the TV, some boat people were coming across from Cuba or Haiti. I flicked the channel and got a magazine show doing a report on the prison system. I flicked again and got singers. I punched the Power button and turned the television off. There was a knock at the door. I got up and answered it. It was Penny, looking for Jen. I told her Jen was downstairs.

"Are you guys all right with this?" she said.

"What? You leaving?"

"Yes."

"I think so," I said.

"It's not because we're not going to L.A.," she said. "It's not because the plan is changing."

"No, I understand that."

"We just have other things we want to do."

"Sure. Of course you do."

She was messing with the paint on the doorframe, using her thumbnail, scratching at the paint.

I said, "We were wondering if you and Mike might want to go to the Grand Canyon in the morning and then leave in the afternoon."

"Hmm," she said. "That's an idea."

"It's not far—an hour and a half."

"I don't know what the flights are like," she said. "But I'll talk to Mike. I'll call you, O.K.?"

"If the phone's busy, Jen's on the computer," I said.

"Fine," she said. Then she leaned forward and gave me a little kiss on the cheek. She patted my shoulder and moved off toward the elevators. I was standing there watching her go when the guy across the hall opened his door to put out his room-service dishes. He was wearing shiny black bikini underpants and a net T-shirt.

"Howdy," he said. "I'm from Van Nuys. Where you from?"

"Alaska," I said.

"Never been there," he said.

"Well, do it while you're still young." We both went inside our rooms and closed the doors at the same time.

———

Jen got back on the Internet a little after midnight, dialing in through a local access number. She wrote a note to Durrell that said we weren't going to L.A., that the plans had changed. That was all she said. Then she started looking at newsgroups and collecting some other mail.

She got a note back from Durrell, who was apparently on the Internet at the same time. His message said, "Please don't back out now. You're one of the few I have contacted with regard to the project. I'm not sure I can carry on without support. Why are you not going through with your plan re Damian Williams? We must stick together. Are you aware of the Church of Euthanasia? Send e-mail to listserv@netcom.com with 'subscribe snuffit.I' for info. An intriguing program devoted to restoring balance between humans and other life forms via abortion, suicide, cannibalism, etc. Definitely in our bandwidth. We are increasing at one million per four days. We must stand together. Please reply at once."

"He's on right now and he wants me to explain," Jen said to me. "He wants me to tell him why I'm not going to L.A. to bust up Damian Williams."

"So why aren't you?" I said.

"Not my job?" she said.

"Just tell him the truth."

"The truth," she repeated. "Let me see. The truth is that we saw this horrible thing on television which seemed more horrible than the usual stuff we see on television, and we decided to do something, only we couldn't think of what to do, so we thought we'd go to the West Coast and either see Damian Williams or see where it all happened, in the hopes that some idea of what to do would come to us then. Is that right? We also decided that even if we didn't do anything about Damian Williams, we would do something else, something less ordinary than our regular lives, so that we could have an impact on the world around us, so we wouldn't just sit there and watch the stuff on TV and complain, so we wouldn't just say the people on TV were assholes, we'd do something about it. And I guess we agreed that the flyers and handouts and all the grisly stories were preaching to the choir, so that wasn't a sufficient thing. Is this the way you remember it?"

"Pretty close. We were concerned about other people, and we wanted to do something and not spend so much time in our own little world, because it's better to be a part of their world than it is to be shunted off into our own isolated one. That's what we thought, anyway."

"We were thinking it was our responsibility," Jen said. "We had a duty or something."

"To make our voices heard," I said.

"To try, anyway," she said.

"So tell him that," I said. "Write Durrell a note and tell him that."

"That doesn't explain what we're doing, though. Why we're not going to L.A. I need to tell him why."

"What's the reason?"

"The reason is that the world is so gorgeous that we can't stop ourselves from going around and looking at it," she said. "The reason is that putting one foot in the Painted Desert is more satisfying, more fulfilling, more rich and human and decent, than all the vengeance in the world. This country is making us into saints, making us feel like saints, and that's worth everything."

She was sitting in the messed-up bed with her knees up and the computer wedged between her stomach and her thighs. She had the telephone cord crossing over the top of the keyboard, plugged into the modem on the other side of the notebook.

"I've got to do something. I'm online here."

"Tell him," I said. "Go ahead."

She started typing. She was typing carefully, sometimes speaking the words as she typed them. From where I was sitting on the other bed, I could see the block of text developing on her screen. She went on typing. The text got to be almost a full screen's worth. I leaned over so I could read it. It said that the world was wonderful and horrible at the same time, that for every wretched thing there was something sublime, but we didn't see the sublime as often as the wretched. "Even the goony tourists are wonderful out here," she wrote. "Their Bermuda shorts and their silly hats and their stupid shirts, carrying their compact cameras and video cameras and Polaroid cameras, with spouses and children in their campers and station wagons. These are all people filled with hope. These are all people who are not spraying somebody's genitals black. These are all people who are trying to be kind to each other. And the best we can usually do is make fun of them in movies, make fun of them on television, make them out to be rubes, jokes. This is not the way things are supposed to be. These people are all lovely and sweet. They've come out of their holes for a little bit. It's a pleasure to be among them, to be one of them, to be like them. Because all they want out of their trips is a little bit of first-order experience, a little bit of contact with the ground, a little reminder of the wonder of things. And that's what they get out here. That's what we're getting, too, because once you're out here, all the easy ways you use to understand the world no longer work, and you're left with a mountain or a sea or a river or a canyon. Suddenly, blowing a hole in Damian Williams's face seems like a small idea. Almost every idea seems small and you can't imagine why we spend our time the way we do. Why we sit in our little houses complaining about people doing things wrong, sit there having our little precious thoughts, clinging to our ideas and opinions, arguing for our 'beliefs.' "

She stopped there and looked at the screen, rereading what she had written.

"It's fine," I said. "Send it. It's right."

"It's sort of the way I feel," she said. "We've got to find some new things to love."

"Good," I said. "I agree. I was telling Bud earlier."

She punched a key and sent her message off into the night. Then, without even bothering to sign off, she shut down the computer, unplugged the telephone cord from the modem, and plugged it back into the telephone. Then she got out her book of national parks and started reading, looking at the pictures, looking for places she wanted to go.

Penny called. She and Jen had a thirty-minute talk that was all whispers and giggles. Jen was on the floor between the beds. I was in the bed near the window, staring at the silent TV, listening to Jen's end of the conversation, the parts I could hear, anyway. When Jen hung up she climbed back into the other bed and said, "You suggested we go to the Grand Canyon tomorrow and bring them back after?"

"Yes," I said.

"She likes that idea," Jen said. "She said Dad will like it, too. She said I shouldn't worry. About her and Dad, I mean. Now I don't know whether to worry or not. I mean, she was real nice on the phone, she made sense, she was like regular Penny. What do you think? Do you think anything? I mean, she's probably not going to hurt him, and even if she does, he can probably take it, right? He's been hurt before, and she seems to really like him, says he's a big improvement on the desk gum she's used to."

"I don't doubt that," I said.

There was an interval, and then she said, "What are you doing over there, Del?"

"Where?" I said.

"In that bed."

"Nothing," I said.

"Oh," she said.

"Sitting here," I said.

"Oh."

"Not doing anything, really. I was thinking I wanted two *l*'s in my name from now on, like the comics."

"Uh-huh," she said.

"Just thinking," I said.

"That's a good idea," she said.

# nineteen

Mike and Penny were pressed up against each other in a jewel-green leatherette booth in the restaurant of the Holiday Inn when I got downstairs in the morning. They were sharing some French toast, which they'd cut in half on the plate. They topped one half with syrup and the other half with powdered sugar. Mike hadn't shaved since the day before. I brought the paper in and sat down opposite them.

"Where's Jen?" Penny said.

"She's coming. How are you fellows?" I said.

"We're great," Mike said. "We got a flight at four-thirty. We've got all day to hang around."

"Great," I said. "We'll eat and then head out. I haven't been to the Grand Canyon in twenty years. It's probably overrun with tourists and junk, but so what?"

"Yeah," Penny said. "What are they going to do, stand in front of us?"

Mike started to eat a piece of French toast with powdered sugar on it, but she gave him a look and he stopped midway between the plate and his mouth and redirected the fork so she could eat it.

"So did you decide what you're going to do?" Mike said.

"Yeah. We're going to keep on going," I said. "There are things we want to see."

"What about L.A. and the triumph of righteousness?" Penny said.

"We decided that riding on into the country is the triumph of righteousness," I said.

The waitress came, and I ordered a short stack of pancakes and a cup of coffee. Jen walked in and ordered juice and toast.

"What's in the paper?" she said to me.

"Arson, buzz cuts, peyote, sacred daggers, wolves, conspiracy, terrorist bombings, fish piracy, sex offenders, needle-exchange funding, white wrath, progesterone, massacres, tamper-proof Social Security cards, junk mail, and a bridge named after George Jones," I said, turning the pages of the paper and tapping the stories in turn as I named them.

"Why did you select those stories?" Penny said. "There were other stories in there you skipped."

"What are you, the story police? I couldn't think of what to call the other ones."

"To be fair, you have to name every one," she said.

"I'm not being fair today, Penny. Or any other day in the near future. You can forget fair as far as I'm concerned."

"It's up to you," she said.

"Easy, you guys," Jen said.

"What would it be like if they published just full-page photos in the paper?" Mike said. "They could still do crime and politics and everything, but they could do cars, too, and rivers, deserts, and regular people, downtowns, suburbs, mountains—"

"Somebody did that a long time ago," I said. "They weren't snapshots, though, they were art."

"Wouldn't you know it," Penny said.

"I did some picture stuff," Jen said. "Not very much."

Penny said, "I like the idea of pictures you can't figure out why were published. Is that a sentence?"

"Close," Jen said.

"You'd have a problem with people looking for reasons all the time," I said. "They'd be talking and explaining, having opinions, most of them obvious, sloppy—twelve column inches of opinion in a media rag, forty seconds of opinion on TV. Analysis would eat it alive."

"That already happens," Mike said. "You kind of have to tune that out."

"Lordy knows we try," Penny said.

"Doesn't work," Jen said. "That's like TV on, sound off. You get the feeling you have to turn the sound on every once in a while, that you have to hear what they're saying. You see a picture, and there's something going on in the little square behind the guy's head, and you have to turn on the sound to hear."

"That's hard," I said.

"Yeah, because the fun's hating them," Jen said. "Like the jerks on politics shows—you spend time thinking what idiots they are. Except Jack Germond."

"She loves Jack Germond," I said to Mike.

"Who doesn't?" Penny said.

"When you find people you like on television, you want to give them everything," Jen said. "You want them to have all the power. You want to king them so they can fire and kill. When someone is sensible on TV, you fall in love."

"Is he that roly-poly guy?" Mike said.

"The exact one," Penny said. "Everything he says is so smart and reserved and thoughtful. He's fresh air."

"He is pretty good," Jen said.

The waitress brought our food. We ate. Jen did not eat my pancakes. I did not eat her toast. Mike and Penny left to go up to their room and finish packing.

"This is O.K., isn't it?" Jen said. "Mike and Penny?"

"It's fine," I said.

When we were finished eating, we paid the bill and went upstairs to get ready. We met Mike and Penny in the lobby and got back in the Lincoln and headed for the Grand Canyon. The drive was quick, and soon we were coming in along the south rim, the touristy rim, because it would have taken us another two and a half hours to go to the north rim, which was too authentic, anyway. The south rim was crowded, and parking was hard to find at the overlooks, but you could pull off anywhere and step out to the edge readily.

The canyon was nice to look at. Reduced a little bit by its flamboyant press, but more lovely than almost everything we see in ordinary life. It was big and colorful, with a graceful apple-green river winding through its floor.

"We ought to take one of those airplane trips through the canyon," Penny said.

"We can't do that," Mike said. "They crash all the time."

"What are you talking about?" she said.

"I read it in the newspaper," he said. "Light aircraft going down in the Grand Canyon. Happens several times a year. Whole families have been wiped out."

"I don't believe it," Penny said.

The people looking at the Grand Canyon were interesting, too. They pointed and stared and yanked on each other's arms and chattered away in various languages. I watched a crowd at the first overlook surveying the canyon. I was watching their backs, wondering what was in their heads. What were they seeing? What were they thinking? I guessed they were thinking just about what I was thinking, something like, "Man, this thing is huge!" Or maybe they were filled with that pleasant vacantness of mind where nothing in particular is thought, where what is before you seems just to float unimpeded through the senses and into, then out of, the brain. Or maybe they had that slight sense of something wonderful but unspecified going on. Or maybe they were filled with their sore throats, their crying children, their onracing adulteries, their legal worries, their sick parents, their credit card debts, their special TV shows, their hamburger desire—the rest of their lives. There were a few who knew too much for their own good, of course, just as there were at the other spots we'd visited—Carlsbad, White Sands—but mostly people were just looking blankly at the canyon, soaking it up. Natural wonder. Big black birds circled overhead, hawks, gliding. People were dressed in Bermuda shorts and plaid shirts, T-shirts with concert logos, funny Tim Conway hats folded down to keep the sun off their faces. A lot of people were taking pictures of each other out on the rocks. Some were more daring than others; they went farther out or farther down. Some just lined the kids up along the railing and shot them right there at the overlook.

We drove the south rim, stopped at a bunch of spots, gazed into the canyon. There wasn't much to say unless you were willing to say what everybody else said, which we were, eventually. So we traveled in a lot of silence before we got to "Jesus" and "Look at that" and "Hmm." It wears you down. We stopped at the big tourist complex and bought T-shirts and baseball caps, then went out and took a path a little ways down into the canyon until we were too tired to go farther. We sat by the side of the path for thirty minutes or so, listening to the wind, to snatches of talk coming from above us, to squawking birds, to rocks skidding down cliffs, to whatever was up there.

# twenty

Mike and Penny didn't get off until almost six. The plane was late. We spent the time wandering around in the little airport. Mike wished us well and invited us to come to Baton Rouge on our way home. I reminded him we had his car, so we were sure to come to Baton Rouge.

"Right," he said.

We all hugged and said how pleased we were to have been together. It was sad to see them go, because it meant the end of something, even though something else was due to start at any minute.

"You get used to traveling with people," Mike said. "You get used to the things they say, the way they talk, their ideas, their jokes. If you like them, going on alone is a loss."

"He means we'll miss you," Penny said.

"Same here," I said.

"I mean sometimes you can do things you didn't know you could do," Mike said.

Jen hugged him and whispered that she loved him, and Mike and Penny crossed the concrete. We watched their small plane push into the sky, then we left the building.

The Town Car, which had been big with four of us in it, was gigantic now. Jen pulled us over in a rest area and got all our junk out of the trunk and put it in the back seat so we wouldn't be as lonely. When she got into the car again, she said, "You want to go back to that same hotel for tonight? What should we do?"

We were headed north from the airport, toward Flagstaff. I was watching the sunset, which had filled the sky with low, thick clouds. These clouds were strung throughout the west and looked like mirrors of the rocks below. Searing yellows with edges in red, gray darker tops. These were deep clouds, swept and striped, thick into the sky with a startling trail of golden highlights. The sky looked like earth, only upside down and more colorful.

The clouds were full of shapes—I saw a ship, some kind of cabin cruiser, mountain peaks like those in the movie about Shangri-La, and the head and shoulders of a man asleep, his face open into the heavens.

"Are you getting all this?" I said to Jen, pointing across her and out the window at the sky.

"Yes," she said. "It's incredibly fabulous."

"I don't want to stop in Flagstaff," I said.

"What do you mean?"

"I think we ought to start now, we ought to go out into the desert," I said.

"Tonight?" she said.

"Yeah, why not? It's just the two of us," I said.

"You're a dangerous man," she said.

I looked at the map and figured a route through Flagstaff, out to Winona just off Highway 40, and then north and east to a town called Sunrise, which was right on the edge of the great swath of the

Painted Desert that ran from the Grand Canyon all the way down to the Petrified Forest National Park we'd been in the day before, hundreds of square miles of open, untended desert. When we stopped at a fast-food joint on the interstate for a drive-through hamburger, I showed Jen the route.

"We'll go to Sunrise, which is an hour, maybe, and we stay there if you want, or head north to this Indian village. Then up to Tuba City and then either northwest or northeast, whichever."

"Right across the center of this Painted Desert," she said, scraping the map with a fingernail. "I like this plan, Del."

We sat in the parking lot of the hamburger place, eating and pointing out spots on the map.

"Red Lake and Cow Springs," Jen said. "Then Blue Hills and into Colorado and over to Mesa Verde. Remember I showed you that?"

"Yep," I said.

"Then we shoot straight up Colorado and Wyoming to Devil's Tower," she said. "I looked it up. It's way up in the corner."

"What about all this Utah stuff?" I said, sipping my drink and wagging my hand over Utah. "All this stuff is amazing—Mexican Hat, Dark Canyon, Rainbow Bridge, Cedar Breaks. We could go there and then shoot back into Colorado."

"Other way," she said. "Since northern Utah looks great too, why not go the other way and then straight up to Yellowstone, and across after?"

"Or Salt Lake City, cut into Pebble Springs, Table Rock, Red Desert, down to Medicine Bow, then north to Como Bluff, where the dinosaur graveyard is. See that?" I pointed to where the map said the graveyard was.

"We could do that," Jen said.

At the Mobil station, she filled the car with gas and I got some peanut M&M's, and then we got on the road for Sunrise. The sky was going deeper blue and the yellow clouds were behind us, leaving only traces of pink and a bit of salmon overhead. The desert in the light of sundown was a pale rage of colors, weirdly erotic and seductive, all thin oranges, violets, apricots, pale blues, even greens popping out on the mesas and river terraces. The landscape was huge eroded knife-edged rocks, irregular peaks and swept washes, arroyos and creased fallen cliffs stretching out as far as we could see on either side of the bare two-lane highway. The sunlight trickled over these rock fields and flats like luminous water. Everything we saw was constantly changing, flickering from what we'd just seen to what we were just beginning to see. An unbroken wind blasted the surface, stirring whirlwinds and sandstorms off the tops of twisted rocks that stood up in the desert like the last ruins of long-gone cultures.

By the time we got to Sunrise, the sky was a lovely deep blue and the clouds had cooled off behind us. There was still light, but it was that odd indirect kind that happens before night finally falls.

"Let's rest," Jen said.

The town was small and dusty, and the first time through we couldn't find anywhere to stay, so we stopped at a frame house that was a grocery and gas station and asked if there was a motel.

An Indian woman behind the counter said, "You want to stay in Sunrise?"

"Yes," we said.

"We have a motel," she said. "It is very old."

"Good," I said. "Where is it?"

She told us where it was, back on the highway in the direction from which we'd come. On our left as we entered the town. We had driven right past it.

We thanked her, bought some diet Cokes, got back in the car. The Ideal Motor Court was a one-story wood-frame building with six rooms and a hand-painted sign in the window of the office. A whiskery guy was sitting in a lounge chair, watching TV, when I walked through the door. The place was like a den, with a big counter jutting out from one wall and cutting the room in two. He was on one side of the counter and I was on the other. Behind him was a door into another room, which was furnished like an apartment.

"Can we get a room?" I asked.

"How long?" he said.

"Tonight," I said.

"You probably want a TV," he said.

"If you've got one."

"Oh, we got 'em," he said. "We got tons of 'em. Some rooms got two or three."

"We just need one," I said.

"Figures," he said. He craned his head to the side in order to look out the open front door toward the car. There was a big scar on his neck. "That your daughter?"

"Wife," I said.

"No kidding," he said, taking another look. "How you fixing to pay?"

"You take a credit card?"

"What do you think?" he said.

"MasterCard," I said.

"Shoot it on out here," the guy said. "Let's have a look-see."

I got the card out of my wallet, and he took it and went to his desk and zipped it through a scanner, then tucked it into a receipt printer, put a blank on top of it, and cracked the handle across. When the O.K. came through on the scanner, he brought the receipt back for me to sign.

The room and the bathroom and the bed were all clean. When we got inside I opened a Coke and turned on the TV, then unfolded the Arizona map.

Jen took a quick shower, then jumped into bed. "We forgot to stop at Sunset Crater," she said, pointing to a photograph on the back of the map.

I turned the map over so we could look at the pictures.

"What if we went to all these?" she said. "Tuzigoot, Keet Seel Ruin, Tonto. Oh, yeah, this Chiricahua National Monument, too."

"I don't know where some are."

"Look at this," Jen said. "There's another town called Sunrise, over there by where we were yesterday, by Canyon de Chelly. Two Sunrises. They're both on this same road."

"It's smaller than this one," I said.

We found the Arizona places she wanted to see. Most were south of us, down by Tucson, just west of New Mexico.

"We'll swing down there on the return," I said.

"You hungry?" she said, getting her computer out. "There's an extra hamburger in the car."

"I could run hot water over it," I said.

"Maybe the manager's got a microwave."

She hooked up the notebook, and after some messing around to change over to pulse dialing, she linked up with CIS.

I looked at the map some more. "We might want to go to the north rim of the Grand Canyon if we're going to Utah first," I said.

"Whatever," she said. "I want to walk around in the desert. Just pull off the road and walk out into it for a couple hours, just get lost in it."

"Uh-huh," I said.

"Look at that," she said. "Nothing from our friend Durrell. Not a word. I guess he didn't like what I said last night."

"Probably shocked him," I said.

"I'll try the Net," she said, logging off CIS and running her Internet front end.

Nothing there, either. Not from Durrell, anyway. She did collect some new messages from the Amazon Women list and an updated index of zines online, and subscribed to alt.buzzards.cracked, alt.putz.bob.bob.bob, and a few other new newsgroups.

"O.K. if I cut the light?" I asked.

She nodded, and I reached and turned off the lamp on the bedside table. It was just eight, but I was tired. I shut my eyes and listened to Jen's notebook keys.

It was after five when I woke up. The room was dark except for the TV. Jen was naked and stretched alongside me belly up, like a cat caught in deep sleep. I rocked her shoulder.

"What?" she said.

"We didn't go to bed right," I said. "We're on top of the covers. It's five-something."

"In the morning?"

"Yeah."

We lay there for a while, not talking, not moving. It was easier not moving. I was staring at the ceiling and letting my eyes close when they wanted to. After a time I got up to pee, then sat down on the end of the bed in front of the television. Most of the channels were infomercials or early-bird exercise shows or religious things. Dick Cavett was on with a guy who was going to help us with our memories. There was a tropical storm down in the Gulf. The Pope was blessing something in some third-world country, selling his book. The home shopping networks were going full tilt.

CNN had some footage of weather in Florida, then cut to a report from some modern-looking hospital. There were lots of ambulances and police cars, lots of lights flashing, and this very elegant young woman was standing in front of the emergency room entrance, talking to the camera. They were having some kind of crisis. When the signature line flashed on at the bottom of the screen, saying the tape was recorded earlier by Channel 2 in Las Vegas, Jen said, "Move over. Hit the sound."

I flicked the sound button and caught the recap. Three people were dead in Las Vegas after a series of sniper attacks in the early-morning hours. Four more were injured. Dead were a local news anchor, a state senator, a casino employee. Wounded: a drug dealer, two policemen, a housewife. The police had a suspect but had not been able to find him; there was no explanation for the shootings. There was a short piece of tape of a cop showing an artist's rendering of a balding man with a ponytail and steel-rimmed glasses. They froze on the drawing. The guy was wearing a plaid shirt open over a white T-shirt. His face was chunky, with a day or two of beard.

"Jesus," Jen said.

"Durrell?" I said. I got up for an instant, then sat down again.

"It's got to be," Jen said.

CNN cut away from the story, so I did a quick circuit of the channels, trying to find something else. There wasn't anything.

Jen was off the bed. "It's him," she said.

"Jesus," I said. I got up again and this time went out the front door and into the parking lot. I leaned against the Lincoln's front fender. I listened to the window units working on the air. Some birds I didn't recognize were squeaking nonstop. In the distance I heard the whistle of a train, then the rhythmic rolling of its trucks on the rails. There were just a couple of lights on in Sunrise. It was still dim out there. Mostly what I could see were low adobe buildings, half-repaired cars jacked up at odd angles, stacks of tires, barbed-wire fences, old signs, whorls of sagebrush, and a few broad-branched trees lining the highway, and everything in sight was covered with dust. I was out there looking around when Jen showed up with her bags.

"Let's go," she said.

"What, now?"

"Sure," she said. "It's almost morning. We got plenty of sleep, didn't we?"

"I guess so," I said.

I went into the room, washed my face, brushed my teeth, did a quick change, got my stuff together, and hauled it out to the car. We stopped to get a receipt from the office and in ten minutes we were rolling out of Sunrise, cutting northeast on Indian Route 2, where we crossed the Little Colorado River and headed into the desert.

The desert wasn't flat, but it was plenty empty. The big Town Car was the only thing on the highway at that time of the morning. We got some miles in, crossing the Hopi Indian reservation, the car washing along the two-lane at fifty-five miles an hour—Jen was going easy. After a time she slowed up and stopped at a spot where a red dirt lane cut north off the highway, straight into the desert. It wasn't a real road at all, just some packed ground where other cars had obviously turned in. We were parked there in the middle of the highway when Jen opened her car door, got out, and stood up on the sill, looking into the desert. "I'm going here," she finally said.

I was out of the car too, standing in the road. There was nobody as far as the eye could see in front of us or behind us on the highway, no lights, nothing but a few insistent stars and the craggy silhouettes of dark desert rock against a still-sleepy sky. I couldn't see anything anywhere. Jen was walking around kicking up dust on the shoulder of the road. The dirt-covered Lincoln was idling there.

"Straight across, huh?" I said.

"It'll come out somewhere," she said.

"I guess," I said.

So we got back in Mike's car and she swung us into the dirt road and in a few minutes we were cutting across open land. Sometimes there was a road under us, sometimes tracks, sometimes just uncluttered ground.

As the darkness evaporated and lifted off the desert floor, the land around us turned into a bigger-than-life topographical map, its colors eerie and surprising as the sun began to brighten the horizon from below. I felt light-headed to finally be off L.A., to be out in the country in this way we'd never planned.

After forty minutes of gliding up the desert, I reached in back for the little TV and said, "I'll try to get something."

Jen caught my hand and stopped me. "Do try the radio," she said. Then she hit the gas hard, picking up speed. I saw it cross eighty.

I punched the Seek button a few times, and the tuner caught a preacher, a sports talk show, finally a news station. The announcer was talking about snakes, how there were too many snakes, and how they were having an impact on the tourist business. He called it a rain of snakes.

"I want to marry you when we get home," Jen said. "Regular married. Just like everybody."

"You do?"

"Is it a deal?"

I punched the little chrome button to drop my window, then stuck my arm straight out into the buffeting wind, flying my hand the way I'd done as a kid. "I guess it's a deal for me," I said.

She waved at the radio and said, "Find some music."

"What do you want?" I punched the Seek button again, watching the numbers flip by.

"Swing," she said. "Western swing."

I kept hitting the button, but I couldn't find anything that made sense to listen to, so I left it on Autoseek—ten seconds of every station. For a minute all I could think of was what we must look like from the sky, the black Lincoln, the two splintered headlights shooting out into nothing, the two taillights glowing red tracers behind us, the big flat space everywhere and all this dust swelling around us like a land-speed-record attempt. We rocketed across that desert sand.